AFTER THE DYING

e. a. rogers

iUniverse, Inc.
New York   Bloomington

AFTER THE DYING

This is a work of fiction. All of the characters, names, incidents, organizations, and dialogue in this novel are either the products of the author's imagination or are used fictitiously.

iUniverse books may be ordered through booksellers or by contacting:

iUniverse
1663 Liberty Drive
Bloomington, IN 47403
www.iuniverse.com
1-800-Authors (1-800-288-4677)

ISBN: 978-1-4502-5931-6 (sc)
ISBN: 978-1-4502-5932-3 (ebook)

Printed in the United States of America

iUniverse rev. date: 10/29/2010

DEDICATION

AFTER THE DYING is dedicated to the fictional people in the fictional town of Sainte Lillian's Missouri.

Or is it? Are they? Check the sky.

Note from author:

The story you are about to read was compiled from research, meticulous notes kept by my family members and copies of speeches made by then President of the United States Inez Brown-Parkinson. Videos of events were an integral part of my research.

When I reference President Zavier Turnbull, President Inez Brown-Parkinson, or any other person, be assured I have compiled and copied to the best of my ability.

I found the spinning and weaving of characters together to make the story as complete as possible, both challenging and enlightening.

As I am American, I cannot speak or write for other people in other lands.

Therefore, this story is the result of my research about this time in the History of the world, and the resulting events surrounding my family and friends. As far as I know, LIFE AFTER THE DYING is the only personalized American account of the birth of a new nation.

My decision to focus on one family and more or less on one community even as it was interwoven with the widely diverse and geographically scattered American remnant, was the knowledge all Americans are (in essence), one family. We are related not by DNA but by faith and resilience and our goal to walk toward wholeness.

It is my heartfelt wish that in every country someone has taken the time to compile, chronicle and compose a more-or-less comprehensive overview of what happened there, what happened when, and what happened after the dying.

ONE

Before the story begins, there must be included a brief review of Sainte Lillian. Not the town in the Missouri Ozarks, but the Sainte it was named after, and acknowledgment however brief of women who modeled her life of service.

* * * * *

For centuries people have revered the 14th century Sainte from Wales, Lillian Marguerite Augusta du Morgan. Known as the Sainte of the impossible, she was canonized in the dark ages by a pope who wanted to give the people another thread of hope.

Towns throughout the world are named after Sainte Lillian. Of interest in this narrative is the small Ozark town of Sainte Lillian, Missouri.

Also of interest is the difference in spelling for male and female saints. When men of merit are canonized, the designation is Saint: as in Saint Francis of Assisi, Saint Peter and Saint Paul. When ladies are so honored the title ends with an e. As in: Sainte Lillian and Sainte Genevieve. Some say it is almost as if their name were not enough to indicate femininity.

Back to Sainte Lillian. The little Missouri Ozark town of Sainte Lillian, Missouri, as well as hundreds of same name towns across the continental United States (was and were) named after a 14th century Sainte from the little bit of Great Britain known as Wales.

Wild and warring the land was then, but that didn't stop love blossoming in the hearts of a dark skinned traveler of Moorish descent and a green eyed Welsh lass, a Jewish convert to Christianity. Both of Sainte Lillian's parents were devout Christians and raised their only child in the faith of, and immersed in the love of God.

Lillian Marguerite Augusta Du Morgan was never known as beautiful.

In fact, she was not pleasing fair to the eye. Some superstitious said she was born with a witches caul and should be burnt.

As her father stood six foot six and was known to keep men about with sharp swords and a ferocious pack of hunting dogs guarding the child, they only said it once. Fools said it twice. Not that the gentle giant ever threatened them, but when he walked around with his child secure in his arms, they knew.

Truth is there was something grand about Lillian Marguerite Augusta Du Morgan other than her size. Something peaceful. Though she seemed put together of spare parts, with unruly coarse dark hair on her overly large head, there was just something good about her that made people pause and a special way. Her right hand was a size larger than her left, she had square mannish feet, and teeth so crooked and discolored she seldom smiled.

Marguerite Augusta Du Morgan's differences were noted for posterity by a village scribe, and then overlooked.

She like her mother had a laugh full of joy. It was said one look into her merry hazel green eyes was enough to bring peace and hope to the most unruly heart.

As she grew into womanhood, Lillian Marguerite Augusta Du Morgan skipped childish games and willingly took on the most menial task. Her hands were so busy doing good works and her feet moving so fast, not one village gossip was heard to compare her to a more comely woman.

The prayers of every mother in the area were their daughters would grow to be like Lillian Marguerite Augusta du Morgan. "Saintly, that's what she is," they said.

In her lifetime, Lillian lived and breathed her faith. It was said she never encountered a situation she considered impossible. Her formula: "First I pray then I work and pray."

It was also said miracles came when she did that bit of work. When plague and the pox came to villages, she was there nursing and curing the sick.

Her telling the good news of Christ was followed by a gospel of cleanliness. She rolled up her sleeves, boiled water and scrubbed everything shining with her home made lye soap. "Cleanliness is next to Godliness, God gave us this earth! Do we show our appreciation by turning it into a pigsty?"

When there was famine she devised ways and means to feed the hungry. Orphaned children found homes. Barren women bore children after she prayed with them. Stray or wild animals tamed at her touch. Festering wounds healed, and warring clans were brought to peace by the cool calmness of her faith and logic.

There was that something good and blessed about that woman they said.

Those that once said evil against her hung their heads in shame and begged her forgiveness.

Lillian Marguerite Augusta Du Morgan was born content. Contentedly, she lived. At the age of 88 she died without ever shedding a tear of self pity.

Her last words were spoken on a gloriously warm May day. The last of winter's cold had left the land and blue sky and green grass, flowering trees and shrubs sang Glorias. She had walked to her favorite resting place near a bubbling brook two days hence.

There, as she rested in the shade, she watched the play of light and shadow like she was watching passing time. For two days then, praying without ceasing she was as she knelt by a bench near her favorite Wych Elm. At sunrise of the third day, she went to pray at the roughly hewn wooden cross centered in the large circle.

It was a simple but restful place, bordered by graceful alder and aspen that loved the water as much as she. Around the circular area where the reverent knelt to pray at the cross, the area near the burbling stream was filled with wooden benches. Sun bleached and grey they were, but beautiful under the blue sky. Smooth pebbles lined the pathway that led to kneeling benches.

News was about in the small thatched roofed huts that made villages and in the surrounding countryside and hillside that Lillian Marguerite Augusta du Morgan was ill. Critically ill. The faithful gathered to be with her. Deep the crowd was, and reverent as they celebrated her life with song and psalms and prayed for her soul.

She heard the prayers and singing and was slipping slowly into eternal sleep when she moved so quickly those ministering to her jumped back in alarm. Lillian raised her twisted right hand and pointed up. Toward heaven. Pointed up so there was no mistake she was reaching beyond the mountains and above the blue sky lined with circular white shining clouds.

The bright sun seemed to grow brighter as she spoke. "Oh, it's so beautiful," she whispered. Then slowly, each word expelled on the faintest puff of breath, each word weaker than the last, she looked into the eyes of the one she called sister, and said, "Oh!... I...Hear...The...Bells...Ringing." Then, she went to sleep.

Lillian Marguerite Augusta du Morgan was legend before her death and canonized in less than one hundred years by a Pope who wanted to give the people hope.

Sainte Lillian became the Sainte of the eternally optimistic eternally faithful ladies who served the Lord. Towns around the world are named after her. As were many young and Godly young women.

In Sainte Lillian, Missouri as there are in every town so named there are women who carry the spirit of Sainte Lillian in their heart and walk hand and hand with mercy as she did.

In the current century, there were few named Lillian. It is her spirit they carry. They are known by many names. To name a few: Mary B., Melanie, Jannelle, Olathe, Samantha, Lynn, Mollie, Cathie, Margaret, Inez, Mother Theresa and the Sisters of Mercy...

They are Missionaries and care givers. Some never leave their hometowns. Yet all work to feed the hungry and love the loveless with their deeds of mercy. Prompted by a soul searing love, they go into hovels, huts, and slums to rescue the perishing from alleyways and from under bridges and viaducts.

They are Black and white, yellow and American Indian, Irishwomen and Germanic, Hindu and heathen. They are mother, sister, niece aunt, grandmother and friend. They are from every country and every nationality in the world.

Some of them died that July 4th.

And that statement is the bridge to AFTER THE DYING. Which begins when you turn the page.

TWO

Congratulations continue to pour in from across the world as the United States celebrates the inauguration of its first female president.

Inez Brown-Parkinson, vice-president under two term world leader Zavier Turnbull, won in a landslide as Americans rallied around the blunt speaking woman. She says what she sees and says she sees no sense in excessive spending just because she's on the hill.

The best example in her private life includes her wardrobe and household staff. Wardrobe first: Her wardrobe for all seasons consists of either pants suits or dress suits in shades of grey or blue. Her accessories are always a combination of red, white, and blue. Her shoes are always three inch bright red patent leather heels.

Until she assumed the second highest office in the land, she shopped at local malls and or discount stores. Members of her staff now check for bargains twice a year.

Gone forever are the thirty thousand dollar inaugural ball gowns. For her Navy blue inaugural ball floor length gown, she paid over seventy dollars at discounts.com only because her husband and five children insisted she was not being lavish. Her jewelry, a single strand of imitation pearls were a gift from her great grandmother Mo Brown. She bought them for fifty cents at a garage sale.

Her household…or house keeping staff including cooks is a diverse group. Some including the immaculate butler have a long history of serving presidents. President Brown Parkinson said she kept him on staff because butlering was the only job he'd ever had and she couldn't stand the thought of his being in the unemployment line. Besides, he was good at it.

As President Turnbull offered his chef and staff positions at his residence, President Brown-Parkinson has engaged cooks (not chefs, cooks) from across the country. She said, "My family and I will not exceed the normal food budget for a family of six. We will have a White House garden and will grow, can, and freeze our own vegetables, fruits, jams and jellies.

My kids spend a lot of time in the kitchen and make sure our cooks know our favorites like vegetable soup, macaroni and cheese and biscuits and gravy. Fried chicken ain't bad either."

Once recovered from cuisine shock, mainline gourmet magazines turned to home style country cooking. Sausage gravy and biscuits, grits, greens, cornbread and buttermilk pie became cover photos.

Major grocery chains and restaurants could not stock enough buttermilk.

To say the ex-president and the current president are studies in diversity is putting it mildly. He preferred elegant dinners with many courses and exquisite wines. She serves family style and beverage of choice is butter milk.

Yet, the tall balding elegant president Turnbull and the plump folksy President Inez Brown-Parkinson who has been known to wear an apron in the Oval Office, have led the nation through eight tumultuous years.

While at first glance they appear as opposites of the spectrum, they state they have been and will continue to be united in their commitments to the American people.

President Turnbull's lineage as everyone knows goes as far back as history is written in both South America and America. His ancestors fought in the war of 1812, and have continued to be patriots and public servants.

President Inez Brown-Parkinson, the descendant of slaves, has traced her lineage to the Southwest coast of Africa, and to the American Colonies.

Family history indicates the first Zavier Turnbull freed his servant John Brown after the war of Independence was won.

The Brown family went on to become average working class Americans, with an abundance of teachers, preachers and factory workers. Also, they chose to work for the Peace Corps around the world.

President Brown-Parkinson's great grandmother, who raised her after the death of her parents, was a florist in Sainte Lillian, Missouri.

President Brown-Parkinson credits her "Grammy Brown" with instilling in her the love of Christ, hunger for an education, and the desire to serve her country.

President Inez Brown-Parkinson is the first female African American President.

Other first: President Inez Brown-Parkinson ran as an independent, merging the best of both Democratic and Republican political parties. "Not a tea party, a FREE PARTY," she said.

She said she was past tired of political infighting and guaranteed pork barrels and bridges to nowhere would not happen in her watch. "Congress and the House will continue to work together for the good of the people. As President Turnbull stated in his inaugural address, pocket padding and favoritism will also not be a part of my administration."

Early in the election process, would be wise editorialist had predicted because she did not lean toward favoritism, accept contributions from big business and outlawed all forms of ear marks she would loose in a landslide. As shown, the opposite is true.

Quoting the President: "Every cent in my campaign came from the people. School children saved pennies and nickels. Families wanting President Turnbull's policies to continue put me in office and continuation is what this administration will provide. I was elected president by the people and for the people and will be the president of all the people.

Tell the world my administration will not waste money. State dinners will be at a minimum and informal. In fact, I'm planning to give some of these world leaders a taste of real American food. To name a few, I'm talking Mac Donald's and Burger King and Taco Bell and Wendy's. If fast food is good enough for Americans, it's good enough for kings and queens; many of whom have never had to stand in line for anything in their lives.

Visiting heads of state need to know real Americans. When they return to their homeland they will have a new appreciation for the grit and determination that makes our country unbeatable and our optimisms unstoppable..

Time, energy and funds wasted by previous administrations on glitz and glamour will continue to be directed toward ending corruption, ending the drug trade, and importantly providing equal medical care for everyone. This includes citizens with pre-existing conditions, and those without insurance. We will not only feed the hungry, we will continue to train and employ them and work with them until hunger and despair becomes a memory."

Acknowledging the fifth round of tumultuous applause, she said, "During President Turnbull's administration, he worked with the stock market, bank presidents and CEO's of all Major corporations. His final act as president was attaining the signature of each on a document that will not only stabilize America but influence the world economy." She paused and looked into the cameras.

"My friends, you're going to love this and may want to elevate President Turnbull to sainthood but he's Lutheran and that won't work."

Laughter rose and President Turnbull, on cue, joined the newly sworn in president at the podium. She then continued.

"Because of President Turnbull's persuasive leadership, all corporate CEO's, bankers and leading businessmen in every state will begin their next working day earning a minimum wage. Like every worker if they want to keep their jobs, they will work to do so. Their scaled down living style is now turning mansions into Hospices. Their works of art, and private jets, and museum pieces and their yachts manned by season crews are now donated for public use.

Their combined fortunes ensure education at major universities including all schools of medical knowledge. Schools of science and engineering, and all trade schools will continue to offer degrees to everyone willing to bone up and pass entrance exams.

We are not giving education away to students that can't read or choose to pay tutors. That will not work. Degrees and graduate degrees will be earned.

President Turnbull was a bit lax on this one, attempting to excuse high school dropouts from educational endeavors. That is not necessary. It was instilled in me by my Grammy Brown that there are skills and there is knowledge available for everyone regardless of their I.Q.

In short, there will be no more high school dropouts. Curriculum will change, but education will not end. It is up to educators to tap into this heretofore bypassed source of intelligence.

This land needs doctors, nurses, architects, workers, musicians, artist and dreamers. We absolutely guarantee there will be no unemployment in America."

President Brown-Parkinson and President Xavier Turnbull stared into the silent crowd. He cleared his throat and said "Ladies and Gentlemen, staring at us with jaws agape is quite unnecessary.

I urge those of you who, think we are leaning toward communism, to dust off two excellent sources of knowledge. The first is the Bible. The second must read is The Constitution of the United States. This country was founded on Christian Principals. It's time we rediscovered truth and lived it.

One further note: While President Brown-Parkinson has given me credit for this economic turnaround, I want to insure you that before we were elected to this highest office she planted the seed. Time and. circumstances watered it, God guided my heart, and she nagged. You can tell by the way she's looking at me I'll hear about that statement later."

Then quickly, " Besides, I doubt any of you could resist anything this president proposes especially when she has you in her kitchen at midnight and is treating you with her hopes along with a side dish of home made Apple Brown Betty old fashioned hand churned ice cream."

Laughter, applause, and a standing ovation filled the room and the TV screens across the country.

At the conclusion of her inaugural address, President Brown-Parkinson asked for complete silence. She then repeatedly stressed that her administration would put the construction of underground shelters and living quarters for humans and animals on the fast track, as threats of a world wide disaster continued to grow. She said her administration and leaders of the free world were united on this project and would continue to issue bulletins and keep the people informed.

President Brown-Parkinson's entire Inaugural address is available on line and in print. Videos are also available.

In the event anyone missed her closing remarks, she said, and this is a direct quote,

"This administration will welcome your comments and criticisms as long as they come with ideas to improve situations. However, if all you want to do is whine and complain, the exit is clearly marked. I suggest you exit quickly before the door smacks you in the butt."

THREE

Dear Mrs. President:

Hello!

My name is Tasha Maureen O'Rourke. I am almost eleven years old. If you answer my letter. please be sure to capitalize the R in my last name. A lot of people don't and since that's the way we always do it, I sure don't want to miss a letter from you. I mean if you have time to answer and I really truly hope you do.

We live in the southwest in one of the experimental mountain homes you've set up. My daddy works at the electric power plant, my momma is a home school teacher, and my sister will soon graduate from high school and enter college. We have a few sheep and all kinds of dogs and cats. I must tell you they don't like living in caves, but we make sure they come in every night.

My momma and daddy voted for you and said you're about the smartest person that's ever been in the White House. They like it that you don't have expensive parties. Daddy said he's glad you don't 'Kiss up" (whatever that means) "to movie stars and have stopped paying the rich to be rich."

Really what I'm writing about is since you said you are the people's president, I have an idea for you.

When we toured D.C. a few years ago, we saw a lot of fancy paintings and pictures all over the White House. I was wondering why you didn't put them in museums and have us school kids draw you pictures of our families and our homes and stuff. You could make it a contest or something, and it would be a nice way to thank kids for saving their allowance and turning in pop bottles and stuff when you needed money for your campaign.

I hope you like my idea. Write and let me know.

Very sincerely yours,

Tasha Maureen O'Rourke.

P.S. Me and my family pray for you and your family every day.

Dear Mrs. President:
    Do you really like my idea? I'm so excited. Now I have to figure out a way to tell momma and daddy I wrote to you and you answered.
    I could write just tons more but it's almost time for the mail, so I gotta run.
    Thank you, thank you, thank you, thank you, thank you, thank you, thank you, thank you.

Very sincerely yours,

Tasha Maureen O'Rourke.

FOUR

EXERPTS FROM SPEECH DELIVERED BY AMERICAN PRESIDENT INEZ BROWN-PARKINSON AND SENT VIA SATELLITE TO ALL COUNTRIES.

JUNE: EIGHT YEARS AGO:

"Fellow citizens of planet earth: I come to you at a time in world history when survival of the human race is challenged more than ever before. Earthquakes, floods, famines, heretofore unknown and so far uncontrollable diseases are on every continent. Wars and rumors of wars are world wide. As you know two years ago in the United States, the entire state of California was made uninhabitable by the San Andreas Fault quake.

For over 800 miles there were few survivors. Rock slides and gigantic tsunamis finished what the quake started. All real estate along the San Andreas quake line is considered unstable. Those families and farmers who choose to live in that area do so without Government sanction.

Some consider the loss of Hollywood good news. Considering their penchant to produce increasingly violent and phonographic movies, as President of the United States, I join with worship leaders to mourn the loss of lives but not the loss of their product. Other world leaders share this sentiment. It is encouraging to note people turning from evil and towards God.

The New Madrid Fault, inactive since the big quakes in 1811 and 1812 remains stable through the Central Mississippi Valley. However, communities in North East Arkansas, South Eastern Missouri, Western Kentucky and Southern Illinois are on constant alert for seismic activity. Centers in Cape Girardeau, Missouri and Little Rock Arkansas continue to monitor.

There are areas of devastation similar to the San Andreas quake around the world. One example is the 2010 Haitian quake that killed hundreds of thousands in Port Au Prince, the countries capital. Seismic activity continues to increase in the far ease and on isolated islands."

Videos of devastated areas flashed across the screen, following one another in rapid succession, each more unbearable, each featuring destruction suffering, and death.

A small mid-Michigan family spellbound as usual by reality TV questioned their father. The oldest boy wanted to know who San Andreas was and why all that terrible stuff was his fault. His father said "He's the second cousin of the New Madrid Fault."

They said "Oooh!. They were so proud of their dad. He knew everything.

"Our cousins live in New Mexico and Virginia. We know it ain't their fault," his three year old daughter lisped and snuggled closer to her dad.

The pictures and solemn music ended and the President's speech continued. "Those of the Christian faith turn to the Biblical book of Revelation and say… and perhaps rightfully so, that we are in the end times.

Perhaps this is true. Perhaps not. We need to remember that in the Psalms, it is stated that to the Lord, one day is as a thousand years or a watch in the night. Militarily, a watch in the night never exceeds four hours. God holds eternity in His hands. We are not that privileged.

Those who do not follow the Judeao Christian ethic cite (over and over again) time and place as predicted (countless times), prophecy by Nostradamus and far eastern philosophers. Others look to outer space, star gaze as if the stars will share their secrets, and ponder the positions of Jupiter, the sun and moon. Sadly, after all we have suffered some of you tune out, turn away, and grab what you call life with gusto.

National Security advisors and top scientist have confirmed the existence of satellites carrying the only weapon known to completely annihilate all air breathing life forms. How long they remain in safe orbit is up to God.

To this end the United States and nations of the free world are stepping up the shelter program similar to that used during the cold war of the twentieth century. Families will be given materials and plans for shelters. Basements of all apartment buildings and homes will be so converted.

Be assured, time is running out. Nationality, faith, origin, military might, or home address, humanity shares a common destiny. It is for all of us to get right with God and prepare as best we can.

The good news and there is good new, the deadly dust has a life span of only fifteen minutes., United, we can save ever life on this planet When we stop trying to kill one another and build shelters, we will all survive.

We stress again that after the deadly dust penetrates our atmosphere and settles on our earth, its effectiveness is a short fifteen minutes. Your life or death will be determined in that short time span by the work you have done to survive.

The bad news and this is very bad news, scientist cannot predict exactly when the dust will fall. It could be five years, or 10, or 50. We do not know. We do know it is the duty of every person to be prepared.

For updates check my web site WWW.the Pres.com."

*　　*　　*　　*　　*

Male response (In every language) "What the hell, another War of the Worlds? H.G. Wells died a long time ago. Who knows maybe Stephen King done come outa the grave and wrote that, or one of them science fiction writers put her up to it! It was bad enough a few years ago when our leaders first started talking about it, but this is getting on my nerves. Why don't they shut up and leave us alone?"

Female response: (In every language) "Honey build us a shelter. It wouldn't hurt and it would be fun, cost of vacations and all, we could camp out sometime. Please honey."

Male response: "Don't nag me woman. I'll get around to it sometime. Gimme another beer"

(Note: Choice of beverage varies. As this is written in America, beer works).

FIVE

FOUR YEARS LATER: UPDATE FROM LEADERS OF THE FREE WORLD:

"My fellow citizens. We are grateful for your suggestions and have explored the possibility of using underground caverns as natural shelters. If it were possible, we would. However, multiple problems exist...

As stated, the extermination period of the dust is 15 minutes. Fifteen minutes does not give sufficient time to transport and off load one person, let alone hundreds. At that time, the only possible survivors in caverns will be those touring. And we cannot move people or animals to these areas for an extended period of time as they would not survive. Creating satisfactory living conditions would destroy the caverns, take at least a decade and create astronomical expense.

Historical footnotes: Over one hundred years ago in the United States, attempts to house tuberculosis patients in natural caves failed. Temperature variations and dampness sealed their doom almost as fast as the disease.

Our solution Project Underground is based on studies done of survival of persons and animals in arid regions. It is fast, efficient and proving successful as farm animals, house pets and their caretakers begin living in man made shelters in arid regions."

Teleprompters flashed.

"This just in scientifically and astronomically, reports show the satellites are gradually veering off course. This indicates predictions are true and time is short. It does not give us a time frame. If you do not have a shelter or have not prepared your homes, there is no better time than now to get it done."

From around the world, the male (i.e. masculine, strong arm, body building aggressive response: "Are they ever gonna shut up?")

(See last chapter for remainder of male/female conversation).

ONE YEAR LATER:

"My fellow citizens, the satellites are in a collision…"

Male response: "Are you still listening to that crap? I swear, if I hear about impending doom and apocalypse, I'm gonna bust that damn TV. Damm crap even cuts into my games. Bring me another beer and shut up with that but honey crap. I told ya I'd get around to it didn't I?"

*   *   *   *   *

President Brown-Parkinson placed the netted White House bird house on the floor near her oval office desk, adjusted her bi-focals, and scanned her folder of letters from Tasha Maureen O'Rourke.

Dear Mrs. President:

I did just what you said, and didn't tell anyone at school I knew about the contest before it was announced. It was the hardest and just about the best secret I ever kept and momma said she was really proud of me because keeping a secret is not the easiest thing for me to do.

Anyway, when our principal made the announcement at assembly he said since our middle school was so big we'd do the contest right here and everyone could vote for the best picture.

I raised my hand to tell him that wasn't the idea, but then remembered in time.

As you can tell, my picture didn't win and I'll never know why a tank with a big red white and blue flag on it won.

Some kids say it's because the principal's grandson drew it and they wanted to score with her, so they got together and voted on it. Is that legal?

There were lots of other pictures prettier than that old tank: pictures of families and flowers and the most beautiful sunsets. You would have loved the pink and gold shafts of light climbing up into the evening sky just as the sun sorta went to sleep. Some sixth graders drew pictures of you and your family at the white house and they did a good job too. The lady even looked a little bit like you except for the hair. Yours isn't grey is it?

I asked my momma if I could send you my picture of the Flag with a big gold cross in the background and beautiful shining clouds behind it and she said "Why certainly, my dear I'm sure she'd love to see it."

My mother always calls me that (my dear) when something I do makes her proud and happy. So the very next day I went to the post Office and got a special envelope one with the bubbles in it because I didn't want anything bad to happen to the picture, and addressed it myself in my best cursive (did you like that?) and sent it to you.

It wasn't two weeks later that my momma came into our room when we were having social studies and said she had a very important message for me. She walked up to Mr. Hale's desk and he looked at the envelope in her hand and said "Oh my! Oh my goodness!" He sat down real fast like he was a leaky tire or something. He looked really funny.

I am glad to see your letter is handwritten just like mine and, I must say your cursive is very nice. And also, thank you for remembering to do the capital R in O'Rourke the way I asked. That was important to me.

I pulled out the letter you wrote and read it to the class and they all applauded.

By the way, I've been thinking maybe I shouldn't have sounded jealous about the tank drawing. I'm really glad you didn't mention it.

Then I felt something else in the envelope and pulled out the picture of you holding my picture. Gosh, that was wonderful and I'm glad your hair is such a pretty dark color too. Momma said she wouldn't be surprised if it turned grey what with all the trouble you inherited in your administration but I said to her "Momma, maybe she touches hers up at the beauty shop like you do." And momma told me we wouldn't talk about that any more.

The school principal called the local paper and they took a picture of me holding the picture of you holding my picture. I'm sending you a copy.

I think my momma is the nicest and smartest woman in the world and you're just like her. I told her when I grew up I wanted to be just like you and her. And she said then I should stop writing this letter and study for my Geography test so I will. Especially since you told me you knew I was a good student and all.

P.S. I like your idea of us being pen pals. If we did e-mail it would save us money.

Very sincerely yours,

Tasha Maureen O'Rourke

Xoxoxoxoxoxoxoxoxoxoxoxoxoxoxoxoxoxoxoxoxoxoxoxoxoxoxoxoxoxoxoxoxoxoxox

That's a lot of love case you wondered

Dear Mrs. President:

Hi! It's me Tasha Maureen O'Rourke again.

I'm really glad to be able to talk to you because right now it seems there ain't too many people listening to us kids

Remember when you started the TV broadcast about families getting ready for something that might happen sometime within the next ten years or so? Well, my momma told my daddy he should listen to what you were saying.

My daddy told my momma he was sick and tired of politicians telling everybody what to do and all he wanted right then was to take his shoes off and have a cold beer.

When my momma tried to reason with him he just said something terribly rude. He said "Shut up and bring me a Bud."

Well, my momma said she didn't marry him to be treated like dirt and if he wanted a cold bud he could get it himself. Then she kissed him on the cheek.

Daddy looked embarrassed. When he saw I was watching he said something about little pictures having big ears and then said since she was so tired, he'd have his sweet little girl get it.

I looked at momma and she shook her head and I kissed my daddy on the cheek momma hadn't kissed him on and told him I wasn't old enough to handle alcoholic beverages.

He said some words I've never heard but once or twice before and don't want to hear again but let me tell you if I used them he'd have washed my mouth out with Ivory soap. He did it once. It tasted awful. But it was funny.

So my favorite pen pal, I hate to add more problems to all that mess you're facing with the economy and foreign relations and arms build up and everything else, but what am I supposed to do?

I do pray a lot like you said in your last letter.

Thank you for sending me a picture of your husband and your twin girls and twin sons and Randy. Does your single son (is that right? Anyway, he's not a twin). Does Randy have a girlfriend?

Daddy says he wishes I'd stop telling you about his nightly can of beer. See in the picture he's trying to hide it with his right hand. He can be silly, but he's a good dad.

I'm next to momma and back of us and momma is my big sister Martha home from college. The only reason momma is not on daddy's lap is our dog Einstein beat her to it. Einstein is just about the prettiest and smartest American Eskimo dog in the world. That's why we call him Einstein. See the way he grins? All we have to do is get out a camera and he's ready for a picture.

Your loving pen pal,
Tasha Maureen O'Rourke

Dear Pen Pal Mrs. President:

You will be happy to know I did it just like you suggested…

I've become pen pals with eight girls all over the world. Two are close by, like Canada and Mexico. They are Roberta and Carmine. Ma-Ling lives in Vietnam and Olga lives in a town with a great big name in Russia. Vladistock I think it is.

Can you believe a girl in Ireland has my name and feels the same way about the capital R? Rosalind, the English girl, says she's finally old enough to have high tea. I've no idea what that means, but trust me, I'll find out and also why they pronounce the name of the River Thames as Tims. Did they forget to use the H?

There are mysteries all around us aren't there?

Yulainne (she pronouncesYulainne like the Y is a J) lives in Burundi, Africa with her mother, father, sister and four brothers in a two room hut. She says they're doing really well, because there's so much more room now the second room was added. Boys and men sleep in one room and girls and women in another. They don't have beds, they sleep on mats. Can you believe that? She says they are lucky to have enough to eat and a church keeps them supplied with clothing and medicine. She's told me stories that make me cry.

Soon I'll have a pen pal in Wales. Lellylyn is her name. When I say her name, it's like I'm hearing bells.

Anyway, what I started to tell you is my pen pals and I are all pretty much the same age and wonder about the same things. Our skin colors are different and we don't eat the same thing and if it weren't for translators in China and Russia helping with out letters we'd be in big trouble. We're different sizes and have trouble with pesky boys, and are serious about our studies. We are all Christians and every day at a certain time we kneel and pray for our world leaders and for peace on earth. Like you said, that is very important. Each of us tries to get others to join us.

I find it almost unbelievable that in our own way, we're all interested in economics. Some see it as a community, while others of us look at the world wide picture. Oh this is so exciting.

Were you really interested in economics when you were my age?

Did you like boys too? Sometimes they can be such a problem. Why do they like to cause trouble? For awhile I thought it might be a good idea to tell them they couldn't have any more of my Krazy Kake (which won a blue ribbon at the 4H bake off at the county fair), if they didn't behave.

Momma said that wouldn't solve the problem. They'd be good, just to eat the cake and misbehave again. We talked it over and decided I should teach them to make Krazy Kake and then together, we could share with kids that never had any. She said butter is better than guns any day. Maybe I get my interest in the world wide economic view from momma. It sure helps to know that you, my number one pen pal were also interested in the subject when you were my age.

Daddy found that magic day he called "any day now," and built us a shelter outdoors. He has something he called a Quonset hut he bought at the army Surplus store. He put it in the biggest hole I've ever seen in the back yard and covered it with the dirt from the hole. Then he planted pansies on top. Purple and blue. It's pretty. In a humpbacked kind of way.

Daddy said his grandpa had one like that about a thousand years ago during what they called the cold war. Do you think he was kidding? I mean about a thousand years ago. We studied the cold war in history class. I think he was kidding.

Momma has piled up a ton of dirt around all our basement windows. She says for the first time she's glad we don't have a sliding door exit in the basement because it sure would be hard to dirt it all in. Or did she say pack dirt around it? Anyway, that would be a hard job.

By the way, daddy very nicely asked me to stop telling you about his beer. He said you had other things to think about. I said you said you enjoyed hearing about family life in mid-America and he said the next time I wrote about him to write about his hobby of building bird houses so I will, but watching his face when I wrote about his Bud was more fun. As you know, his bird houses are really nice. Do you think Randy would want one?

Momma wants to know if you'd like more Apple Butter. Did you like the spicy or do you prefer the plain? I know Randy ate almost a whole pint of the spicy before you stopped him. That was so funny!

Momma says most Apple Butter recipes just add cloves and cinnamon but she likes to add ginger and nutmeg and just for fun sometime she adds red pepper flakes. That's the kind Randy likes. Tell you what, we'll send a couple dozen pints of each so you won't have to fuss at him. I wish you could all be here when we make Apple Butter. The house smells so good.

Daddy's getting a lot of over time at the power plant. He says when school's over for the year he plans to take you up on your invitation and we'll come visit again. He says the Fourth of July would be perfect although I wanted to see the cherry blossoms but he can't get off then and we'd have to hurry home.

We'll probably have more fun than we did last year. Remember how we brought our portable grill and daddy did burgers and dogs right on the back lawn. Your Secret Service people really enjoyed the hot dogs.

Remember the picture you took of me sitting in your chair? Remember? Oh gosh! There's so much to remember.

Daddy said he'd never forget the look on your face when he gave you the White House Bird House. You said you'd never seen anything like it and the detail was perfect. Randolph senior, and Randy agreed it was real art and should go to the Smithsonian or to your Presidential Library, but you said as long as you were sitting in the Oval Office it would be out doors where you could see it. You said when your administration ended, you'd be sure to take it with you. By the way, did the Orioles have babies?

I said if we really get to visit, you have to promise me you'll take a few days off and relax. You were so busy last year it's time you took a little at home vacation. You do so much for all of us.

Please, oh please, let us take care of you for a few days.

We could do all the fun things you remember doing as a child at your Grandma Brown's house in Missouri. Except fishing for catfish of course. I'm sorry the Mississippi river isn't closer so we could.

Maybe you could tell those important Washington people some people that voted for you are coming to visit and they can come back later. Oh! I wish you could! Why not? Just because you are President doesn't mean you have to work all the time does it?

I am really looking forward to visiting Arlington again, and I do love all the Presidential monuments. Especially President Abraham Lincoln. There is something so grand and heroic about that. And isn't it wonderful that President Roosevelt's dog Thala is by his side. What would be great is spending more time at the Smithsonian. Especially the historical wing.

There's so much history to see in our capital. Momma says I need to make a list of what we have not seen.

Momma says I'm a curious young woman loving history and economics and classical literature, but I said so did she and so did you and why shouldn't I?

We read 1 Corinthians Chapter 13 and 14 last night at family devotions and talked till almost midnight. Tonight I get to pick and, I'm reading from Romans, my favorite book. I like the ending of Chapter Eight because it says nothing, not even death can separate us from the Love of God. That promise helps me sleep at night and keeps me singing during the day. I know no matter what happens, the Love of God is with us, and because we have you for a president, America will pull together in any crisis and be better.

My goodness, I've really rambled this time but all this seemed important. There's a lot more I wanted to share but it will have to wait.

Momma is calling me to supper. We're having baby back ribs, and momma's famous potato salad and corn on the cob, and fresh Big Boy Tomatoes and cukes from our garden and, for dessert, momma used your recipe for Apple Brown Betty. She says making the crumbs out of English Muffins and using real butter makes it perfect.

Wish you could all be here with us.

With all my love, your pen pal
Tasha Maureen O'Rourke.

Dear Pen Pal Mrs. President,

I am so excited.

We start our vacation soon as daddy gets home from work.

Momma just came into my room. She was crying. She said you called and said we should camp out for a few days in our shelter.

I cried with her though I'm not sure of everything, but I know it's scary.

Daddy came in just then and said they had the word at the plant (he didn't say what word) but they had to get the animals into their shelters. He said me, my sister Martha, and momma should get the cats and dogs and go to our bunker.

Momma said I shouldn't cry for what we're missing, but for should pray for your safety and the safety of everyone all over the world…

I was afraid for awhile and then remembered my favorite Bible verse at the tail end of Romans Chapter Eight. You know the one that says "Nothing will ever separate us from God's love." I'm holding on to that.

Whatever happens, I want you to know how much we love you and how proud of you we are for handling all the crisis this country has gone through. Personally, I think with God and you taking care of us, we'll survive and eventually we'll be a better country.

God bless you my favorite pen pal and your husband and your twins and Randy, and give you courage and wisdom and strength in the days ahead.

Maybe we won't come this next year, but look for us when the Cherry trees blossom.

With all my love,
Tasha Maureen O'Rourke

          *   *   *   *   *

President Inez Brown- Parkinson wiped her tears and looked out across the beautiful rose garden and up into the clear blue sky. It was July 3rd.

She opened her cell phone as she took the net covered bird cage and left the White House for her underground headquarters.

SIX

The following is a brief but true history of life:

In the beginning (before I pod and Spiderman, before wars and rumors of wars, before Black Plague and AIDS, and long before Bodacious the biggest dog in the universe and hand churned vanilla ice cream on Maple Brook Road in Sainte Lillian, Missouri,) God created the heavens.

The heavens as everyone knows are a great big place full of stars and planets. He made the sun to guide us by day and moon to sing us to sleep and make us wax poetic.

There are solar systems that thanks to the dust will never be discovered, black holes, and greatness out there up there, somewhere beyond the sunset and our weak ability to comprehend the vastness of creation. In short, God created everything.

God really liked what he created because He called it good. In fact, if I had been around then, I'd have begged God to create Ludwig Von Beethoven first thing so the rest of all the beauty He created could be done to Beethoven's music. Especially the Moonlight Sonata. But, I wasn't. Oh dear! I'm laughing at myself now because God being God not only had and heard the music of great composers, He also heard the stars singing.

How infinite is the reach and glory of God and how small and finite that of humankind!

Eventually, taking His time about it because God has an eternity of time and we have no idea how long that is, He separated land from water, fire from ice, sand from dirt... that kind of thing.. On this small speck of cosmic dust, God created all kinds of animals and mammals and fish and flowering and green things. Then he said something along the lines of "Man, that's cool, but..." (I wasn't there, I made that up, but He said something like that.)

That's where we come in. On this small speck of cosmic dust God created man and woman in His own image. We don't have pictures of God, but I know none of us could look like Him, because we're all so different. I finally figured out our God image is our eternal soul. Made sense to me and I stopped worrying about it.

Back to the story. God took these created people and placed them in the most beautiful garden ever designed.

All was perfection. Free food, free water. No headache or toothaches or PMS, or men griping because they wanted women to bring them a beer and politicians to shut up. All was peace. . Beauty.

Until Adam couldn't man up and blamed Eve for his own weakness.

The rest as has been said is history but a brief look shows man always in pursuit of killing and women wanting to know why we couldn't just get along. Man said "Shut up. Stop crying. Give us babies. We kill to stop killing."

Rich said "What else are we to do with the masses? We create weapons of mass destruction, train the poor, and let them kill one another and every 50 years or so stop long enough to clear the land before we start again

Yeah we know the intellectually illiterate call us war mongers and capitalist but how else are going to make money and run financial institutions?

They are so stupid. Don't they realize war makes money? A little trickles down to them. They get cars and mortgages on homes they can't afford because we have war. They get to travel and see the world. Why don't they just shut up and die the way they're supposed to?"

In the meantime little bitty wars in far away places with strange sounding names keep war on the tongue and, as the saying was long long ago, (thanks to warriors) "The beat(ing) goes on."

Around the world it was like "Rwanda? Iran, Afghanistan? Oh yeah, weren't they somewhere between the crusades, Hitler, and Sadam? Or was that after? Don't matter much, they all wound up dead. What with all this instant reporting and watching people burn to death, we get used to it. Let's party."

The irrefutable truth ignored by male ruled democracy, monarchy and dictatorship was scientist around the world had perfected one weapon that would end wars forever. The threat of it was enough to bring peace, because if it were unleashed, life of all air breathing creatures would end. Peace would come if ruling powers believed and acted accordingly. Earth could again become Eden. If the people believed, if they gave up selfish pursuits and worked together for world wide peace.

They didn't. Not in America, Russia, China, or the Far East. Around the world, male leaders scoffed at the idea of world wide destruction and pushed it aside. "Impossible. Ridiculous, Not in my lifetime," they said.

Ladies behind the reigning monarchs, presidents and dictators studied and believed. They lobbied for shelters and public awareness.

In their own diplomatic way, their men said what men have always said when ladies presented irrefutable truth and logic. Their 'diplomatic' response began with stonewalling and, when wives persisted they cut to the chase with "Shut up!"

Through whatever means at their disposal and these shall not be documented for the weak at heart would have trouble with women being so devious, almost a century ago all lethal dust was sent into the farthest reaches of outer space.

The ladies confident their mission was accomplished stopped talking about it. For uncounted years, it was considered mission accomplished. Then scientist began probing and talking to the ladies again.

Men in charge bearing a striking resemblance in paunch and manner to their predecessors lit their cigars, opened hundred year old bottles of scotch and went on with the profitable business of war.

Some warriors came home. Some, along with the innocent, died. Wives, mothers and fathers, sisters and brother, kith, kin and friends cried, and prayed, and begged and lobbied for peace. And men in charge said what they've always said.

Some warriors they say were healthy, unscarred and unscathed by what they had witnessed. Unscathed yet, everywhere, in every country, those who fought had the habit of constantly checking the sky.

Every day, they looked up, east to west, north to south. They looked up and felt a dread pushing at their hearts. Something was out there, up there somewhere, and they didn't like what they felt. But they couldn't name it.

SEVEN

The life of medically retired 100% disabled Army Sergeant Major Mark John Thomas, courtesy of the Veterans administration honoring his service to God and Country was comfortable. If being harnessed to a motorized wheelchair could be considered comfortable.

Life threatening injuries in the last little war in some place people hadn't heard of that killed only 75,000 insurgents and a few hundred peace keepers; made sure he would be comfortable for how ever long it took for his body to wear out. They didn't tell him their best guess was twenty years max. Why should they?

Sergeant Major Thomas' faith in a loving and merciful God kept depression away. He said he was lucky even though wounds that all but severed his spine ensured (barring a miracle) all but guaranteed he would never walk again.

Surgical and neurological experts at the VA and Universities said he'd never have kids either, but Evangelina took care of that. They had three: nine-year-old twin boys. First born Mark John the Second and the surprise package his identical brother, John Mark

All along the docs had said Eve was carrying one. "One Big boy," they said.

He said impossible she was as big as a barn.

She swatted him.

He was there when Mark John snapped to attention and he said to the grinning team, "You'd better get ready because here comes number two."

They looked at him and laughed. They knew better.

Evangelina pushed and said "Now!" They were the talk of the hospital for weeks.

Small as Eve was the second time he knew she was carrying a longed for daughter and the birth of Anastasia Evangelina his red headed freckled faced soon to be eight- year- old daughter made his life perfect.

It was the Fourth of July. Day to celebrate American Freedom. Day to party at the beach. Day to laugh and forget trouble and threat of trouble the President always talked about. Invisible things and dust from the sky was not on the mind of anyone this glorious Fourth of July. Not today.

Anastasia teased her brothers as they struggled with an overfull picnic basket. Mark cleared his throat and in his best commanding voice that they loved to hear, he issued orders that stopped sibling grumbling and brought smiles to their lips. They loved it when he called them troops. Loved the deep strength in his voice and knowing he was in charge and they should obey.

Anastasia giggled. "Daddy if we forget that watermelon momma will really give some orders."

They all regretted the Memorial Day picnic incident when the iced melon sat lonely on the front porch while they wheeled out to Lake Michigan. A repeat of that day was not in their game plan.

"Corporal Anastasia see to the melon now!" he ordered. And she hurried away while the boys began to load the van.

Evangelina snapped one more picture, told the boys to turn the military marches blaring from the radio down to less than ear splitting level, applauded Anastasia carrying the melon across the grass, and said "I forgot the beach towels. Meet me at the door hubby."

She hurried into the house, heard the voice of their president on the TV but did not then register words. She sighed, thinking of the hundreds of warnings, the endless speeches, and their perfect survival plan. "Not today," she said and reached for the remote.

She jumped over their golden retriever August snoozing on the landing, and hurried to the basement. With folded beach towels stuffed into her green and white beach bag, she started toward the steps. She remembered she'd promised the kids they could wear their dad's hats (but not his campaign ribbons) and rummaged in the old trunk in the sub basement. Which hats? Green Beret? Ranger? Regular Army? Special Forces? He had so many.

"Enney, meeney, miney, mo," she said and solved the problem the tried and true way. She closed her eyes and pulled hats and stuffed them into the bulging beach bag. Starting up the stairs again, she remembered the need for extra sun tan lotion and turned to the storage area. Feet finally on the steps, she paused. Eve said to Eve "Child you're getting as forgetful as your momma and you're only 30 years old. Snap out of it."

One last thing. Where was the white envelope from the VA? Her searching hand plowed through bottles, beach towels and tubes of suntan lotion, down into the bottom of the green and white beach bag. Searched, almost gave up, and finally at the last moment claimed the treasured envelope.

She knew its contents by heart but had to read it again. Skipping the overly wordy legalese, her eyes focused on "To discuss with your doctors and therapist the next phase of your therapy." She knew and he knew the only 'next phase' would be walking. First the bars, then baby steps alone, until finally he'd round home plate.

VA doctors wanted to tell him about the long road ahead but she said no. She was the one who'd wanted the surgery, who watched him struggle. She was the one who saw his toes move and legs jerk when they did that thing with straight pins.

She was with him when doctors talked about impossibilities, the long struggles and what if's? They said he had to understand the chances were slim to none. They were both tired of it. They dreaded the mumbo - jumbo more than they did the surgery and waited for results. Because they knew he would win.

It would be her job today, on this marvelous Fourth of July to tell him it was time to get a for sale sign on his motorized chair. To tell him their prayed for waited for miracle was happening.

Prepared to again maneuver over August, she jumped and only the grace of God kept her from falling face down. All that was left of August was his Spartan Green collar. "Darn dog!" she groaned and checked the door. Closed like she left it. That meant he was hiding in the house. "O.K., you dirty dog, don't be a coward" she said in her best Edward G. Robinson voice. August always watched Turner Classic Movies with her. His ears always perked up when she imitated voices. Not this time.

She tried again. Her best James Cagney "I'm a Yankee Doodle Dandy Born on the Fourth of July." She said it. Nothing. She sang it. He always sang along. Always. Golden head back, amber eyes gleaming, he'd nudge her first and then with a wag of his bushy tail, snuggle against her on the couch and sing.

The kids said he did it because she howled but she knew he did it because he loved to sing. She settled on the brown leather couch and sang. And waited. August did not come.

She switched to a plaintive whining Scarlett, the one that always brought him out to kiss her face. "But Rhett, what shall I do? Where shall I go?" Tears of a lost and frightened soul were in her voice.

Nothing.

Slowly now, cautiously, she opened the back door and stepped onto the deck. Her eyes scanned the back yard. Empty. She listened and heard nothing. No bird song, no squirrel chattering, no music from the radio. No kid noise from the pool across the street. She walked to where her favorite chauffeur should be waiting arms outstretched to pull her into his lap. He was not there.

She remembered the TV and the voice of President Inez Brown-Parkinson. A voice as commonplace as buzzing blood sucking mosquitoes. But different somehow. Sadder like she was crying. She'd cried before and begged Americans to prepare. What was different this time? What had she said? What? Her mind was as blank and dark as the darkest night, as dark as night without stars or lights anywhere. Dark.

She remembered the music blaring after she'd told the kids to turn it down. Had they? Did they? What then was that long long rising note on a tenor trumpet? It seemed to follow her indoors. Was it music or the warning siren? Her heart, her breathing, her thinking stopped as she stepped into the silent empty yard.

When Eve raced to the basement for the forgotten head gear, John Mark called to his waiting kids. "Turn the music down and pack em up, we're moving out troops." He laughed at their salute. Then he heard the siren long and loud cutting the air with its urgent warning. Something drew his eyes toward the clear blue sky.

Together John Mark and Mark John said "Daddy listen. It's like the President is crying. She wants us to repeat after her the Twenty Third Psalm. We know that don't we daddy. We can say it: Listen to us daddy."

"The Lord is my Shepherd
I shall not want.
He makes me lie down in green pastures
He leads me besides still waters
He restores my soul
He guides me in paths of righteousness
For His names sake.
Even though I walk through the valley of the shadow of death
I will fear no evil
For you are with me…"

Their voices muted that of the president. "Daddy you always said we were supposed to obey the President but you're not. Why are you crying daddy?

Anastasia looked up and squealed in delight. "Look daddy the stars are falling and they're all pink."

She said "Daddy" again question and amazed wonder in her voice. Then the "pink stars" touched them, blanketed them and they were gone. He had time to cry "Oh God!" before he felt its touch. Then he felt nothing.

Evangeline walked into the side yard. His chair was empty. Momentarily, a surge of joy. She thought he knew. She thought he'd waited to surprise her. She took countless jerking almost automated steps forward and stared. Not empty. His clothing was there; crumpled, sleeves over the arm rest. Blue jeans like he'd stepped out of them. Old straw hat the kids loved there, on the thick green lawn. But empty. Everything empty.

She watched Mark's new dark blue jeans wrinkle and slowly fade into the braces that held his legs; leaving only the slightest suggestion someone had been there.

As she watched, everything seemed to fold onto itself. Empty. She looked toward the van and saw her kids clothing, crumpled. Empty.

There in plain sight her watermelon on the driveway, spread open as if hit with a hammer, red flesh embedded with black seeds. Next to it, the fallen Tupperware bowl of potato salad, the green top loosened in the fall and spilled chunks of potatoes, green celery and yellow eggs splayed onto the driveway.

She moaned and thought, It's like body parts, like someone has been murdered chopped up, and tossed aside.

Packages of Kosher Hot dogs, jars of dill relish, bags of buns and two containers of their favorite Klingers sweet hot mustard were scattered like toys from a hurriedly emptied toy box. A box of graham crackers, bars of Hershey's chocolate and a big bag of marshmallows looked like they' been tossed aside and the picnic basket like it had done a double roll as it fell from the hands of her sons.

Minutes ago, a lifetime ago, when she went indoors the boys were there with the basket, teasing their sister, and she was giving it right back. Giggle for giggle. Now? Where were they? What happened?

Where was bird song and barking dogs? Where were the kids across the street? Where were other families and the cars? Why did she smell burning rubber? Why was there so much smoke? Smoke meant fire.

She screamed and the only sound was her voice. It echoed and bounced from house to house down the wide empty avenue, crossing from brown house to blue, to the house with cranberry shutters and the little green house always decorated for every holiday. Sometimes the family forgot which switch was the switch, and Halloween and Memorial Day and Christmas and Easter and Fourth of July lights blinked their message of cheer and fun at the same time.

Eve ran into the street screaming names of her family and friends. They became a bouncing echo, rolling like marbles down the emptiness of space.

EIGHT

"Go to Medical school boy. Be the best you can be." That was the song his mom and grandma sang every since he'd been a boy and started fixing things. "Fine, I'll be a Marine," he said and they laughed. They knew every boy fell for the Marine Corps posters. They knew it was his way of joking.

He went to Medical school and absorbed everything. His professors had him on the fast track for The Mayo Clinic and or John Hopkins. He didn't care as long as he could work to heal...

He saw every surgery, was at every autopsy. He questioned everything and found answers that didn't exist. When they said tumors couldn't be excised, he found a way. When they said brain surgery was next to impossible, he did it.

Now on a Fourth of July break from his end of residency at the Mayo, Thaddeus Greer spent every spare minute at the hospital, which was going through yet another name change. Hometown folks, so tired of the rigamarole associated with different health corporation ownership decided to call it The Local.

The story made headlines and TV newscast so even strangers knew when "The Local" was referenced, it didn't mean a restaurant or bar. Though it was rumored the best subway sandwiches and chili in town were to be found in its cafeteria. Salads weren't bad either, the ladies guild and volunteers said. Especially when you could put on as much low fat turkey or cheese as you wanted. Same price. Free coffee or tea for adults and milk for the kids. Somebody in town who loved the hospital and was grateful for miracles performed on a family member donated the beverages.

"I got my money on you headin' up the Mayo" Rosie, his favorite aide said. She'd know him forever, every since his momma brought him to take your kid to work day. Watched him. Liked the way he asked questions. She helped him get a job on the surgical floor when he was in high school.

Hey Rosie this is America. We got us a black Jewess president."

"Hold your horses boy. Get your stories straight. She's a Baptist. Ordained Minister matter of fact. It's her husband that's Jewish. Judeao Christian he calls it. He's a kid cancer doctor. Thought you knew that."

"I did. I mean I do Rosie. Problem is I've been up nearly 48 hours and need a nap."

Rosie snorted. "Even when you was a kid, you never was much for sleep. Your mom said you would study all night, take a shower and head to school while other kids were still in bed. Never saw such a one as you so interested in everything. Now you got yourself through your years of residency, you need a break. Why don't you go home, crawl into bed and rest your overworked brain."

Rosie don't sidetrack me like that. Let me start over. As President of these more or less United States, we have a lovely Black lady."

"Right so far boy, now how about the rest!"

"Coming up mam! You want fries with that?"

As usual, he made her laugh. My, she did love that boy.

After clearing his throat theatrically, Thaddeus continued. "Our President, the lovely and esteemed world renowned Inez Brown-Parkinson is not only an ordained Baptist Minister. No sir and Mam! Our president at the very youthful age of 45 also holds degrees in economics and foreign languages from Harvard." He paused and grinned at Rosie.

Knowing full well she'd unlocked his brain, she sighed and waited

"Her husband is the world famous Randolph Parkinson head of children's Oncology at leading Washington D.C. Hospitals. Her teenage son is a brainiac, her twin sons are nurses working with their father. Now that we're onto her family, I might add Donna Lynn and Doreen Lainey her twins in medical school are about the cutest…"

"Praise the Lord, he's noticed girls."

Thaddeus ignored Rosie's wide grin, and hoped she ignored the blush taking over his cheeks. Wasn't his fault the Parkinson girls were adorable and intelligent and a fair match for his enquiring mind. Not to mention the way they looked in bikinis.

"Both of them sharp as tacks and cute as buttons" his grandma said.

"As I was saying, Rosie," he said and paused maybe 10 seconds. Now her eyes were focused on his.

"We got ourselves…"

"Doncha go there boy. We done established the faith and leadership of the greatest president this country has ever seen. Move on boy. Move on."

"Thanks Rosie. Thought you'd never ask.

"Along with our illustrious leadership in D.C., we Americans have native born Russians and Iraqi on the Supreme Court. I find it only natural that I agree with your assessment of my capabilities.

Considering my bloodline, it's about time America had a quarter Chinese, quarter Blackfoot Indian, quarter full blooded Afro American and a quarter Irishman heading up The Mayo.. B'gorrah they need all the help they can get." It was their joke. Their secret laughter.

"Boy when you get to that ethnic line and you mark other, do you have room to put all you is made up of there, or does you really put Golden?" Her brown eyes twinkled. "Last time you was home you couldn't decide between that or 100% American." Laughing she shooed him away.

Responding to his Indian heritage, he danced warrior like around the corner and paused to stare into the long wall mirror reflecting the empty corridor. Thaddeus ran fingers through his kinky gold curls. "Golden." As usual, he laughed at the thought, although his six foot three muscular frame more than fit the image. He was golden. Skin, hair, eyes. Maybe the only golden boy on the earth. His amber eyes completed the picture and if girls had their way...but they didn't.

Thaddeus walked the hospital halls, comforting frightened patients, ringing for meds when his prayers and words of comfort didn't help.

He thought about the stone wall of auto immune diseases, the cancers that invaded all age groups and races; all the unexplainable horrors medical science couldn't cure.

Sometimes, he wished he'd never entered medicine; that he'd stuck with his childhood dream of being a mechanic. It was still his sideline, and there wasn't anything he couldn't fix. Spare parts made machines run again. New batteries replaced old. It didn't work that way with people. Try as hard as he could, he couldn't keep leukemia from taking a three year old or stop heart disease ending the life of a promising ballerina.

Thaddeus sipped green tea in the hospital cafeteria and hurried home to walk Bruno. Wait a minute. Brunoette. Ma said sharp as he was about most things, he'd surely missed when she wrote him about the stray black and tan German shepherd that adopted them. . "Walked up to the back porch one day, sniffed my hand and kissed grandmas and took over".

He said. "Mom, you're the one who told me she was a he. I don't claim responsibility."

Grandma laughed. "Adam and Eve all over again," she said.

Downstairs, down deep in their cool basement, he showered and crawled into his summer cave. Three of them were cut into the deep basement wall. Seven feet long, wide enough to hold box spring and mattress, lined with brick and under tons of dirt. He and his mom and granny had each dug their own, piling dirt above their caves, planting roses and vegetables over each one.

Sometimes, he spared a thought to the city fathers--Like once every year or so, around, Christmas, or maybe Easter. As long as he thought about what they would think once a year, he was comfortable with it. Their caves were their own business. They sure beat high electric bills for air conditioning, and as long as they were comfortable, it didn't matter. Nothing penetrated their caves.

Knowing his mom and granny needed a few hours extra sleep after working all night cooking up fried chicken and baked beans and their world famous potato salad loaded with secret ingredients for the church picnic he set his radio clock for 9:30. Then Thaddeus called the whining dog to his side and was instantly asleep. Whining dog? She doesn't whine, he thought and reached down to pet her. It was 7:30.

NINE

Submarine Captain Adam Dimitri Bladgovicz ordered coordinates set for Hawaii, and turned the helm over to his XO.

For eight months they'd patrolled the seas and now the USS Dove had one more stop before she headed home. One stop after months of secret missions and secret messages sent to the U.S. and the Pentagon. Thanks to the Dove, the shaking world peace was more secure than it had been in years.

Now the world knew the truth. Now the world knew the nuclear power of every Dolphin, Akula, Han Class Victor and Samson.

The world knew everything, and countries that called America war mongering aggressors were laughed off the air. The world knew. That was important.

Now his kids and kids all over the world stood a better chance of growing up in a safe world. Rather than become statistics, they could use their skills and intelligence to keep it safe With threats of war diminished this up and coming generation could truly represent the Christian faith as they fed the hungry, housed the homeless and saved lives for now and for eternity.

He stepped into the narrow passageway just as a crew member passed singing the last verse of the Navy Hymn. Its words echoed down the corridor:

Bless those who serve beneath the deep
Through lonely hours their vigils keep
May peace their mission ever be
Protect each one we ask of Thee
Bless those at home who wait and pray
For their return by night and day."

"Amen and amen" he said, and ran his fingers through his salt and pepper hair. He turned slowly toward his spartan quarters and was surprised to find his eyes moist with tears. Captain Adam squared his almost six foot frame and entered quickly.

The thought any crewman would see his tears was more frightening than hiding from depth charges or out smarting known enemies.. They had run silent and deep for months and been through more than anyone would ever know. They didn't need to see his tears. Why tears?

He knew his girls were getting ready for his homecoming. He could hear his daughters calling; their voices full of joy as he knelt to embrace them. "Daddy, daddy, daddy," their sweet trusting voices said and his arms ached with the need to hold them again

Zoe would be standing behind them smiling, waiting for his embrace. This was the year he would tell them he was home for good. They would live on their farm in the Blue Ridge Mountains of Virginia.

Life would unfold. He would be there for dance recitals and graduations and proms. He and Zoe would grow old together. Home. He was going home. Resupply in Hawaii, and home.

Adam remembered handpicking his crew of men and women from every sea going country. The pentagon said men and women couldn't crew together. China Offered to sterilize every member. Russia let them know any member disobeying crew orders would be terminated. Germany shared the sentiment with a twist: A barren wind swept hill in Germany near Weimar. Their isolation in a camp not used since liberation after World War Two would be permanent and a long life span doubtful. Great Britain sent "Chins up lads" and a 16 page booklet on the proper purchase, preparation, serving and drinking of afternoon tea. He kept that one. The others he read to the crew and shredded.

Addressing the crew before departure he was brief and to the point. "I hand picked each of you, worked with you as a unit for over a year and when we go on this top secret mission, you will obey my orders! You know what they are and why. If you are unable to obey, leave now, go directly to debriefing and remain there until we return."

"Sir! Aye Aye Sir!" they said as one.

The Dove started with 90 members and would complete its mission with 90 members.

Captain Bladgovicz sifted through his family grams, his eyes resting on the last from Esther his youngest "Peanut butter daddy. All you can eat, and my own special Krazy Kake. Like Great Grandma Mollie Kate taught me to make. I promise you won't have to eat any more lobster or T-Bone or Prime Rib till you absolutely want to. Hurry home daddy. Hurry home."

He looked at the Barbie Doll Clock securely attached to the bulkhead. His gift from his daughters would not be hidden. It was there for every man and woman to see. They knew it meant home and family. Doubtful a one of them had questioned or thought to comment.

His girls said no matter where he was, he would know what they were doing when it was 10 o'clock in the morning Blue Ridge time. He knew and when that hour came he joined them in prayer.... He knew this morning after prayers they would hurry home and pack up for the church picnic. Again tears stung his eyes.

Adam knelt by his bunk and bowed his head, thinking about Zoe and his girls. Remembering how they'd searched until they found the perfect place for their prayer bench. It was an uphill run, but that didn't matter.

They bought the bench at Lowe's, sprayed it three times with burgundy colored Rusto-leum and waited impatiently for it to dry.

Esther and Cheyenne used small fans to hurry it along and led the cheers when it was no longer sticky. He and Zoe loaded it onto the back of their ford pickup, secured it with strong leather straps and very slowly drove the gravel coated narrow road the winding quarter mile to the top of their mountain. Blue sky as far as they could see up and green earth as far as they could see down.

Now it was securely anchored there around the narrow lonesome pine bordered curve. "Perfect" they said, and perfect it was. In the most perfect place on their mountain, he would give thanks on their prayer bench for safe delivery and for their safe, secure and happy future.

Before he left this last time, they took a picnic lunch absolutely loaded with s'mores and apples and little else and sat there and prayed. His girls stared down into the impossible depth of their beautiful valley and he told them to remember him when he was down at the bottom of the sea.

Little Esther looked look at him with her big green eyes and pointed down into the morning mist making a wonderland of their valley. "Is the sea deeper than that daddy?"

"Oh yes my little one, deeper than that because wherever we go, the sea is home to fish and whales. Sailing ships and tankers and all types of marine craft are on top of the water. Daddy and his crew and other submariners are down with the fishes.

"Don't hurt the fishes daddy," she said and he promised. "Never," he said. "God gave the fishes their own radar, and it keeps them away from us."

Zoe said "No matter where daddy is every day at 10 o'clock our time, the time we have right here and right now, he will be at the bottom of the sea praying for us, and we will be up here on our bench praying for him."

Cheyenne his red headed freckle faced 11 year old said "And the bestest part is we may be jillions of miles apart, daddy down there with the fishes and us up here on our mountain top closer to the stars, but God will hear our prayers at the same time. It's totally cool."

Once again, he felt and tasted the salt of his own tears.

As if Zoe were there with him, he heard her calling the girls. "Time to gather your water bottles and snacks and hit the trail. We don't want to keep daddy or God waiting."

They raced for the bench, and collapsed laughing and breathless. At precisely 10 a.m., Zoe said "Let's pray for daddy and the crew." On the prayer bench and deep in the ocean depths, heads bowed and they repeated their favorite verses in Romans, Chapter Eight. "I am convinced that nothing can separate us from God's love. Neither death nor life, neither angels nor demons, neither our fears for today nor our worries about tomorrow—not even the powers of hell can separate us from God's love. No power in the sky above or in the earth below --- indeed nothing in all creation will ever be able to separate us from the love of God that is revealed in Christ Jesus our Lord."

They were there staring up into the heavens. He was near the bottom of the ocean. Nothing could separate them from love. Not God's, or theirs. Why then was he filled with sadness?

It was 10:20 on the pink Barbie doll clock when Adam ended his morning prayers.

He did not know then what happened on the prayer bench. That waited.

TEN

President Inez Brown-Parkinson leaned on the birthing stall wall and watched Veterinarian Selaine Blue finish cleaning the area after the birth of yet another healthy heifer. "Sixth Charlovoix this week. Sturdy little gal, and the longhorns aren't far behind. We keep this up and we'll have the finest herd this side of the Pecos."

Inez said four words she never wanted to say; four words that changed the face of humanity forever. She said "The dust has fallen."

Selaine sank to her knees. Her dry lips formed "When?" but she didn't wait for an answer. She thought of her husband probably making his usual stop at Arlington before he went to yet another emergency meeting of congress. The words they'd shared that morning were not I love you, but anger.

He did not believe as she did. He called everything she'd worked for a fool's mission. "You've got cattle and sheep and farm animals, and pets and bee hives and food crops in man made caves all over this country. You're supposedly part of a great scientific experiment, training school kids about other environments and methods of survival. You and your troops keep them underground for months and then send them home to their communities with plans for construction of shelters and environmentally safe living quarters.

And why? I'll tell you why!" His face was crimson with anger as pent up frustrations and questions exploded like shotgun pellets around her. Hitting her. Hurting.

"All this expense, all this media attention, this cave dwelling and underground shelters and list of things to do and don't do came about because some idiots convinced our president almost twenty years ago death would come from the sky and only those underground and under the sea would survive.

Presidents before Turnbull bought into it and now your beloved Brown-

Parkinson is stuck on that idea and all we're doing is spending tax dollars. People are tired, and sick of scare tactics and waste.

I bought it at first, but years of this crap is too much. I don't believe it and I'm not wasting any more time with you or the project. I'm done. You want me you know where to find me."

Other words, Anger. Disgust. Dismissal. Now their years together were empty memories. Now their kids and their home on the beaches of South Carolina were nothing more than videos and pictures in an album. Memories. Only memories. Now all things that meant life all over the globe were snuffed out like grains of sand in the Sahara, to never be counted.

Selaine found voice. Her question was an odd mixture of hope and fear. Hope they survived, fear they would be unable to cope. "The students?"

"Safe by God's grace, when it fell they were boarding underground for the trip. Their mothers are with them."

*   *   *   *   *

With the exception of prepared families, submariners at sea, vacationers underwater or underground, of Holy places in Jerusalem and around Israel, Enclaves of Christians in China, Russia, Iran and Africa, all over the Christian, non-Christian- uncommitted to anything except self, high society tobacco chawin' heroin shooting, drunken, sober, sophisticated unpolished democratic monarchies tyrannized world at 10 a.m., Blue Ridge Mountain time in the United States of America, life as it was for most men who had told women to shut up, ended for some. The dust fell. They died.

Latitude and Longitude didn't matter. Earth rotation didn't matter. Nothing man had labeled as "must have, to die for", or "The epitome of pleasure," over the centuries mattered.

If it was dark in Russia or the glorious golden sun was rising in the South Pacific. Nothing mattered.

Brides and grooms never kissed.

Mothers never held their newborn.

Shoppers and beachcombers disappeared.

Boys carrying picnic baskets and girls carrying watermelon became as vapor. Vapor that wavered for a heartbeat above the earth and was then away on a soft gentle breeze.

*   *   *   *   *

In Las Vegas Bacchus-King Midas, one of the richest men in the world, and owner of more strip joints and women than he could count, pushed the last of ten wheelbarrows of diamonds from his underground vault...

He scooped hands full and laughed as diamonds his gloved hands threw into the scented air reflected their shining multi faceted beauty. Blue, white, yellow and rose prisms filled the vaulted room.

His plans to draw more people into his empire would go on line today, the Fourth of July. They were better than the Lottery, much better than Publishers Clearing House, with its one twenty million dollar winner and a lot of people sorry they'd bought magazines they didn't want wouldn't read and had to literally sneak into hospital waiting rooms doctor and dentist offices because each year they were gifted with tons of the crap.

Better than any contest, because everyone enrolling in his diamond a day scheme would win. And want more. And follow him into his heaven. How could they resist? The first million people who sent him ten dollars in gold coins would receive their choices of a perfectly faceted one caret diamond; ring, or necklace set in platinum. For five more gold pieces he'd throw in a one caret ruby or emerald good luck charm.

When the diamond supply depleted; and he knew within three months it would be, 10,000 names would be drawn at random and each Grand Prize Winner and their families would win a trip around the world and opportunity to work and live near his island resorts. The poor unfortunate losers would beg for another chance!

He, Bacchus Kings Midas would give them everything. They would give him their devotion. He, the little dirty kid who ran away from home before he had chin whiskers, would be their god.

The self styled king spoke into his blue tooth and waited for the TV studio to answer... The answering machine, voiced by his favorite bedmate of the week, purred like a sexy starlet. Each word was softly expelled in a whisper of suggestion. How she could put so much sex in such common words would forever be a mystery, but she could do it. And he loved it. Sometimes, just so they could watch his excitement grow, he'd punch in the numbers while they were at his side.

While the message was always "I'm so glad to hear your voice. I'm so busy right now I can't pick up the phone, but leave me a message and I'll call you right back," each word was an invitation to pleasure, to dine on exotic fruits. He would never understand how common overly mis-used every day words could stir such excitement and lust.

He cursed. Tried the number again. Heard the same voice, the same message, felt the stirrings.

He called security. Tanned muscular Hercules, another bed partner, gave the same message in a strong all masculine voice of command. It had the same effect.

Cursing and yelling for guards that did not appear, Bacchus- King Midas ran from the vault.

*   *   *   *   *

Since I seem to be starting a cast of characters like the playwright I always wanted to be, Bacchus-King Midas, appears because he and his followers play a very brief but still major role in this story.

*   *   *   *   *

It would be too time consuming to list all air breathing creatures great and small above ground or water. Suffice to say, for over three fourth's of all the earths population (including over 10,000 species of butterflies), life ended. If in the predicted 15 minute time span they inhaled a minute particle of the dust, or if it touched them, they died.

In training camps, college campuses, prisons, hospitals, shopping malls homes of hope and homes of hatred. Life ended. In verdant pastures green and sheep with shepherds, in jungles with lions and tigers and bears, in homes with cats, kittens, puppies and dogs; for creatures great and small, life ended.

Great whales surfaced and nothing hit the water. Planes fell from the sky. Everything ended. In Sainte Lillian Missouri and everywhere.

Merciful this death and quick and pain free. Not always the aftermath, but that was a personal choice.

Not so fortunate the aquarium dwellers or underground reptiles and rodents but eventually they would turn on one another, eventually they would die of starvation. Eventually sewers would spill decayed bodies into rivers and oceans and eventually earth would be clean again. Eventually.

*   *   *   *   *

At 10:45 a.m. skies darkened and rain started. Underground sleepers woke, those searching for answers ran for cover, and the President of the United States sent the coded message to all submarines at sea.

ELEVEN

It rained. Sheets of water, great gusts of wind, more thunder and lightning than Evangeline had ever seen washed her, washed her earth, turned everything bright and clean.

It rained. Fires sputtered, smoked, soaked to the last ember, and stopped leaving skeletal hulks of planes, trains, automobiles, cars, busses, motorcycles and SUV's. In short, any motorized vehicle on land or water, anywhere, everywhere, on this lovely green and blue planet earth, that had crashed and burned, stopped burning, smoking, sputtering; and became wet soggy ash.

Some fires had engulfed city blocks. Some threatened forest. But there were no voices to cry out, no one to hear trees fall in the forest. Eve didn't know, and never would because this death ended that type of need to know.

She knew the chill of rain the lashing of wind and, she knew fear. Lost and afraid, she searched the streets of Jackson.

When a terrific white zigzag of lightning struck the massive oak tree across from the dairy she ran for cover through its revolving doors.

She saw a young man behind the counter tidying up what had been fun and celebration for families. She saw puddles of ice cream slowly oozing across the counter and onto piles of empty clothing.

There, a Winnie the Pooh baby seat, a pacifier, an empty Pampers, a bottle of formula. There shoes big enough for a four year old, a red bandana, sunglasses, blue jean shorts, a halter top, a straw hat. Formless articles of clothing like that in her yard, lay everywhere. She saw wedding rings, earrings, and a Barbie Doll pony tail holder on the floor almost on top of a pair of genuine imitation polished silver cowboy cap guns in their brown leather holster. Because her boys told her all real cowboys wore boots and a red bandana, Eve found herself looking for the cowboy boots and red bandanna.

In her search, she looked across and around the winding counter and found she focused on small American flags. Once the crowning glory to patriotic Fourth of July ice cream creations they made her think of the flag raising on Iwo Jima that showed a well won victory in a long ago WW11 battle for freedom. Flag supported and raised by brave men fighting for freedom there, and here, flags without support of any kind slowly sinking in the melting ice cream chocolate syrup whipped cream with chopped nuts and a cherry on top muddle.

Men fought and died so that flag could proclaim freedom. Her beloved husband was one of the brave men who put his life on the line to support all it stood for.

Now she watched as these confectionary little flags without support slowly slipped down a sugary chocolate ground nut filled maraschino cherry topped slope into the white mass of dissolving whipped cream.

Thunder. Loud, like a thousand kettle drums, and lightning golden and brassy. Both like the Fourth of July fireworks waiting at home in the van. The kids were so excited.

Another flash and she saw the boy again. Registered his golden hair and tanned golden arms, and thought of the mimes they'd seen on the Magnificent Mile in Chicago: silver, chocolate and gold. Like this boy. But he couldn't be a mime. He was moving towards her, his mouth was opening and closing. Something, some sound...words.....words she'd heard hundreds of times thousands of times somewhere, someplace far away from where she stood... came towards her like she was underwater.

Chilled to the bone, shaking uncontrollably, she stood dripping enormous puddles onto the black and white tile floor.

She sputtered, coughed, cleared her throat, did not recognize her own voice; yet she heard a flat monotone: "You... you, you're real, you're alive?"

"Yes, mam, I am," he said and Eve did the one thing she'd never done in her entire life. Not through all the fear and pain and suffering. She'd held her head up, supported her husband, fought for his right to a good life, cheered him on, and prayed with him. When his parents died in the house fire and he blamed himself for not saving them. She was his rock. She was always strong. Regardless.

Everything, through it all, she'd been steady and strong. Faithful. Dependable. Even today in the faceoff undeniable evidence, she'd held on to hope. Now faced with the reality she might be speaking to the only other living person on earth, she felt her knees crumple and welcomed the darkness. She desperately wanted it to be permanent.

A thousand years later, she woke fighting the sheets, calling her kids, reaching for her husband. Only it wasn't sheets, but a thick pile of red and white aprons. She pushed them aside, still believing she was in caught in a horrible nightmare. She had to wake. They had so much to do. Where was that silly dog? Why wasn't he nudging her, demanding she get up and busy? She didn't need an alarm clock she had August. Where was he?

"Drink this." A voice she'd heard before said. Tapered golden fingers held a steaming mug of sweetened coffee to her lips. She held onto the lifeline with shaking hands and gulped the hot liquid feeling warmth and her heartbeat return, feeling herself reach for anything resembling normalcy.

She heard something, a familiar friendly sound, a Fourth of July family fun type sound and turned to see this unknown unnamed but definitely golden boy scooping ice cream. A lot of ice cream; pistachio and black cherry and vanilla and chocolate, lemon and raspberry swirl and butter pecan. He topped it with red maraschino cherries and whipped topping, paused, added a sliced banana, looked at her.

You forgot the pineapple, the kids always want pineapple, and caramel syrup, and my husband Mark John has to have lots of chocolate and whipped topping," she said. As if expecting them, she looked toward the door.

His eyes did not follow hers. He busied himself with ice cream. For her he added the crushed golden pineapple and brown caramel and dark chocolate syrups, and an overly generous swoosh of high caloric full of country cream whipped topping. For her he made a showman's entrance with his creation. He took her empty cup and placed a long handled silver spoon in her hand. She stared at it. She needed four more spoons. Didn't he know? She turned toward the closed door. His voice brought her back.

"Me and mom and grandma we always pray before we eat," he said and obediently like a little girl she bowed her head folded her hands and waited. Waited for this unknown golden boy to find in this most horrible hour she had ever known some way to thank the Lord. He did.

"Father in Heaven we know you have plans for us or we wouldn't be here. We don't know what they are. We don't know what happened. We don't why our loved ones were taken so suddenly from us. We do know they are with You in heaven. We thank You for the promise of eternal life and the assurance we'll be with them someday. We do not know what tomorrow will bring but one thing we do know right now is we're sitting in front of a heap of ice cream and we'd better eat it. Amen."

Evangelina laughed. Suddenly, from somewhere deep down inside, she found laughter and with it came a strong stirring of hope. She would go home. She would gather their clothing and their videos and photo albums and a broken heart full of memories and she would mourn. Eventually, she'd head home to the hills of Missouri. Eventually. Farewells first, then home.

But right then and there, she had ice cream to eat. "Amen," she said and took a firm grip on the spoon. She peered intently into the mountain of ice cream. Her search was now as always for pistachio and cherry vanilla. They could have the rest. "Ah ha," she said and pushed a mound of whipped topping aside, and laughed at her kids sitting beside her, watching her, looked at her husband and winked. Because she always did.

Thaddeus did not see a defeated woman. He knew after the shock wore off, she'd grieve. But the way she sat and looked at him, and past him, he saw a resolve building. He saw a strong capable woman. He saw a survivor.

She was too busy eating ice cream to talk. But she could listen. He told her of waking at 10:30 wondering why the radio alarm was silent.

His bedside clock worked, but where was the talk show from Family Life Radio? He'd planned to phone in about the President, wanting to tie in her predictions with the Bible.

He woke his mom and grandma. They stumbled upstairs to the spotless kitchen, filled with the aroma of fried chicken and baked beans. There on the counter mounds of biscuits. There the jars of dill and sweet relish piccalilli and their favorite peach and spiced apple butter ready for the picnic.

He noticed Grammy had done it again, dipped into her coffee can savings to buy the red white and blue special plates and napkins and glasses. She'd bought the twenty ounce glasses, the tall ones because she knew her thirsty crowd. Everything was lined up on the counter ready for sweet iced tea and lemonade. Everything was so normal.

He went to the TV and radio. Nothing.

His mom called sister Eustice, Sister Charlene, Sister Maude, and ten other sisters, choir members, and every member in the First Baptist Church directory. She heard voices she would never hear again and, "At the sound of the beep, please leave a message."

She didn't. Giving up on local calls, she called relatives out of state and the mission team in Brazil. It took longer to hear nothing from Brazil.

While his mom worked the phone, his grandma worked the kitchen frying up potatoes bacon and eggs. "Thaddeus I'm gonna make you a pan of pepper gravy for your fried potatoes and fill you up and then you're gonna go out there and find out what's happened. You take the van. Me and your ma will wait. You might call us from your cell phone should you find anyone."

"Thank you Grammy" he said and sat down and prayed and ate what she put in front of him. Not because he wanted to, but because she loved him enough to do this for him and he loved her so much he could clean his plate for her. Twice. He did love pepper gravy over home fried potatoes with just the right amount of sweet onion. Bacon, ham and sausage on the side. And the way she did easy over eggs! Oh my!

When his defeated mother came to the kitchen, he was ready. "That boy dog of yours is fixin' to have a litter of pups" he said, and caught the flicker of her smile. "He'll need you around today," he added and she threw her arms up in mock surrender. "I'll name every gal after you," she said, and reached for her favorite dark blue coffee mug in the maple cabinet.

This time it was his turn to give in, give up, and get busy. "I'll go to the hospital first. Every time I find someone, I'll call," he promised. Hours later, he'd been to the hospital, the clinic, the stores and churches and parks. He'd broken into homes and driven past empty pastures. Lush green grass, fields of corn and soy beans, Orchards nearing full fruit.

With the air conditioner off and all windows of the van open, Thaddeus strained to hear bird song and animal noises. He heard nothing; no sassy chattering squirrels, no cawing crows or arrogant blue jays stealing from feeders; no soft cooing of the peaceful morning doves.

Thaddedus listened and looked and searched until his mind became a picture frame with nothing in it. Thinking maybe he'd find a policeman somewhere, he raced down Michigan Avenue until every building was a blur and the engine screamed for mercy. He ran red lights, went the wrong way down one way streets.

He walked into an empty jail and prison. On Michigan Avenue he broke the biggest brightest window of the most expensive jewelry store in town and stood drinking in the noise of the shrill alarm. Wasn't someone supposed to call? Would the alarm ring forever?

Once desperately needed noise drove him away. Everywhere he looked everything was silent and empty. Even the wind forgot to moan. Everything, where there should be noise and bustle and hurry, empty, vacated as if inhaled by a giant suction.

Yet what supported life, green grass and trees in full flush leaf of a ripe summer, sweet air and gurgling water fountains, hanging baskets of perfuming pink and white petunias, roses at the park, flower stands everywhere, all that and more was untouched. The silent world was beautiful. Thaddeus told her everything

Green and white ice cream made little spots on the corners of her mouth. Eve was staring at him as if his long convoluted tale had finally found a home in her mind. She dropped the spoon. Thaddeus used a napkin to gently wipe a stray cherry bit from her cheek. She turned and looked out the big window now full of blue sky and white dancing clouds.

No outdoor sounds penetrated their quiet haven. There were no bird songs or barking dogs or laughing kids racing for the parlor door. No cars screeching to a halt. She was therewith the golden boy, and the mounds of empty clothing and gobs of ice cream. Nothing more.

"They're gone." Her voice dry and factual. "They're all gone," she said, and ran from the booth and almost made it to the bathroom.

Thaddeus reached for his cell phone.

He took Eve home and watched as she stooped in the yard gathering small piles of clothing. Once, twice, three times, she bent to retrieve shirts and jeans and held them to her heart. Once she went to an empty motorized wheel chair and added the clothing to the wet empty pants and shirt there. She had so much to do.

TWELVE

Captain Bladgovicz had started his tour of his sleek vessel when Lieutenant Stephanie Reynolds, Communication Officer-in-Charge called him aside. "Priority, Sir," she said. The look on her face, the tone of her voice told her captain he didn't need to read the message. He returned the crisp salute and under a bulkhead light read words that confirmed his knowing.

Hawaii would not be R and R, but search and rescue. Code told him to expect no survivors. Duty told him to hope against hope and obey. It took them less than 12 hours to send the president their new coordinates

In the United States, and around the world submarines berthed at almost alien landscape. Quiet. Landscapes Full of buildings and familiar landmarks, void of life. Flags from every nation were raised and slowly lowered to half mast as Taps sounded over silent waters.

After two days, Lieutenant Reynolds reported her only contacts were with the president and other submariners. It was then the stupor of disbelief and hidden hordes of hope ended. Each Submariner turned to his or her own God and then towards what had been home. Some had many underwater miles to go before they slept.

Others, including crews of the DOVE and her sister sub the EAGLE and peace keeping crews from Europe turned to their CO's. Search and Rescue their mission, and in America, their destination the great gathering ellipse near the Washington Monument.

Long ago Martin Luther King had led a march there. "I have a dream" he said.

Hippies and yuppies and stoned out drunken peace loving war hating protesters had gathered there. Forest Gump found his true love there. And so much more.

Now that hallowed place waited for submarine crews and the remnant of a great nation. He knew whoever they were, wherever they came to light and air, they would be the new beginning of a new country. He found the thought terrifying.

Two weeks later Captain Bladgovicz stood at rigid attention in front of the great mahogany desk in the Oval Office.

He saluted the president.

"Captain Adam Bladgovicz reporting as ordered Mam."

"Welcome home Admiral," she said.

"Mam?"

"You heard me."

"Mam I appreciate the thought, but I came to resign not to be promoted."

"Admiral!"

He looked around the room for someone else. For anyone else. His eyes rested on the seal of the President of the United States. They traveled the walls traditionally covered with expensive artwork, now filled with drawings from school children. His right eyebrow twitched.

"With the exception of a few favorites, I have them changed every month. They are my constant reminders of the task ahead. Look at them Admiral. What do you see?

A slow perusal followed and he smiled at the thought of his daughters sending her picture

Cheyenne had written "I drawed her a picture of Esther watching the corn grow and of all of us on our prayer bench. Momma said I did the best job ever. Do you think our President liked them daddy? Do you think she'll hang them in her office?"

"I see what was and what someday may be again," he said.

"Exactly, she said and then, "I took these down this morning, would you please replace them in the vacant places near the Rose Garden Door." She beckoned him closer and handed him Cheyenne's pictures.

A memory of a childish scrawl carefully kept in the lines in her favorite pink bubble ink melted his heart. She had written: "I drawed them for her daddy. I drawed them for her daddy."

He took them quietly, held them reverently near his heart and after a pause replaced them in the vacant area near the Rose Garden door.

His eyes traversed the length and width of the Rose Garden. An old man bent over a brilliant red rose looking at green leaves, spraying them with something. Water? Why?

His attention was drawn to a birdhouse replica of the White House situated for the President to see as she sat at her desk. "Nice," he said. "A gift, a treasured gift from another young friend. Last year Orioles nested in the oval office" she said, and smiled.

Somewhere in the Rose garden…he liked to think near the walkways where children ran and families delighted in beauty, somewhere under that lush green lawn over 10,000 Civil War Soldiers were entombed. They were together, Union and Confederate. Deep, under tons of soil. Dead for a cause not now remembered. All now dust.

Was it there, near the pink climber his girls called Powder puff, or near the portico where blossoming roses named after first ladies sent sweet peppery perfume into the room?

In a heartbeat he knew there would be no Rose Parade or Rose Bowl or high school Rose Queens in rose hued formals smiling as they waved at family and friends from their thrones on rose floats. No more roses for Zoe on their anniversary.

Yet at the Rose Garden, every beautiful hybrid rose in the catalogues graced pathways. There were day lilies, daisies, Hostas of every shape and hue. Combined the flowers of summer made a beautiful yet sad picture he tucked into his heart.

Newly designated Admiral Adam Bladgovicz remembered his girls loving roses. Just like their cousins. He looked again at the art work of his daughters. How had she known where to place them?

When he again faced the president he noted that what passed for a smile was on her lips. Yet her eyes were rock hard… Harder.

"Am I not the President?"

"Yes Mam," he said and saluted again.

"As president of the United States am I not the Commander- in-Chief of all armed services?"

A question that was not a question stared him in the face. Rather than salute, he bowed.

"Madame President, as a loyal member of your armed forces, I respectfully request the honor of tending my resignation."

"Respectfully noted, and respectfully denied."

He snapped to a rigid attention. "Madame President I have served my country in peace time and in war and defended her against all enemies foreign and domestic. I am a warrior. There are no wars left to fight. Again, Madame President, I request permission to tender my resignation. I want to go home."

"Close the door Admiral, we have serious plans to discuss."

If he walked away, what could she do? Shoot him?

It was his choice to turn and walk toward the wide open double doors. His choice to continue walking. He could escape out the East Door and the rose garden, or easier still the North West Door and the closest exit. He could walk past all the imposing portraits, and under the gleaming chandeliers.

The heels of his polished dress uniform shoes could sound a final tattoo as he a hurried over the shining- even now- immaculately polished parquet floor. Across the red carpet, and out; away from duty and responsibility. He wanted to go home. Home to Zoe and his girls and their life together. More than want, he had to, he was compelled, he was pulled toward that beautiful log cabin and those dearest to his heart by forces greater than any he'd ever known. He had to go home.

OR, he could obey, and shut himself in with the President. They both knew it. When he closed the doors and turned to face her, his eyes were as hers.

He had said there were no more wars. She proved him wrong. This battle or world wide survival would be the longest in history, and the most difficult.

Two hours later his orders and responsibilities were clearly outlined.

"You may choose members of your crew, or keep them all. Give them a choice and give them five minutes to decide. More time than that is wasted."

He answered for the crew of 90. "They will stay."

"Admiral within the next ten days I expect a crowd to descend on D.C. That gives you and your crew seven days.

Your crew is waiting in the Formal dining Room. If you will escort me, we will join them for a light buffet and immediately afterward, your crew will be flown to their homes. They may bring anyone back with them. Take those that do not wish to make this journey home with you."

He bowed and offered his arm.

After the buffet, she promoted every crew member to officer rank, taking time herself to pin on the insignia.

The most awe struck new Lieutenant junior grade stared at her. "Mam iffin you don't mind me saying so, I was just a Seaman."

She frowned. Question in her voice as if she'd never heard anyone describe themselves as just an anything. "Just a Seaman? I feel…"

He interrupted. "Beggin' your pardon Mam but that means I was about the lowest enlisted rank. I had two little white diagonal stripes on a patch of cloth that was sewed onto my dress whites and pea coat. Otherwise, Mam, I just ironed them stripes on my official blue Government issued work shirts."

He took a deep breath. She, knowing a born talker when she encountered one, stood patiently smiling and waiting for what came next. She was not to be disappointed. He looked at his shipmates and grinned. "Well, Mam, what I said about the lowest rank wasn't exactly God's truth. They'se probably Marines and Army and Air Force guys got a lower rank, because they didn't do what I did and where I had to do it."

In spite of their resolve to be formal in the presence of their president, the entire crew of the USS Dove broke into spontaneous applause and cheers for submariners.

The president did her best to control her laughter as she waited it out and then asked, "And that was?"

"Mam I took care of the trash and cleaned the heads. Heads is bathrooms Mam and they had to be cleaned bout twice a day. And please Mam don't ask me what that was like. Since I'm an Arkansas farm boy, I kinda got used to the smells and such but Mam, if you don't mind me saying so, seein' as how I just wanted to ask what for you promoting me to Lieutenant Junior Grade, I done talked too much. Mammy always said I talked too much. I'm plum sorry Mam. Honest. Ask the fellas if you don't believe me. But anyways Mam if my question got lost back there, what for you making me a Lieutenant Junior Grade?"

"If I could, I would do more but I'll tell you what for. For your devotion to duty, for your ability to fight the good fight: For your determination to stay with your leader in the face of insurmountable odds that's what for and why.

Lieutenant Junior Grade Joe Jones you may not be a graduate of a prestigious school, but you have passed the test of honor and integrity with highest honors. America needs leaders of your caliber. That was part of my speech but now that it's said, I won't repeat myself except to say it goes for all of you.

Choppers are waiting on the lawn to take each of you to the airport where you will board jets that will take you to your homes. It is my hope and prayer you will find survivors and offer them the opportunity to return with you. Ladies and Gentlemen, do what you feel must be done. On the eighth day, we will all meet in my office."

Before they were dismissed, she said "My gratitude and prayers to the Almighty God go with you. I wish you safe journey, God Speed and strong hearts as we face this momentous task together."

They saluted. Tears in their eyes?

Admiral Bladgovicz wasn't sure, his were too blurred.

THIRTEEN

In the hunt for areas the dust would not penetrate, then President of the United States Zavier Turnbull had assigned members of the geological community to research the feasibility of creating a refuge for farm animals and their keepers inside national caverns.

On paper, the caverns seemed a perfect solution. However, plans on paper and reality were eons apart. Their report naming caverns in virtually every state, listed year rounding temperatures, unexplored depths and other issues was condensed to this conclusion:…"Natural and historic caverns found in nearly every state are part of God's work of art and worthy of visit, but they will not house farm animals or families. As we do not know the exact date of the coming satellite collisions, and resulting death dust hitting the planet, we cannot depend on these caverns. They are too deep, too unexplored and potentially dangerous for such a venture."

Scientist and engineers concluded man made underground bunkers where lighting, temperature and space were controlled was the lifesaving solution.

Work on underground shelters intensified as reports became more troublesome. Science could not say when, but they could say sooner than they expected. The way they said it was information enough for President Brown-Parkinson to speed up the underground program.

Instead of the six month training program, she shortened it to three, and after these months of exhaustive training, companies of Army engineers, Navy Sea-Bees, and Marine guards descended to rural regions in the farm belt and southwest. They set up shop, employed locals and established friendships as they dug deep and long. In each area manufactured homes and barns were perfectly climate controlled, for man and beast.

The working plan was to house, breed and feed farm animals and household pets. Employed families learned to live in underground bunkers.

Animals roamed and grazed hillsides and pasture lands by day and sheltered in underground barns at night.

National Geographic did a spread. School children studied the progress in weekly news reports and families slowly joined the parade. Too slowly to suit President Inez Brown-Parkinson.

To encourage American interest in underground living, the President moved her headquarters to an underground white house in the hills of Virginia. She gave virtual tours (without disclosing the location), and encouraged all Americans to pursue underground living. As always, she stressed the coming threat from the orbiting satellites and the need to save lives.

In the dry southwest, luxury adobe hotels were built deep into sandstone mountains. Advertised as the Great American Adventure, they drew families and school children. Visionaries, believers and historians took over and worked non stop attempting to educate a skeptical population; a population tired of political double speak and war.

They worked with a skeptical population, attempting to save lives as she and her predecessor had done.

Government worked. People watched. To a jaded population this mass movement was yet stupid government expenditure to raise taxes... It gave them pleasure to shake their heads and walk away. They walked faster when they encountered Marines toting guns and looking ornery when they got close to equipment and blasting caps.

One rumor was the lost city of Atlantis was out there somewhere, betcha your paycheck on it. Wasn't America once completely under water? Some men began exploring on their own but gave up when hillside caves collapsed.

Another, rumor that there was gold in them thar hills was replaced by the all round favorite; the caves were actually linked underground tunnels for movie makers. As rumors had it, "The movie was a "a sci-fi kind of thing and would revitalize the long silent Hollywood."

Every month of every year, scientist told the president and the president reported to the people that death was closer.

Every month of every year, earthquakes rumbled under every continent.

Every month televised charts, satellite positions and warnings became as common as sunrise and fuel for political cartoonist and pundits.

Every day, every week, every month, every year the people chose. Some dared to hope. Some turned away. "Too much information," they said. They ignored warnings as they ignored parameters set by traffic lights and speed limits.

With great reckless abandon, the over informed tired of war, talks of war, threats of death and fear of tomorrow Americans and people around the world chose the fast food pleasure seeking credit card spending "don't give a damn about tomorrow" life they knew.

*   *   *   *   *   *

The prototype fully functioning underground animal, insect, beekeepers farm (known locally as Noah's Ark) was in its seventh year of operation off Maple Brook Road near the little Ozark town of Sainte Lillian Missouri.

To see if they could, on which the basics of scientific wonder is often based, scientist from the University of Missouri and Michigan State University Agricultural School grew corn and soybeans underground under artificially controlled conditions. They created their own day and night, sunlight and shadow, their own seasons. If they did anything else, it was secret.

Gentle brown doe eyed Jerseys and black and white Holstein milk cattle seemed to have their own contest for most milk production. One month Jersey's won by the pail full and pound and the next Holsteins took over producing more; with a higher fat content per cow plus more sweet rich milk.

Agriculturist checked their notes and stirred ground soy into grain and congratulated themselves.

Polled (hornless) big Black Angus beef cattle ruled the west pasture and polled red Herford the East. At first they resisted underground stalls, but something about the aroma of grains drew them in and kept them content.

Brown-grey draft horses with feet as big as dinner plates, Palominos and Shetland ponies roamed at will in pastures among the cattle.

A basement hatchery housed a thriving flock of chickens and pigeons. Barn cats and a steady stream of gigantic Ozark only bodacious dogs roamed at will.

Problems were solved as they rose but one the college boys couldn't solve was the penchant for pigs to seek cold spring water and mud for their daily bathing. Pig puddles were never covered in labs. But caretaker and Farmer Noah Owen solved it in less than a heartbeat.

"Simple," he said "give them porkers a few heat lamps, some mud and decent water to roll around in and they'll be happy as any pig in a mud puddle."

His genius was applauded by the college boys.

Noah's questions that began with What? and "Why? As; "What are we doin this for? And, "Why are there so many kids here all the time? Day and night we get more kids to board and ship more out to who knows where, and I want to know why?" were answered in a document with such political double speak and signed with the seal of the President of the United States, he

56

couldn't decided whether to destroy or frame the whereas and therefore and in conclusion for the good of humanity and the furtherance of science."

Noah, being Noah, finally decided to put it with the old Sears Catalogue in the outdoor privy. Only it wasn't used as a privy. He'd just built it for the fun of it. Besides, in this smack dab marvel of a farm a feller had to make his own fun cause he had all he needed except company.

Them science guys didn't know how to talk and kept their noses in books, their eyes stuck in microscopes, and heir hands full of little test tubes.

Noah snuck back there one day whilst the college boys was at breakfast. He found something called a centrifuge whatever that was, and a sterilizer, and bottles and potions like he'd always thought witches kept in their secret lair. He looked once, and said "Boy howdee!" Noah up and promised the Good Lord iffin he got outa that place alive, he'd never go back there again. He did and he didn't.

Didn't take long for Noah and the wife to shed their lonelies by inviting their church group for Sunday afternoon potlucks. Birthday parties and such too helped.

Always they'd have a great big spread, tables plum groanin' under all the home cookin' and whilst the women folks were clearing the dishes, him and the fellers would sit on the bench and chaw and stare out the thick plate glass window and wonder about a lot of stuff. Sometimes, even the college boys joined them. Found out they could talk after all. They always got to arguing about sports. Far a Noah and the fellas were concerned there was only one sport and that was baseball. And there was only one team, the Saint Louis Cardinals.

College boys talked tennis and rugby and football. Noah and the fellas rolled their eyes and listened cept when they got to goin' on golf. Noah up and said how any grown up man could consider hitting a little white ball with a fancy stick a sport was beyond him. The college boys took the hint and talk went back to baseball.

Once the Michigan fella said something Noah didn't rightly like to hear about the President and Noah set him straight right off. "Inez has roots right here. We're kinda partial to her," he said.

"Inez who?" The smart young Michigan man stuck his nose right up into Noah's face and tried to stare him down, acting like he'd never dreamed common ordinary people who knew about pigs' penchant for mud baths could know much more than that.

Noah blew onto his tri- focal till the young fella couldn't see diddly from squat, and nudged him aside. "Inez Who? you asked. Whatcha matter with you boy? Doncha know the first name of our President?" While the educated boy stared open mouthed Noah reeled him in. "She's a home town gal. Next time she drops by I'll introduce you."

Give him credit though, once he recovered, that Michigan boy laughed along with the rest of the gang.

Coming up to summer, and already hot enough to fry an egg on your Chevy or sidewalk take your pick, one of the church deacon Will Williams he thought it was, said it'd be a fun thing to have their Fourth of July celebration underground where it was natural nice and cool. Bring their wives and kids and grandkids and have a real whiz bang time. After dark they'd sneak out and do up fireworks.

Noah didn't even think to ask Laney. He knew she'd go for it, liking to have folks around as much as he did. "Done deal," he said.

They gathered early that Fourth of July, about a hundred of them hurrying in to escape the heat maybe more counting husbands and wives, kids, grands and greats plus the passel of kid boarders and the smart young fellas.

Good thing they was all loaded with picnic baskets and such, each of them carrying enough for their own families plus five or ten more count of it was going to be a long day even with all the watermelons Noah had back in the spring and the freezers full of home made ice cream Once the women got busy, him and the fellers sat back on the bench and watched coon dog pups playing in the driveway.

One of them said "What' the heck fire is that stuff?

They watched pink dust fall and the pups disappear. The group of men sat as if frozen for over 20 minutes.

*   *   *   *   *

Laney Owen wife of Noah, mother of Evangelina Thomas, grandmother of twins Mark John the Second and John Mark and Anastasia one of the cutest red headed granddaughters in the world, plus a whole passel of kids and grandkids all over the country, eased the last of the ten breaded chicken breast into the bubbling Crisco oil and yelled to Noah to answer the phone.

He didn't. Fact is, he acted like he hadn't heard her. That man!" she said, and wiped her battered smeared fingers on the ever present red white and blue dishtowel tucked into her apron.

She called him three more times. Each time her voice went up a notch. After the third try, he managed to give a mumbled response. And it sounded like "Oh my gawd!"

She knew he didn't talk that way. Then it was like he yelled her name.

She couldn't be sure. He had the dangest way of calling her anyway and the way he sounded wasn't the least bit normal.

There she was with frying chicken turning golden in the vat of Crisco oil, salted water boiling for corn on the cob, listening to kids running back to the barn caves, and just full to the brim with the sweet harmony of busy women cooking and talking and laughing. She had no choice but to answer the insistent phone.

"Noah Owen, I'll deal with you later," she said. Her friends laughed. They knew the day would never come when she dealt with that man. One look from his big brown eyes was all it took for her to forget even thinking about being mad at him.

Laney made faces at the women and headed for the nagging phone. Funny the way it kept ringing. Usually after seven long shrill attention grabbing lengthy clarion calls, the answering machine picked up

She turned to the alcove and then saw the blinking red light. The thing was red enough to light up the whole dang area. Noah had told her about that. Said he hoped to high heaven they'd all be inside when and if that happened.

Then he wouldn't tell her no more. He hemmed and hawed and cleared his throat while she stood arms akimbo watching his eyes search the room for a hiding place. Backed into a corner, he head down to his chest he mumbled "Inez used to be Brown."

She looked at him. "Inez? You mean to tell me…"

Noah cut her off. "Yeah you know, the President, not Inez the baker, or Inez that plays the organ at the Lutheran church, our President, Inez Brown Parkinson, raised by her Grammy Brown, now President of the United States."

His head snapped up and laughter at her reaction was in his brown eyes. "Inez told me not to tell you that much. Said it was enough she'd scared me purt near to death. Didn't want me doing that to you with your weak heart and all."

She gave him a swat and laughed till her sides hurt. "Noah Owen you do beat all! You know a touch of angina is the only thing wrong with my heart. And you're telling me the president was concerned about that! You can do better than that Noah! '

"O.k. o.k., but its God's honest truth she told me not to bother you with that news."

"You need to stay out of that hard cider!" she said and then looked at him. Long and hard.

He looked back, didn't wink or crack a smile or nothing. *She thought if anyone ever asked her what a poker face was, she'd tell them about Noah's whopper, his face as serious as a heart attack and all. Seems like that long dead Jethrow Parker gave a little bit of his yarn telling' skills to his great grandson.*

Her hand reached for the phone but her mind directed her to find Noah. Last she knew him and the fellas was out on their hermetically sealed front porch talking about whatever men talk about and coming up with ways to stay out of the kitchen. Big as it was, three stoves and all, with a passel of women in there, they knew they weren't needed.

*   *   *   *   *

Since this was in the diary, it is included: "It *took folks in Sainte Lillian quite a spell before* they heard *about the wind that blew dust away from most of Israel. However, in some parts of Israel and places around the world that dismissed the truth of God as creator of all and of Jesus, the only way to true salvation and life eternal, life ended. Snuffed out like a candle by the wind*

There was no dying on Calvary Hill, where Christ was crucified and in simple homes in Bethlehem and around the Church of the Nativity. They said people lived because they were on Holy land.

Accepted thought was the Angel of Death had once again passed over the Israelites. Christians included. Which reminds me, if there's anybody alive who hated Israel, we haven't heard about it.

Seems like no matter which part of the world they lived in the dust got them and the earth swallowed the dust.

Petra, the rose red city carved from rock outside of Jordan didn't loose a person, a mule or a camel. I can't figure that out. They're just simple nomad people. Hear tell when tourist stopped coming to buy their genuine camel bone jewelry and the stuff they made out of stones, they kinda ambled out. It didn't take them long to move into kibbutz and start farming and tending sheep. Their saved lives cause me to wonder about their Biblical ancestry...

Eventually it was reported that in Africa and China where honest Christianity flourished, life went on as it had when Christianity began to spread those long long years ago. The people were like those recorded in the Book of Acts, Chapter two. "They were overcome with a great sense of awe, and were of one accord."

Chinese Christians survived while heathen neighbors didn't. Stories like that keep popping up. One I really like is the deserts are blooming and for the first time ever, there's enough food to go around. Balance is what is needed. Y'know, like before the dust we had people but not enough food. Now years and years after the dust, we have food but not enough people. All of this, truth or lie, don't know much what we can do about it from down here in Sainte Lillian, Missouri.

My thinking is where evil flourished it was snuffed out and where grace and mercy flourished they abounded even more.

However, I'm convinced our life won't be an easy street. History records in times of warfare when civilians were killed their deaths were referred to as collateral damage. In other words their dying couldn't be helped.

This catastrophe seems to me to be a war pitting good against evil. While so many Christians survived, I feel God's plan made sure there would be collateral lives (i.e. survivors of all religious, political and economic persuasions) to populate our world.

I know there and more dead than we'll ever count but the president said a pretty fair guesstimate was over ¾ of the world population was gone.

My diarist quoted Abraham Lincoln, who said it was "up to us to living to ensure those that died did not die in vain and that this nation under God would not perish from the earth." She said we had to get busy and work together to make that happen.

But I'm getting ahead of my story. Because, as I wrote in the beginning, this is my story; the story of my family and all who survived in and around the little Ozark town of Sainte Lillian, Missouri.

Maybe someday we'll know more about the rest of the world.

FOURTEEN

Again, I'm quoting from my great grandma's diary written two years after the July 4th when the dust fell, but this is part of my family story so it's o.k.

"As it has been since man was created and Cain had a jealous fit, there are men who, regardless of what rub life tries to teach them cannot, or will not will not pursue the path of peace. Therein lies the rub."

I'm not sure, but I think that part has something to do with the way some men acted after the dust settled.

"A group of them wound up at Noah's Ark. Without being asked, they blamed God. Second on their list was the president. "She shoulda told us what was gonna happen," they said. "Lookit what we lost. We ain't got no jobs. We ain't got no money. What we gonna do when we run outa free groceries?"

Laney stood hands on hips staring them down. "Noah, c'mere, them flowers you were talking about just arrived."

"Lady are you nuts? We didn't bring you no flowers and we sure ain't flowers."

"Stink weed, more like it."

Noah stood behind her surveying the rag tag bunch. "You're right Laney, it they ain't a bunch of blooming idiots I don't know what they are."

It helped Noah had a double barreled shotgun cradled in his arms.

The whiners and complainers didn't get a chance. First up, Laney; "You got eyes in your heads. Look around. The only jobs any of us has is keeping this country together. First thing you do is clean yourselves up. After this when you make messes you clean them up. You need food and clothes. What? Are you idiots? You're surrounded by food and clothes. Ain't none of us got money but money doesn't matter no more. Grow up for heaven's sake!" She took a deep breath.

Noah hit the ball out of the park. "And if you don't want to stay in

Sainte Lillian head to D. C. President Brown-Parkinson's put out a call. She has jobs for all of us. Course you'd known that if you'd sobered up and paid attention."

Whiners whined. The smart ones threw their shine and absolutely perfect Tennessee whiskey in the dump, looked truth in the face and got busy.

As always in the game of baseball and the game of life a few vowed to kill the umpire. They began slicing and dicing ingredients that would lead to insurrection. Slowly. While they had beer and good Tennessee whiskey, they were in no hurry.

When women pointed to articles in magazines and newspapers, when they played copies of the President's speeches and reminded the men what the President had said and how their requests were ignored; their men said what men always said to reasonable request backed with reliable information.

History repeating itself, the male response began with "Shut up!" Followed by the less than polite request for beverage of choice. The gentlemen (to a man) always prefaced their 'request' with "Shut up," and the litany beginning with, "Gimmee another."

She wrote "it just goes to show you, the way men were is the way men are."

It bothered her that some of these men were calling Sainte Lillian home. Some migrated there. Their accents were pure Alabama, Tennessee, New Jersey, and Bostonian. Some were Missouri men who listened and believed but were now lost in the first flush or disbelief and grief.

Great grandma and great grandpa caught a few rednecks trying to slaughter a pig and in no time the fat was in the fire.

I asked great grandma what a redneck was and she stuttered and stammered and said maybe it was men folk who worked in the sun and got their necks sunburnt.

Great grandpa looked at her and cleared his throat and she shot him a look but he said it anyway. "Rednecks is what folks who didn't care much for black people or anybody else that wasn't white was called," he said and looked like he was gonna say more but great grandma said "That parts purt near all over Noah so hush." He did.

Anyway, we never learned exactly what was said, but since it was backed up by double barreled shotguns and Sainte Lillian's own contingent of U.S. Marines and 82nd Airborne, all toting mean looking repeater rifles, the message got across.

Grandpa said he'd never seen grandma so mad in all his life.

"I've been putting up with you stragglers for awhile. What ails the lot of you? We listened to the president same as y'all should a done. These here pigs and cows are the starting' in of repopulating the animal world. Ten years or so, when there's enough to harvest, we'll do er. In the meantime, grocery shelves are full of food. You can eat canned Dinty Moore stew and Blue Belle chicken and dumplings and peanuts and, you can fish for lake trout and cat fish like the rest of us. Got some corned beef too, if you're interested, and a whole passel of Slim Jims. Heck, loaded as they are with preservatives, they'll be good when we finally have fresh meat."

It didn't work.

They cursed God, They cursed her. They cursed the president.

Sainte Lillian's county jail known for its habit of encouraging ne'er-do-wells to follow the straight and narrow, and world famous for its diet of oatmeal breakfast, peanut butter sandwiches lunches and chicken noodle soup suppers helped reform a few. They stuck around, willing to learn and earn. The rest drifted off and promised revenge but somehow or other, for some reason or another, most of them were never seen again.

Their leader, a short wiry man with long black hair and burning black eyes had his plans. They absolutely and positively did not include gun toting square jawed military and a mad as a wet hen hillbilly woman. No sir. Not with everything he ever wanted out there waiting. He spat on the red gravel road and turned away from slim pickings. He was going to D.C. Him and his crew and his dogs.

Those first years, similar tales about marauders in the farm belt and deep south surfaced. People got in the habit of wearing six guns and carrying shotguns in their trucks even when they went to church. It seemed a natural thing to do considering.

FIFTEEN

Eve, Thaddeus, his grandma and mother saw nothing wrong with bringing four small stones with ovals for pictures from the monument works. These were centered in Eva's front lawn.

Home Depot had enough quick dry concrete and shovels. It didn't take long to finish he memorial. The red cedar cross Thaddeus fashioned was permanently secured in five feet of concrete. Ever blooming multifloral red roses surrounded the stones and cross.

As if money were of no consequence, Eve plunked four crisp brand new one dollar bills on the desk of the Vanlare dealer and walked out the door with the keys for a four million dollar luxury motor home in her pocket. Beautiful thing, this luxury home Red, white and blue just like the flag sliding down the melting slope of ice cream. There the similarity ended. Their flag represented life, liberty, courage and freedom.

This "hunk of junk" as she named it, was at the other end of the spectrum, representing nothing but selfish excess. It was full of imported Italian leather and marble. Everything including can openers was top of the line stuff she would never use.

She laughed till her sides ached when she saw the gold toilet. "As if," she said, and Thaddeus had presence of mind to not say what he was thinking.

Eve opened all windows to get rid of the new car smell that never failed to make her dizzy, filled the 70 gallon tank, and after a crash course from Thaddeus drove home and parked most of it in their big old back barn. Seemed like it stuck out half a mile.

The next day she plunked 16 silver dollars and fifty new pennies on the desk of the local Ford dealer and claimed ownership of the truck John Mark always wanted. A bright red four wheel drive four door super crew cab XL pickup.

"Four dollars for a four million dollar piece of junk, I figure four times and a little change for a 40,000, dollar truck I'll use is fair," she said.

Thaddeus laughed. "Lady, you sure do beat all at horse trading," he said and compared gas mileage of the two" You'd get 8 mpg with that house on wheels up to 25 on the highway with this truck," he said. "Me, I've got five whole dollars to buy a VW bus. Me and the family are gonna see the country."

They agreed to meet again in four weeks and Eve began her drive across Michigan. En-route to the great bear dunes she took every exit. Houses were the same. Everything was the same. Silent and empty. Good driver that she was, she signaled every turn and stopped at every red light.

Albion was empty. Marshall and its beautiful historic homes, its renovated downtown, was empty. She said goodbye to fallen heroes at the Fort Custer Cemetery in Battle Creek and planted a red rose on the hill looking toward the row of white stones marking the German memorial. Mark had claimed that spot as his own. Now it was. His medals, and a family album wrapped twice in thick plastic and sealed in a tool box were under the rose.

Eve turned onto highway 69 for Coldwater and Sturgis remembering high school graduations and festive parades there. Remembering the beautiful park where children played and families spread checkered cloths for picnics. Remembering the Amish farmers, their simple life and beautiful homes.

Somewhere miles north of Sturgis she spotted a picture perfect large white frame farm home. Red barns were to the side, and fields, gardens and beds of beautiful flowers made her pause and turn into the long winding gravel driveway. Near a gas pump she spotted an empty black buggy its harness, bridle and reins lying along traces in the gravel. In the drivers seat an empty black gabardine suit, high collared white shirt, and a straw hat were laying as if discarded. Glancing down slope to the right, Eve saw a garden hoe handle topped with a simple white bonnet, its ribbons waving slowly in the breeze. Crumpled beneath the hoe a black dress.

Row upon row of sweet corn, potatoes, melons, peppers, squash and tomatoes once carefully tended was now surrendering to nettles and crab grass. Weeds were winning.

Near the house, a beautiful rose garden. Rose trees seemed to herald the wonder and climbing old fashioned yellow roses wound their green vines up and onto the railing around the wide porch. After the climbing gold, ever blooming multiflora reds in a long symmetrical line drank in the sunlight. Then alternating white and pink dwarf bushes and at the base the spreading pink tea roses now free to take over the lawn. She knew the sweet scent of roses would have filled the home from early spring until late frost.

Hoping against hope, Eve knocked and called and waited. And hoped.

Maybe they'd been *down cellar, maybe they'd been out in the root cellar.* She walked around to the back where a large blue zinc dish pan hung on a ten penny nail near the door. Still calling out, she tiptoed in, and was overpowered by sour odor of spoiling food.

In the kitchen she found seven crumpled piles of varying size black dresses, bonnets and white aprons. One, the smallest, displayed a pair of long white bloomers with pink ribbons. Every garment was lifeless, empty.

Eve walked to stare out the open front parlor window before looking down at the Bible open to the last verses in Romans chapter Eight. She read aloud "Nothing can separate us from God's love. Life can't, death can't…" She turned away and bumped into the handmade walker that told her this chair and this dress had belonged to a grandmother keeping watch over the child in the garden.

Eve buried spoiled roast beef, spoiled pork and dumplings, spoiled vegetables and molded things she wasn't curious enough to identify. She labeled the entire mess spoiled food, and buried it deep in the back garden. Pots, roasting pans and all.

She opened windows to air the house, and placed bouquets of roses on the crumbled clothing and one long stem white rose on the Bible in the rocking chair. Tears blurring her sight, she gathered every pink rose from the garden and covered the little dress her baby could have worn. Her little girl loved pink roses. Her baby with the curly long red hair and laughter. She took four loaves of home baked bread from the bread safe, three quarts of apple butter and then left a note just in case someone came, just in case, she wanted them to know she'd meant no harm. Her tears stained the note and the counter.

Her last thought was to lower the windows and lay a fresh fire in the wood burning cook stove. Just in case. She knew she could not, that she would not go into another empty home. That one home site so orderly and serene would live forever in her memory.

She drove over familiar and unfamiliar roads through the night and into the morning. Little towns: White Pigeon, Mullvale (or something like that) she didn't turn back to check. Besides it was just a spot in the road, like so many little places in America where people had lived and worked and dreamed their dreams. All over America. Empty now. Burger Kings and Dairy Queens.

She laughed thinking of a king queen merger and remembered one of their favorite jokes the kids brought home from school. It started with Burger King and Dairy Queen marrying and naming their kids Little Mac.

Then family jokester John Mark took over. "Hey mom, did you hear Fed Ex and UPS are merging?"

Mark John: "What's merging mom?"

Her daughter "Even I know that, it's like getting married right mom?"

Their dad "Interesting idea, what will they call it?"

John Mark's laughter. "Fed up. Get it dad?"

And the giggles that sputtered and floated and blossomed around the supper table. She remembered.

At sunrise she was near the Michigan Indiana border and turned to drive up past Juno Lake and what the kids called her baby sister Eagle Lake. Driving to remember, not expecting anyone or anything. Just looking and driving.

Always, for two days, on a diet of apple butter and getting stale bread, she drove on two lane roads and major highways. Everywhere orange cones and signs warned of construction ahead. Reduce Speed to 45. Be alert for lane changes, Jail time and fines up to 20 thousand for injuring or killing a worker. One lane traffic ahead. All so familiar and once a bothersome distraction now were nothing. Empty earth moving equipment and cranes sat lifeless on the roadside. She wove side to side and drove against what should have been traffic but was not, would never be again.

They always went to Warren Dunes State Park, and they always parked in the same place near the bathrooms and refreshment stand. Problem: No spaces available.

No problem. She eased the big truck up onto the sheltered concrete covered refreshment stand and sat for what felt like hours staring at Lake Michigan. Water washed the sand and drew it into itself. Driftwood rolled the crest of one wave along with empty surfboards. Red, blue, Yellow. They came to shore and rode out along with dead fish, inflated life preservers, black inner tubes, the long green—they always choose green-- styrofone tubes the kids loved and assorted bits and pieces of another time, another place.

Eve heard the familiar voice after she lit the signal fire and did not turn. "I'd about given up on you my dear, but I knew you'd come and light the fire." His brogue as thick as ever, his hunger for s'mores as fine tuned as was hers for his champagne and caviar.

Both agreed theirs were acquired taste.

"And what will you be reading us today Professor Mac," she asked. The kids loved his voice, the stories of old Scottish heroes and Robert Burns Poems a part of their time as much as the fireworks and sunburn.

"Lass you said us. I dinna see your husband or the bairns."

"Mac the first time you said bairns I had to tell the kids you weren't calling them barns do you remember?

"Aye, I do."

On the off chance he did not know, she started to tell him everything but a warning finger hushed her grief. "Sure and I've been a believer in the president for years and was more than prepared.

When the dust fell brother Harry the staff and I were in the wine cellar taking stock. We rowed over after," he said and she smiled at his dry humor and the image of him rowing an 80 foot yacht.

"Docked at the Navy Pier and walked inland a bit. Saw a few people just wandering the streets and a lot of looters loaded down with TV's and games they'll never use. Blethorin idiots in those streets."

His Scottish blur grew thicker as he quoted Robert Burns, "Here Holy Willies sair worn clay takes up it's last abode. His saul has taen some other way, I fear the left hand road."

He sighed. "Not much sense in the lot of them. They took in me scraggly beard and stooped shoulders and figured I wasn't much use or harm. Left me to meself.

She rose to add more logs to the blazing fire, rubbing her dirty hands across her jean covered legs before joining him.

"Sure and I'll be missing the windy city." He sighed.

She thought about his shops on the mile, his restaurants and the museum, the Sears Tower, the beauty of the architecture, the city rising above the lake. So much to miss. "Let me guess. You'll miss the museums and the cathedrals most?

"Lass are you forgettin' who you're talking to? It's the thought of Chicago Hot dogs I'll never eat again. There was this little shop on Ohio Street where the folk never stopped smiling and whatever I wanted, they doubled at no charge. I went by to pay respects and couldn't stop the tears." He paused and scratched his chin and looked longingly across the water. "People like that were so much the heart of Chicago, tears come to my eyes just thinkin' aboot all we lost."

Then a sudden change of mood, "Speakin' of my favorite foods, you'll be so kind to prepare my feast whilst I do us a wie bit of bubbly."

When she turned from the fire he was pouring a liquid gold into glasses that sparkled like diamonds. She discovered later they sparkled like diamonds because they were diamond encrusted. But that was later, after she'd rested and thought to ask.

Greenish the Champagne bottle was and white flowers a bit like almond blossoms climbed from the base.

"You didn't buy that at Wal-Mart," she said and turned the bottle to read Perre-Joet 2000 Belle Epoque. She mumbled to herself more than asked, "What the heck is that?"

He heard.

"Taste," he said.

"Mac it's kinda old?" Meaning "Is it fit to drink?"

"Good champagne is never referred to as old. Aged, perhaps, seasoned, but never old. Grand champagne is complex like a good woman."

Before she could raise an eyebrow, Mac continued his lesson. "This grand champagne seasoned under controlled conditions has a flavor intensity that inspires my dear, but we shall not call it old. People grow old and crotchety. Good champagne on the other hand…"

He paused and smiled and proffered her glass. "Taste," he said, and pulled tins of caviar and gold spoons from his pocket. Gold that caught the firelight.

Eve remembered their first meeting. Twilight four years ago, their signal fire blazing gloriously, red sparks whetting their appetites for fireworks. Hot dogs and potato salad devoured, and S'mores almost ready, and suddenly they heard hauntingly beautiful music as if it were coming from the water. Then he was there, at waters edge, marching proudly in his red white and blue kilt piping the Star Spangled Banner in his salute to America.

The kids pulled him to the fire. They plied him with S'mores and he gave them of himself. It was love, and trust pure and simple. Old Scotsman richer than Midas though they didn't know that then; and scratching the dirt and cutting coupons to get by Eve and her family. Kindred spirits to the core. She remembered. They remembered.

Now as wind from the water blew smoke in their faces, they sat in silence, he devouring S'mores and she doing justice to diamond encrusted glasses of champagne and caviar without crackers, onion or sour cream. Just light brown Iranian Caviar from a solid gold spoon.

She drank the liquid gold that took pain away. Lost to memories, they spoke little but watched moonlit highways across the water and street lamps of the stars. Without children's voices their music was the soft rush of the tide and the pop and snap of burning wood. Night drew him away and left her alone; but not alone. Left her solitary, a silhouette. Breathing, but not moving.

'Sure and ye won't bide the night?"

No, I cannot," but if the invitation for breakfast is still open I'll be there come sunrise."

"Aye, a good bowl of porridge, and some of Scottish eggs and I'll bake ye a bannock." He cleared his throat.

"Lass I feel like your own mother should be talking to you, but before ye dine and get back on the road you'll be needing a shower and a change of clothing."

Realizing personal hygiene had not been near the top of her list for almost a week, she gave a self deprecating shrug. "Probably stink to high heaven," she said and he said "You people from Missouri do have a most unique way of expressing yourselves."

When he turned "Mac could we make it a champagne breakfast?'

"That and more for you lass. There's a magnum of Roedrer Crystal Brut just waitin' for a time such as this," he said, and opened his cell phone. As he began a lonely treck toward his beach home, she heard the pipes long and mournful on the wind. Nearer My God to Thee came across the beach, past the fire and water and reached up to the stars as brother Harry paid tribute to her and her loss.

She had mourned for her city and her friends and her country. Now alone, and wrapped in the music she gave herself permission to feel. To cry. To remember, And then strangely to seal the memories away.

Like Mac had said, they were with her forever in her heart.

In the morning, with reference to the new champagne, she said, "I thought the other bottle with flowers was prettier. This gold paper makes me …oh, I don't know…makes me feel like I shouldn't be drinking it, like it's wine made for presidents or royalty."

Brother Harry poured." "Today you are queen of our universe," he said.

"Well, since you put it that way, and I do like pink champagne," she said. And did not notice their raised eyebrows or soft smiles. Ten years later she learned that one magnum cost more than her first four door Saturn sedan. After taxes and closing cost.

Their farewell bitter sweet and, as they all knew, permanent. Brother Harry shy and soft spoken hugged her and prayed for her while Mac hauled three heavy suitcases to the truck. He secured them under a heavy tarp, and to her unspoken question said, "They were for the bairns the middle one a dowry for the bonnie lass. Someday ye may have a need so keep them safe, he said. Strong arms drew her close. "Lass, do not bid the ains lock thine heart," he whispered. And more.

She did not look back because she could not.

SIXTEEN

At the White House, Eve pictured her kids sliding down the long banister. She smiled at the thought of their laughter, and didn't say anything. In fact, every since she'd traveled to the Owen farmstead in Sainte Lillian, Missouri, and then to D.C., she'd had little to say.

Make no mistake, she worked and worshipped and lived but food was tasteless. Praise songs she'd recorded with John Mark and the kids and the Bible she'd loved to read and quote were like soggy cotton in her mind.

Getting to D.C. was another story and someday she'd sort it out and figure out what they were doing there. She remembered the invitation, the decision. She remembered staring out the tour bus window as they passed through many small towns. Empty, everything so empty.

Now and then people lined the streets. "Hell no, we won't go," some said. Others promised to come on their own. "Cars aplenty," they said.

She remembered highways with burned out hulks of cars and trucks pushed aside almost like guardians of the roadway. She remembered stretches of clean pavement. She remembered cities where potholes made her feel like she was a pioneer riding a Conestoga wagon. She laughed at the idea. The pioneers had a dream.

Eve looked at her tired mother doing her best to ease her back pain on the cramped Greyhound seat, and whispered "Have the elder races halted?'

Lainey Owen looked out the window at the barren landscape, padded her pillow just so and eased it to her mid back before answering. "Whitman was another time and another place. How would he speak now to this struggling dispossessed population of every tongue and every nation? President Brown Parkinson liked to quote him. Let's see if she does."

Lonely in a crowd of wonderers, they stared silently out the windows, lost both of them; lost all of them in their thousands of yesterdays.

Eve focused on years of hope and laughter and love. And that Fourth of July, and the suitcases they pulled from her truck and the hullabaloo their contents caused.

"Take them to the back barn where we stored the medicine and clothing and other stuff he sent. We'll figure it out later," her mother said, and she said "That's a good idea. Mac said we'd best keep them safe."

In the deep cavern of the man made storage vault, they stacked the gold coins and useless diamond and emerald trinkets in shelves already loaded with dried foods and herbal medicines. "He gave us enough out door clothing from L. L. Bean to last a hundred years and fur coats and all sorts of senseless stuff," her mother said.

Eve heard the sarcastic ridicule threatening to break through her mother's resolve. "Mom he thought of everything, or tried to. He said we were to take care of it."

"Well, daughter he did send a coupla 18 wheelers full of toilet paper and cleaning supplies, so I reckon his heart was in all the right places."

Eve laughed at the expression on her mother's face and turned away to be alone.

Mac said he had loved her and her family from the beginning, and that he wished he were younger and could be her protector. He said he felt love for her that was not family love but love of man for woman.

"Dear Mac, dearest dearest Mac," she said and hushed his lips with her own. It was a soft kiss, full of understanding and the love she had for him, the love of family. "I know," she said, and placed her hand over his beating heart. "That which cannot be is sometimes better than the reality," she said.

"Oh lass, you'll ever be a joy to me" said the old man with long flowing white hair. Then was time for her quick exit. She remembered the sweetness of their mixed tears, sobs from the staff and brother Harry as she turned away from what could have been and headed into the unknown.

Countless empty miles across Michigan, to the UP, across the big empty bridge separating upper and lower Michigan. Wind whistled through it and beneath it, and the waters churned grey and blue. She missed the birds, the ever present begging birds. She missed the noise of life.

Eve sat on the veranda of the Grand Hotel, sipping champagne from their private stock. Knowing now the difference she raised her glass in toast to Mac and Harry and poured a magnum of what The Grand would consider the best and Mac and Harry inferior over the veranda.

After two nights in the presidential suite she was again on the bridge. It was like she was there, but not there. She was conscious of bits and pieces of empty miles. Sometimes lonely lost people struggling along roadsides. Blank faces, dull eyes. Like zombies they were. She saw them. If they were aware she existed they gave no sign.

Finally she pulled to a stop at the white farm home on Maple Brook Road and walked into her mother's arms. "Welcome home daughter," she said and looked only once for her son-in-law and grand children. Eve shook her head and said nothing. That was answer enough. Regardless of Mac's hope, the lock on her heart could not- absolutely would not- be forced open.

SEVENTEEN

Wasn't his fault the gol-durn dog didn't like being chained up. Wasn't his fault his pappy beat the crap out of him when he found old Pete shivering and shaking in the rain.

"That there dog be yourn. Your responsibility. Got that word boy? Responsibility. I'm gonna teach you boy!" His old man pulled a buckled belt from the loops in his dirty jeans and folded it over. Slowly and deliberately he smacked the dirty leather against his callused hands. The sound was harsh, like wood on wood. Loud and harsh.

W.D. hung his head and looked through thick matted dark hair for a place to hide. There warrant none. Couldn't run. Couldn't hide. Couldn't do nothing' but stand there and take it.

"Like I'm responsible for you boy teaching you right, you're responsible for that dog. Like I keer fer you, you keer for that worthless piece of crap you keep chained up. Lemme teach you a thing or two," he said and his beefy arm rose and fell, rose and fell

The one time he hollered and begged "Pa don't. Don't hit me no more pa." and the old man laughed, W. D. knew to stand silent. Always when the blows fell he remembered the time he begged for mercy and the old man laughed. It was like the old man took pleasure from his pain.

W. D. knew then that no matter what he did or didn't do to set the old man off, his best bet was to stand and take it. Blow after blow cut across his legs and shoulders. Hate blazed from his dark black eyes. Urine and blood mingled and ran down his bruised and bleeding legs and, because he did not shield his face, one sharp cut from the belt buckle cut a jagged wound down his right cheek.

W. D. decided to teach old Pete the way his pa taught him and went out with the biggest stick he could find. He yelled and cursed. Old Pete didn't move. He waited. He knew what was coming. First few times W. D. beat him senseless Pete whined and cried. Not mo more He just lay there in his own mess and looked at W.D. Not moving. Not whining. Just looking at him. Only there warn't no hate in that dogs eyes.

Eye to eye abused boy and abused dog. W.D. raised the club and screamed and threw his weapon out of the woodlot. "You're just like me aintcha boy?" he said and unchained the dog and carried him to his hideout in the cave by the creek.

As he walked Old Pete licked W. D's wounds.

It was the first time since his ma died that W. D. cried.

His cave started out little more than a hidey hole for rabbits and such but then it went way back in the hillside. Scrub brush grew over the hole not covered by big boulders. His place was way to the back near a natural chimney where he kept a low fire, bedroll, pots and pans and whatever else he wanted including bottles of his pappy's shine. He diluted that to wash old Pete's wounds.

Then he brewed a stew of rabbit and squirrel... Old Pete couldn't do much more than lap at broth for a day or two but it didn't take him long to get interested in bits of wild turkey with potatoes and carrots mashed up in the thick broth.

Within a week Old Pete wagged and woofed. W.D. knew that meant more. A wagging tail brought W. D.'s laughter. Like tears laughter was again part of his life.

W.D crept from his cave every night at sunset and snuck to the two room tumble down tar paper shack his pa called home. Wasn't much in there. A big four burner cast iron cook stove smack dab in the middle of the room, shelves where he stored food, his old bed far over to one corner, the one window his ma liked to keep clean and prettified with curtains and flowers in the window sill. Her hope chest, a big iron box the old man kept locked and all his guns. Lord a Mercy, that man had a wall full of guns. About the only thing he kept clean. Musta been a fortune tied up in them guns.

Night after night he watched the old man stagger out drunk as a skunk and heading for the still. When W. D. was dang sure he was gone, he'd sneak out back and raid the hen house. He never once took a chicken but there were eggs aplenty and they wouldn't be missed.

Some nights he'd sneak indoors for whatever he wanted; clothing, his hunting rifle, ammo, knives, and books. For some reason his ma had a collection of geography books and a Bible and books on first aid. Now they were his. He'd kept them upstairs in his loft and doubted the old man had ever seen them. Drunk as he was most of the time, he wasn't about to climb that rickety old ladder anyways. They were his.

W. D. took beans too and taters from the pantry bins. And soap and rags to keep Old Pete clean and blankets from his ma's hope chest.

Time or two the old man didn't go out at night but acted like he was. Like normal, he'd just walk off. W. D.'s clue was the old man was walking. Didn't have a stagger in his shin bones. And he made a big show of leaving. He's stretch, walk around, double check the locked door-- All of it stuff he didn't do for normal. Then he'd kinda amble off and half an hour-hour later come sliding back like he was looking for something, like maybe he wasn't as dumb drunk all the time like W.D. thought.

Two months, then three, then frost and an early snow. W.D. learned to walk backward in his pa's tracks. Slow going from woods to house, faster when he left and headed to the cave. Every step measured, every move guarded. Until he got to the rocky hillside where he could move in the brush and follow animal trails. He knew his pa didn't have sense enough to figure that out.

About Christmas time, on one of them star bright nights his ma loved, him and Pete was in no big hurry, just walking out by the creek, waiting for the old man to make his move when W.D. heard the voice he hated. "Been gone a long time aintcha boy?" it said and hatred was in every syllable of every word.

Old Pete growled low in his throat. His hair bristled and every muscle of boy and dog tensed as they turned. W. D. heard the rifle bolt click, saw a white blur and heard the old man curse as his shot went wild and his foot slipped on the iced rock. Old Pete growled and lunged again. Man and dog went over a small cliff into the rocky water.

It took W. D. one day to carry the body of his old man to the cave. Laid him out just like he'd fell and hit his head on a rock which he thought to bring from the creek and added to the rock pile. Blood smeared and all.

It took W. D. two days to bring everything back to the shack. And he was glad it didn't take no longer. Cold as it was in the cave, the old man was changing and the smell wasn't exactly right. He was glad to be shed of the places.

Took W. D. three days of boiling water and scrub brushing every board and wall with lie soap to get it as clean as his ma had liked it

Then he took an extra week to pamper Old Pete and fix up his bruises from the fall.

It was another week before he hitched up his britches and walked to the sheriff's office and said he thought his pa had took off. Again

Sheriff Putman said he "warn't surprised none. Seems as how the old man did what he wanted when he wanted. Specially this time of year about the time your ma took bad and died. Check back with me come spring."

W. D. said "Thanks sheriff, preciate that," and turned to leave.

"Say boy whatcha doin since you got outa school? You got a job or anything? Need one?"

W. D. remembered his ma always said to respect the law. "Look em in the eye, stand up tall, but above all be polite," she said.

W. D. smiled at Sheriff Putman and lied like he had practice. "Well sir, me and pa been talking about me maybe going into law enforcement. I ain't all that big, but I'm tough and seein' as how I can shoot the head offin a nail at a hundred yards, he figured it might be a good calling for me. Either that or joining up with the Army y'know like Audie Murphy did seein' as how we're from the same parts."

"Tell you what boy let's wait for your pa to show up. He's not home come dogwood blossom time, you come see me. I'm fixing to train me a few deputies and you'd fit right in. Getcha some good training, purty good money, and all. By the way boy that's a handsome scar on your face you been in a knife fight by any chanct?"

W. D. laughed fit to be tied. And since he was good at lying, told another. "Knife fight? Who me? You know pa'd never put up with that. This here scar courtesy of a ring tailed coon blindsidin' me and leading me into the sharpest dadgone branch in the county. Bled all over the place. Pa had himself a real fit." He smiled inwardly. That part wasn't a lie. "I couldn't figure out if he was mad at me for being outsmarted by a coon or scared count of all the blood".

Sheriff Putman looked like he had a question or two, but then he shook them aside and bought the whole story hook, line and sinker.

W. D. couldn't help himself. He smiled all over his face and promised to show up for training come spring.

It was some time in mid February when W. D. decided to break the lock on his pa's iron box.

He didn't quite right know what to do with all that money but he figured seein' as how it was legally his, he'd best keep it. Spend a little here, little there. Sure would be nice to replace his pa's old truck but that had to wait till he got that Deputy job.

One thing led to another and all. He'd be right smart to fix up the place a little. By dab, an indoor toilet wouldn't be a bad idea. Course there'd have to be a drain field or some kind of septic system but he'd figure that out.

Then he'd board up the house put some shingles on, and build a big room with a fireplace. His ma always wanted a fireplace. He'd do it up pretty for her, with beams in the ceiling and all and a winder overlooking the mountains. In the meantime the money stared at him. Chest smack dab full of green and all of it good as gold. What to do with it?

His mind said wait it out and he listened. He kept some. The big chest practically loaded with greenbacks, went into his cave. Fast. Up front where he didn't have to look at the old man.

What he couldn't do around the home site before the dogwood blossomed, he didn't. Changes were minor, but all were good and pleasing to the eye and the place was looking up before training began.

It took W. D. over three years to get it all: the truck, the indoor toilet, the great big room with a fireplace and a brand new kitchen to boot. That kitchen with a refrigerator and electric cook stove and all came to being because this pretty little thing down the holler decided she'd be his wife. He wanted it for her, wanted everything brand spankin' fired new for her because he knew he'd never treat a wife the way his pa treated his ma.

Peggy Sue wanted another bedroom or two or three and a couple more indoor bathrooms and a run around porch and she got them too. Folks all over talked about what a good man he was and how proud his pa and ma would be.

Sheriff Putman asked about his pa now and then and finally got tired of asking. Plain to see the boy was keeping the place up for him and from the looks of things him and Peggy Sue was gonna make the old man a grandpa soon.

Peggy Sue took him and his growing family to church and together they found faith and grew in it. They taught Sunday school and worked Nursery duty and started a food pantry and a baseball league for kids that didn't have much to do but get into trouble. Sports worked wonders with them kids. Summer baseball grew into football and that into basketball.

Life went on for W. D. Old Pete got older and one evening long about sunset, just laid his head in W. D.'s lap and looked at him with all the trust and love in the whole world in his eyes, and lay down at his feet and died.

W. D. never knew losing that dog could hurt so much. All the memories rushed back and W. D. mourned for his best friend as much if not more than he had for his ma.

He wrapped Old Pete in one of Peggy Sue's best quilts and sat by the fireplace cradling him in his arms and bawling most of the night. Peggy Sue put the kids to bed quiet like and then sat beside him in her rocking chair. She kept the fire golden, and cried right along with him.

The next morning come sunrise, they buried old Pete besides his ma. He bordered the new grave with stones he hauled from under the bluff at the creek. They were together; stones and a dog with a story to tell and neither could.

W. D. was the first deputy to get interested in Karate and in no time had himself a black belt and trophies from tournaments. Short and wiry and solid muscle, he taught self defense at the Y and excelled in weaponry.

Peggy Sue said the first Shorin-ryu masters must have learned from women with a houseful of kids because they taught focus, ability to handle stress, strength and balance and above all patience and self confidence.

Sensi Ahi, grand master and owner of the Dojo, said "Pretty momma most wise. Deserves a red belt for her knowledge and experience." He made her one with six stars. She wore it everywhere, even to church.

Remembering his ma's encouraging his interest in medicine; W. D. completed the paramedic course in record time and was so good he could work side by side with ER doctors and more than once delivered babies. Lots of guys called him Little Doc.

His promotions in the sheriff's department were rapid: Deputy, to Corporal to Sergeant to Lieutenant to Captain. He played politics like he was born to it. Next election with Sheriff Putman retiring, W.D. was a shoe in for the job.

Healthy and strong, their six kids grew.

So did the tar paper shack. W. D. wouldn't tear down where his ma lived, but he changed it till she would have been proud. It became a great big main room with a fireplace and the loft that had been his bedroom a secure place for all her books. Sitting on a hill the way it was W.D. and Peggy Sue's house was the talk of the town. Always there was love. Always the door was open for friends.

On the Fourth of July While Peggy Sue and the kids got ready for the town picnic; W.D. and Pete's two pups Little Pete with his blue collar and Repeat with her pink and a fluffy pink bow in her silver hair, made a quick visit to the cave.

With ten and twenty dollar bills stuffed in his back pack, W.D. was ready to leave when on sudden impulse he walked toward the cave back and used stones to cover the skeletal remains of his pa. Decomposition and rats had left very little. Even his clothes were pure rot. A gnawed tibia near the old mans worn work boot bothered him and W. D. thought it was time he did something to in some way to show respect to the old man.

After all, he hadn't gone completely nuts till after his ma died so all the meanness could have been pure grief. He didn't know. Didn't want to know or wonder. Since the natural chimney was packed tight with dirt, he thought to make the grave site look like a cave in and recklessly tossed rocks over what was left of his old man. . Big ones near his head and neck. That took more time than he wanted, but a bit after 11:30, he grabbed the backpack and exited. He crawled from the cave into a new world. A quiet world.

Within an hour he felt as if his heart had been cut in smack dab in two down the middle. Bloody chunks of it then put in a meat grinder, poured out on the floor and stomped on.

Inside where he couldn't scream or see he felt a hate like his pa had festering on the left side, with all the love he'd known glowing solid and good and strong on the right. Hate and love were at war, and that war was pulling him apart.

W.D. asked God why? Why did it happen? Matter of fact, what exactly happened? A man doesn't go about his business and head home to find everyone he loved and worked for gone. Nothing left but bundles of wet clothing scattered about the yard.

W.D. could quote the president's speeches but he figured they were off target because the Bible didn't talk about anything like that. He had read and re-read the end time prophecies: War and rumors of war, the anti-Christ, earthquakes in diverse places, sickness and death.

Thinking about all that gave him pause. There was always war. There was always disease and *hunger. Families in Burundi and Africa and India were always starving. No matter what the churches did, no matter how the world helped people starved to death. Why did God let people starve to death and die of cancer and incurable diseases AIDS?*

Natural disasters? Earth quakes? Lord yes! There was the big quake that ruined California a few years back, the one in 2010 that all but devastated Haiti, quakes in China and other quakes all over the world, not to mention, mudslides, floods and volcanoes. That part of prophecy was sure playing out. But where was this fella called anti-Christ? Where were the soldiers for the great big battle at Armageddon?

Was the anti-Christ really just one person or was it a way of life that so many lost souls followed? He read from the prophets and turned to 1 John and read "The spirit of the antichrist which you have heard is coming and even now is already in the world." EVEN NOW! Heaven help us all! That was written thousands of years ago! No wonder the world swallowed the lies and got itself in such a mess.

Was their hope?

It was like he could hear Peggy Sue singing.

"Our hope is in nothing less than Jesus Blood and Righteousness.
On Christ the solid rock we stand. All other ground is sinking sand."

Yes there was hope. But why did all the innocent people just disappear?

Again, W.D. read his ma's collection of end time prophecies written years ago by LaHaye and Jenkins and shook his head. Broke his heart when that little gal got her head cut off but God was there all the time and they were resurrected and reunited with new eternal bodies. That was his hope. He knew he'd be with Peggy Sue and the kids again but wanting it and not knowing when was the torment. Believing with all his heart the reunion would happen was the hope that kept him sane.

W. D. packed his gear, his dogs, pictures of his family, his guns and his oldest sons Student Bible and took off cross country looking for answers.

EIGHTEEN

JULY 11, ONE WEEK AFTER THE DUST FELL:

Helicopters flew over every major city and small town and covered the landscape with pamphlets authored by Inez Brown-Parkinson, President of the United States. Exerpts follow:

"My fellow citizens. July fourth will forever be remembered as a day of disaster not only in our country but around the world.

Now each nation is faced with the monumental task of rebuilding. Our future consist of long years of education, hard work and personal sacrifice.

In order to prepare our country for the task ahead, the next thirty days will be devoted to a time of mourning, remembrance, and rededication. All chapels, churches and cathedrals will hold on-going services.

Starting immediately, Memorial services will be broadcast from the Washington Cathedral, Arlington National Cemetery and the Ellipse. Throughout the country we will gather together as a family and mourn and remember our loved ones.

After our period of mourning and rededication, mandatory schooling will begin. Food preservation, farming, medical, mechanics, electrical and engineering, are but part of the curriculum.

As Washington D.C., is the center of national government, the remaining members of congress and the house have passed bills that will turn our area into a hub of education and survival training.

As your survival depends on attendance, your presence at these sessions is mandatory. Tour busses and trains will begin the journey within 24 hours. Families who wish to provide their own transportation will find unbeatable prices at local dealerships. Claim the car, truck, bus or van. Fill out the form,

Keep the carbon copy. Attach your dollar to the original. Place form and dollar in the pickle jar on the counter, get the key and drive away. Follow these directions and ownership is guaranteed.

When you arrive in D.C., register at your state centers set up in the national mall. Luxury apartments, hotels and motels are available and will be assigned on a first come first served basis. Historic campsites are also available. After your training is complete and before you leave, you are required to check out. All records will become a permanent part of the Smithsonian.

I am aware there are some survivors who have always thought milk came from a carton and corn from a can. Not only that, your sweat came from workouts at the gym…or the beach, or laying out on rooftops on sunny days. Some of you have never handled an ax, a saw, a shovel, a rake or plow or planted a seed. America Listen up. Those days are over! If you want to survive you will work.

On an even more serious and somber note, rumors have already reached us about unrest and insurrection. I caution you once and once only this will not be tolerated and remind you who plan such that nothing good will be accomplished. If you are unhappy and want nothing to do with reshaping America, you will soon learn there are mountains you cannot climb and rivers you cannot cross.

Long ago, the great American poet Walt Whitman called the people of this growing nation pioneers. He said:

Come my tan faced children
Follow me well in order. Get your weapons ready
Have you pistols? Have you sharp edged axes?
Pioneers. O pioneers."

Now I, your president say to each and every one of you:

We cannot tarry here
My wan faced children.
We must rise up and build.
Have your dreams ready. Keep your memories sacred
March on.
O pioneers, O new pioneers."

* * * * *

`That was most of page one and two. The rest of it was about throwing away I pods and blackberries (whatever they were), the end of indulgence and preparedness for the future.

The president covered medical care in one paragraph: She said "There will be no more transplants. Abortions are outlawed. Medications for heart, cancer and diabetic patients will be available. Every small town will have old fashioned circuit riding medical professionals. The ten year battery cell phones issued to each family unit will reach only one number as they are for emergency/medical purposes only."

She said large cities would become a thing of the past, as the declining population made it impossible and unnecessary for their existence. There was a lot more of the same. Mostly her pamphlets covered rules and regulations that would turn America into a self sufficient country.

*   *   *   *   *

Two days later, every TV and radio in the country began to carry her complete speech every hour on the hour. Full volume. Everywhere across the country.

When dissent reached the stations, news commentators said, and it is quoted for posterity: "The president warned us more than once and we didn't listen. Time for us to get off the couch and get our lazy asses to work. She hasn't said "I told you so" yet, but it's overdue and anyone with a lick of sense knows it.

Around the country, as time passed, people bowed their heads, bent their backs and went to work. It was not that they had a choice. Those that thought they did soon learned the truth. The hard way.

Days became weeks that became months. Grasses browned. Frost nipped the trees and nature's showcase did what it always did, filling the world with beauty.

*   *   *   *   *

It was a wild and stormy November night following a wild and stormy November day. Rain lashed against his truck and overfilled the roadway. Longevity and severity of the storm had not stopped newly promoted Admiral Adam Dimitri Bladgovicz.

He was finally going home for a much needed break and had driven in the threatening weather from Arlington on the Blue Ridge Parkway. Seeing, not seeing the historic sites he'd loved from childhood. His journey was one of remembrance and reverence, and his personal time to say farewell.

At Arlington he stood at parade rest as the tomb guard sentinels continued their solemn march. Twenty One steps down the black mat. Sharp turn. Face east for 21 seconds. Sharp turn. Face north for 21 seconds. Pause. Repeat. After each turn a sharp shoulder arms movement to place their rifles on shoulders closest to visitors. This move signifies the sentinel stands as guardian between the tomb and any possible threat. The 21 steps represent the highest military honor given fallen heroes.

He'd heard the call "Ready! Aim! Fire!" countless times at Arlington as seven riflemen (and women) stood over graves and rendered the 21 gun salute. Now he heard sharp precise footsteps on pavement. Twenty one and Pause. Twenty one and face East. Pause. Twenty one.

He knew the tradition would continue 24-7, 365 as long as there were men and women of C Company, the elite 3rd infantry At Fort Myer. And he knew all but the four who refused to follow their Presidents order to seek safety had died when the dust fell. The names of these dead were on plaques secured to the tomb. Two men. Two women. Young. Seeing duty to country more important than duty to self.

In the cold November rain Admiral Adam Bladgovicz stood at rigid attention and called out the Marine honor salute "Semper Fi!" (Always Faithful).

As one, the soaking wet young soldiers broke protocol and returned the salute of the soaking wet Admiral. They knew him. He'd been at HQ two days before as the President presented each member with the tomb guard permanent badge. They would wear this badge, a simple upside down laurel leaf surrounding a depiction of the front of the tomb until death and then into eternity.

In the cold soaking rain, Adam walked the grounds of Arlington. There on the hill overlook of D.C., the graves of President John Fitzgerald Kennedy, his wife, their baby. Others.

Beneath this historic hilltop, Arlington's 1,100 acres was the final resting place of American military dead after the Civil war. Where once children played and life was a dream, dead now lay row upon row, and visitors walked and wondered.

The white columned Greek Revival home designed by George Hadfield who worked on the White house, and at one time home to Confederate General Robert E. Lee and their family, now seemed a watchtower above hills and fields of the dead.

Two yeas ago when his family toured and witnessed a funeral procession, Cheyenne asked "Daddy why do they plant dead people?" Zoe didn't give him a chance. She said "They aren't honey they're planting hope."

"Momma you can't plant hope. Hope is something we have inside." She looked at her mother and then understanding, said "Oh!"

"Yes Cheyenne. Hope is something we have inside. Hope America will always be safe. Hope we'll live in peace. When we see these graves we remember their

hope. Your daddy and men and women like him remember their sacrifice and do their best to keep America safe."

"Oh momma! Let's never bury daddy. Promise me."

He remembered.

Man with a broken heart, Adam walked until his legs begged for mercy and still he walked. His favorite and he thought the most graceful monument remained the thirty foot long thirty five foot tall aluminum World War Two Memorial to Navy and Merchant Marines. There winged sea gulls skim crest of waves and fly into the known and unknown and wished for glory, and peace; the victors prize.

Monuments to those 16 million who served and died in World War Two, the Korean War Memorial, the 8.4 million dollar VietnamWar Memorial designed by Yale Student. Maya Lin.

So much controversy over the simple memorial yet it drew Americans every day. Every year.

The eloquence of names of brothers, fathers, sisters, sons, grandsons, friends and neighbor etched in stone said more to the American heart, than any forgotten speech ever could.

There, the recently completed Iraqi-Afghanistan memorial where each night names of the fallen flashed up into the night sky. Beyond the stars.

Overlooking it all in peaceful fog shrouded serenity the white column Washington Monument. He was glad the original design had not been completed. The simple obelisk gave more grandeur to the site than could have the planned statue of George Washington on his dashing charger.

He thought of the wars fought and heroes whose hopes for a better tomorrow ended in long ago and present day conflict. Lost grief. New grief. One and the same. Wars. Death. Cities grew where blood once soaked earth and grain fields. Battlefields now opened to tourist.

He had watched tour guard faces and wondered what they knew, if they thought; *"Careful where you walk little boy. Could be you're standing where Johnny Reb and Billy Yankee fought to the death. Hurry to the gift shop for a souvenir. Have a coke and a burger before you leave."*

At the Jefferson Memorial, he paused to read: "We hold these truths to be self evident; that all men are created equal; that they are endowed by their creator with certain inalienable rights. Among these are life, liberty, and the pursuit of happiness. That to secure these rights, Governments are instituted among men. We solemnly publish and declare that these colonies are and of right ought to be free and independent states…And for the support of this declaration with a firm reliance on the protection of divine providence we mutually pledge our lives, our fortunes, and our sacred honor."

Cheyenne's voice" Daddy did that woman who lived here in the United states and enjoyed all these freedoms…you know the one I mean daddy, the one who said there was no God? Do you think she ever read this? And if she read it did she understand what a lie she was telling? What do you think daddy?

He read Eleanor Roosevelt's words; "The structure of world peace cannot be the work of one man, or one party, or one nation. It must be a peace which rests on the cooperative efforts of the whole world."

He turned from the statue of this American woman he'd always considered a twin to Sister Theresa and with bowed head and slowed steps, walked back to Arlington and his waiting truck.

Orchards dotted the landscape as he escaped suburbia. There to the North both Antietam and Gettysburg. How many dead there? 51,000? More? And Manassas 32 miles NW of D.C. and Monocacy, where Confederates last invaded the North.

For three endless days without food or sleep, he had walked them all in the cold rain. He walked and thought and wondered why. He thought about soldiers from both north and south dying on cold wet ground because there was no food and very little medical care. And he wondered why? So we could come to this? So we wouldn't learn? Finally, more than chilled to the bone, but so lost in reverie he was unaware, he turned at last toward home.

So many dreams ago he couldn't remember, but he was going home and that memory brought a smile. The family filling out address forms. Gregory Barnstable, the postmaster scratched his stubbled chin, looked at his awe struck girls, said "Guess you'd best get in the idea of calling me grandpa. I know, I know, I ain't your kin, but I'd be an addelpated old man if I didn't claim you purty gals as family. Here, have a sucker."

"Thank you grandpa," they said in unison and each found not only a sucker, but a welcoming hug. Barnstable hitched up his suspenders and said, "Your address? Why sure, your address is Rural Route, Warren County, By God West Virginia. Welcome home."

That was good enough for Adam, Zoe and the girls. They and their neighbors knew home was in the best place on God's Green earth.

Adam was going home. Home to the sprawling golden log cabin set in the hillside with a front porch view of mountains and valleys too beautiful to describe. Every season full of surprises, full to the brim and running over with Gods created wonder and peace.

He parked back side of the winding gravel road, grabbed his waterproof back pack with papers signed sealed and delivered by the president (Call me Inez) delineating his new duties as Commander of the Department of Homeland Security.

The way he understood it, the country was divided into sections and each section had a security force and each security force had a sectional commander whose voice was his, and his voice was that of the president. He'd said "Madame President" and saluted and accepted the briefcase as he accepted all orders, knowing the time to read them would come when he was alone.

Adam adjusted his gear and began the long uphill walk in the pouring cold rain. He did not ponder why a nearly disintegrated nation needed a Department of homeland security. Or why he was one of the chosen leaders. If awareness he was wet and cold had penetrated his consciousness, that awareness ended long hours ago.

Exhausted by the steep climb, he stopped at the prayer bench. He would rest a minute and remember the way they were. This was where in August he had found their clothing. Empty, formless, and bleached by the mountain top sun.

Cheyenne and Esther either side of Zoe. Zoe's Bible was in her lap, and her wedding and engagement rings were marking Romans Chapter Eight.

Cheyenne was always on the left of her mother with Esther always on the right… unless they'd traded places that morning. He didn't think so. They never traded places. He'd checked to be sure and found on the right Esther's lunch bucket filled to the brim with S'mores. By this time the Chocolate and marshmallow had melted into the graham crackers but still they were recognizable as her favorite treat.

Cheyenne's mesh bag of now wrinkled and depressed Golden Delicious and Winesap Apples had rolled toward the Bible from the left… No they hadn't traded places. They had been that morning as he would always remember, on their prayer bench near the lonesome pine a quarter mile from their log cabin home. He buried the treats there, beneath the bench.

When he claimed them that long ago day in August he'd taken their clothing and Zoe's Bible and rings home. Their clothing, the girls shorts, Zoe's Jeans and their matching patriotic T shirts he hand laundered and stored.

Even though pages of Zoe's Bible were so glued together by days of rain and climate change it would be almost impossible to separate them, he put it on her nightstand by their bed. Her rings rested near his heart on the chain that held his military tags. Inscribed as was his," till death and then eternity."

Memories of events in D.C. replayed in slow motion in his tired brain as he curled up on the prayer bench: In Mid July, as the crowds grew, Inez (he forced himself to use her first name) had grills set up in every available space and the people ate steaks, slow cooked southern style ribs and prime rib of beef until they were sick of meat. Yet chef's kept the grills hot.

Survival training, a 24-7 program provided not only basics in medical care and food preservation but covered mechanical, electrical and construction. Do hickeys and thingamigs became lug nuts and wrenches, "I can't" became

"I will" and men who'd never washed a dish or pulled a weed became experts in the kitchen, and more or less competent with a hoe. Calluses and all.

Six plate wood burning cook stoves with reservoirs for heating water were lottery prizes until it turned out every number drawn was a winner. Reality took its own time smacking doubters in the face.

*   *   *   *   *

FORD THEAER. Teen voices raised in protest when President Brown-Parkinson told them to leave their personal communication devices in baskets at the door.

Mutterings. Voices. One clearer than the others. "How we suppose to play our games and talk?" one asked.

"You won't," she said.

A long haired boy in the front row gave her their best argument. "Listen lady I know you're the president and all but that don't matter much no more."

Small round of applause. Quieter gasp as agreement and disagreement met in the middle. She let the tumult of doubt run its course until finally silence filled the room.

President Brown-Parkinson allowed herself the luxury of laughter. "You remind me of someone I know. He told me I should spend more time being his mother than being president. I told him he should spend more time minding his mother and listening to his president. We had quite a discussion.

Because he listened to his mother and believed his president, he is still alive. Because he obeyed his president he was the first to dispose of his toys. He asked me to remind you that work is not a dirty four letter word.

A slightly nervous cough came from near the back row. A roving spot focused on a slim teen. He shaded his eyes and said "mom" in a voice that meant among other things, son of the President of the United States or not, he was still a teenager and didn't enjoy that kind of spotlight.

A cute blonde seated next to him gave him a friendly hug and others near by laughed and applauded.

"Take a bow Randy." she said and because he had decided after the 4th of July to be very obedient he milked the spotlight for all of five seconds before sliding as far down into the plush red velvet seat as his long legs allowed.

Laughter was a pleasant sound in a room where once a single gunshot stunned a recovering nation.

The President cleared her throat. "As Ben Franklin a famous statesman said, "By failing to prepare we are preparing to fail." He also said, "A life of leisure and a life of laziness are two things. There will be sleeping enough in the grave."

A chorus of voices "Ben who?"

Before she could answer a voice came from the crowd "Mr. Franklin lived about the time of the first revolution. He was kinda fat and ugly, always needed a haircut, and said a lot of stuff and wrote a lot more. He was a lot like Will Rogers only he never saw a woman he didn't like or, a drink either for that matter."

Dozens of voices "Will who?"

Before the sweeping spotlight found the girl, President Brown-Parkinson tossed a question to the milling teen agers. "I'm more than curious. What did you kids study in school?"

Boys said "Girls.". Girls said "Boys." When laughter and snickers abated, a voice answered her question with a question. "Not too many of us came from private schools. We're city kids. Why should we study when everything we wanted to know was on the net?"

"What did you want to know?"

"Miz President mam, you don't want to know but it sure wasn't history or prepositions or poets that died before thermal nuclear bionic kill everybody war was around. Lady in our own way, we studied survival!"

Other voices chimed in. "Yeah, what good is that history stuff anyway?" and, "We kept our books open and did a lot of texting. It was more interesting to check scores and stats than study.

For one of the few times in her life, President Brown-Parkinson was at a loss for words. She hung her head and waited them out.

A sweeping spotlight found the tall heavy set girl. Unlike Randy, she enjoyed the attention and milked her opportunity for minutes of fame. She held the room spellbound with her upbeat version of American History. Her rap with a clap and a shimmy and shake brought more laughter.

"Stick around young lady. You've just become an American History Teacher."

"And they said my reading all the time would never amount to nothing. Lookit me now!" The girl laughed along with the recovered president who turned again to the group of teens.

"Those among you, who just might have been interested in the sciences, or math, economics, or any form of literature, architecture, mechanics, or any of the trades, register at the appropriate tables in the forum. School is now in session. One more thing. This time around if you want to survive, you must learn more than you ever did on the net."

They looked at one another, looked at her. One voice "Dam, she's sure as hell somebody's mother."

NINETEEN

Oh God!

She was so beautiful! Her long curly red brown hair *caught in a diamond studded coronet, the sheen of her veil shading all but the sparkle in her green eyes. On the arm of her beaming father, she was walking toward him. Smiling. Their eyes locked.*

He whispered her name. "Zoe. Zoe. Zoe. Over and over he whispered her name and each beat of his heart echoed

They stood together in front of the robed minister. They said words. Beautiful words they had written themselves. Promising life long love and devotion in sunshine and in rain. Promising to always be as one. Till death and then eternity. They knelt. They sipped from a communion cup. They took two long white tapers and used the flame to light a center candle. They were one. They were Captain and Mrs. Adam Dimitri Bladgovicz.

Words from a lofty place: Shining words. "You may kiss your bride." He did. She laughed and threw her arms around his neck. "Forever and forever and forever," she said and pressed her lips on his again.

Cold lips. Her lips were so cold. His heart beat was low but steady. Laughing green eyes. Her name.

Fast forward the way dreams can. The little unknown child lost too early to name but not too early to mourn. Two beautiful daughters. Cheyenne and Esther. Esther and Cheyenne. Their laughter.

S'mores daddy?" We'll have lots and lots of S'mores.

"It's so cool God hears us at the same time. No matter where we are. God knows doesn't he daddy?

As a family they shared hope that next year there would be another child. Boy or girl didn't matter. Cheyenne and Esther told him so. "We want a baby, but momma says we can't have one till you come home. She does nearly everything else, drives the tractor, works on the truck, even shot us a wild turkey but she says that don't matter. We have to wait for you to have a baby. Hurry home daddy. Hurry home."

The rain.

Warm summer rain Memories. *It was…it was. . . August 5th the first time he kissed Zoe in a shaded flower filled park. Warm summer rain was a soft sheen of wonder enveloping them. One year to the day they married and once again warm summer rain was there. Beautiful warm summer rain. Beautiful bride.*

Their climbing roses thrived. Considering lack of experience, their first mountain top vegetable garden wasn't anything to write home about. But, what they lacked in knowledge they made up with curiosity and excitement. A green tomato was source of wonder as it grew, ripened to delicious deep red, and became a delight, a pleasure, a moment to remember. A fully developed green pepper was priceless.

"Daddy look! We growed these ourselves. They didn't come from the store.
They're real green peppers daddy. I tried to get one and the whole plant came out of the ground. Did I hurted it daddy? Can you make it all better?"

"Daddy How come there's so many rows of little green stuff? What is it?"

'Corn daddy! You mean great big ears of sweet corn will come from that? Does it come all ready to eat with lots of butter and salt and pepper the way we like it?

"Daddy why do you laugh so much?"

Esther brought her favorite green chair. "I want to watch it daddy. Watch it become corn. Will it take forever daddy?

The rain.

The wind.

Zoe's lips. So cold.

His arms wouldn't open. He couldn't. He had to hold her.

"Zoe" he mumbled through blue lips.

Something small and warm and wet probed his face. Then noise was long and howling like that of a lone wolf. It went on and on, keeping him awake. He wanted to sleep. His aching tired body and weeping spirit yearned for the wonderful relaxing peace of sleep.

A voice. Words jumbled together. Strong arms lifting him, supporting him, making him walk.

Disjointed sounds became words thickened by dense fog. "Dennis you take his head and shoulders. Franklin you get both his legs. Don't bend em any more than you have to.

Easy now. Dammit, don't let him fall. Watch the ice!"

Why was he being helped along like he was crippled and couldn't walk on his own? He could walk. He could. But why should he? He was warm and comfortable and so in need of the deep sleep.

"The voice said "In you go buddy." Adam felt something different. Not cold. Not wet.

The warm *spot again on his face and hands. Licking his eyelids. Why wouldn't his eyes stay open?*

More voices: "Good Lord! Never seen a blue man before. You reckon he's one of them fellers from Mars?"

"Idiot! Every kid that ever red a comic book knows Mars men is green!"

"Yeah, I know, but for just a minute there I kinda wondered."

His wonder brought ridicule. The silent staring kind.

Defensively, "Well, if he ain't from some other planet, you reckon he's alive?"

"Damm straight! All the way up the hill He was mumbling the strangest word like he was calling a deer."

Adam said "Zoe" loud and clear and mumbled a word they couldn't understand; a mumbled incomprehensible sound beginning with "ch" ending in "er."

"Chair? Cheer? First he calls a deer now he wants us to cheer a chair?"

Adam cursed. They jumped.

The leaders voice again. Not angry, but filled with humor. "If I didn't know better I'd swear you guys was a bunch of idiots. Now, any more questions?"

He gave them two seconds. "As I used to tell my deputies, we've established a few facts. Now we gotta work on a solution. Number one, he ain't from Mars. Number two, he's alive."

They groaned. O'Fallon to MacAlleny, "Betcha we won't live this down."

"Now we've gotta keep him alive, get some movement and sense out of him. Have to cut his clothes off. Can't take chances. Look at his boots George. Any way to save them?"

"Tell you what boss, I'd took them off and his feet weren't even wet. Once I got the boots dry on the outside, they didn't feel wet or look wet Best yet, everything he's wearing either zips or has Velcro so we don't have to cut anything off. Must be that new survival gear we read about. Lucky bastard. All this stuff probably saved his life."

"We ain't there yet boys. What we gotta do is warm him up nice and slow. Bonnet you and O'Fallon strip down to your skivvies and crawl in that down filled sleeping bag with him."

"Boss!"

"No pictures."

"Buncha clowns! Not to worry, you will all have a turn. Once we get some knee jerk reactions, we'll do warm water bottles in his arm pits and groin and knee joints."

"MacAlleny I didn't say hot! I said warm. Not as hot as you'd do to warm a baby bottle. Too hot would be as bad as too cold. One thing for dang sure, we've got a long night.

"One of you fellas… Yeah Klemstein you! Get me the emergency phone. I'm gonna call Doctor Greer. Come morning, he can high tail it up here with stuff we'll need because we ain't moving this guy."

While he waited: "Where's Gibbs?"

"In the kitchen boss. He figured the feller might need a hot toddy."

W.D. groaned. "We need a hot toddy. That's the last thing he needs."

"Soon as he starts making sense, doc says to give him some warm cider. The bad news fellers is you can crawl outa the sleeping bag. Doc says that's old school way of thinking. If he's shivering, he's warming up on his own. We ain't supposed to rush it. We're supposed to talk to him and give him some warm cider, warm Tang, warm Jello juice. C'mon doc what's Jello juice? Oh! Yeah, it's been awhile. We'll keep him awake."

Gibbs stood in the doorway with an open photo album in his hands. "Boss, you ain't gonna believe this. Look at him. Cept for his all white hair, I'd swear this fella we rescued is him. And boss look at that redheaded woman at his side. I'd swear on a stack of Bibles I seen this woman in D.C. at that food preservation school. She was teaching people to build dehydrators outa 2x2 boards and screen wire.

'Think about it boss. We worked with her. We made pies outa dried apples and squash just a couple weeks ago."

He took the album closer to a Coleman lantern. Yeah, I'd swear it wuz her. "Course it ain't exactly the same, but considerin' what she's been thru!

Lookit her hair. It's the same curly kinda red as the gal in D.C., but her hair was tied back. Plus, the gal we're talking about was skinny as a bean pole and pale. She didn't talk or smile much at all. She'd kinda stare off into space if we wasn't talking to her."

" She shore did know how to make dried apple pie."

From across the room, "Hey boss, he's trying to sit up. Maybe we'd better give him something to drink."

Adam said "Zoe! Cheyenne! Esther!" and fought to free himself from the restraining cocoon prison.

Where was he?

What was going on?

Deep coarse coughing took over and blood streaked mucus came out of his lungs.

"Get Doc Greer back on the phone O'Fallon! Looks like we've go more than a long night ahead. Saving this man might give us the fight of a lifetime."

TWENTY

FOR TWO DAYS TV AND RADIO BROADCAST NEWS OF THE
UPCOMING PRESIDENTIAL ADDRESS.

AS PRESIDENT INEZ BROWN PARKINSON WAS THE ONLY
SOURCE OF RELIABLE INFORMATION AND THE PRESDENTAL
NETWORK WAS THE ONLY ONE WORKING AROUND THE
CLOCK, PEOPLE TUNED IN.

As was her habit, the President delivered each address from a different location. Her first address after July 4th had been from the Oval Office.

Subsequent addresses came from Arlington National Cemetery, the National Cathedral, the Convention Center, the Hershorn Museum and Cultural Center, and various other historic sights around the capital.

Because the President felt it essential to keep memories and patriotism alive, each address was preceded by virtual tours of the city. Known and almost forgotten monuments, all that was part of America's beginning and struggles for freedom and equality were featured.

Cameras walked up to the face of Lincoln, went back stage at Ford's Theater, and silhouetted Washington's monument in sunset and moon glow.

She stressed these tours were not only to showcase beauty, but also to highlight memorials that marked America as a great nation. "We dare not forget our heritage," she said.

This day President Parkinson chose to speak from the Congressional building. Screens were set up in the Mall and in every public building.

Although she normally insisted pomp and circumstance be cut to the minimum, on this occasion she sat through Hail to the Chief, the applause and rigid attention and words that more than anything indicated the formality and serious nature of her coming address.

Giving a nod to proper protocol, she turned to chairs (some vacant) and spoke names. "Mr. Vice President, Speaker of the House, Members of Congress and the House of Representatives Honored Guest, My fellow Americans. My friends."

Noticing everyone still standing President Brown-Parkinson smiled, and extended her hands in welcome and gratitude. "Please be seated," she said and waited for the rustling and sighing to end.

She started again: "My friends. Many have asked if we are in the end times. Believe it or not, we've been there for a long time. Refusing to honor and worship God, degrading morality,

selfishness, and rampant sinfulness have brought the world to this standstill. We have created the problem. The evil, the innocent, and the godly died together when the lethal dust fell. Yet, God in his infinite mercy spared lives in every country.

Before 10 a.m., on July 4th, America was a nation full to the brim of every nationality under the sun. New arrivals to our hallowed shores came for a variety of reasons. I like to think all were peaceful but history has shown that is not true.

Americans, perhaps by nature of our inbred national preferences, have always been a quarrelsome people; each culture intent on their own way, each with their own agenda. For the present time we stand united facing the unknown with a sense of purpose that makes me prouder than ever before to be your president."

Applause echoed. She silenced it quickly.

"Look at your neighbor. Look at yourself. Look at me. And ask why? Why did he, why did she, why did I, why did the President survive? I don't know why we were given another chance, or why God didn't remove all evil. or how long our lives will last.

But I do know it is not for humans to know the mind of God. I do know He has a plan and a purpose for each of us; the good and beautiful, the bad and ugly. We are alive because He has a Plan. I know some will reject others will accept and ultimately, one will teach the other.."

She paused and stared into the camera "I do know the plagues in the book of revelation are being played out.

The Bible speaks of seven years of devastation. What I do not know is this; Is what we have experienced the beginning, or our time now the end of the beginning and a fresh start?

God has heard our prayers!

Is our survival His answer? If so, what will we do with it? Will we wander in the wilderness for forty years? Or will we be responsive to His will?

To add more wonder to our already overtaxed thought processes, we don't need to poll the remaining members of the scientific community for answers... They cannot predict if we have days, years, or decades left.

It is my personal feeling we've been given another chance to get it right. The Bible tells us to the almighty a thousand years are like a few night hours. If you don't know what I'm talking about you'd better find out."

President Inez Brown-Parkinson stopped reading from her prepared speech and stared intently into the camera.

"Brothers and Sisters, whether you like it or not, for the next few minutes, I'm speaking not only as your president, but as an ordained Baptist Minister. In other words, I'm gonna preach.

I've listened to the grumbling that boils down to shame on this administration for not telling you, for not preparing you for this world wide disaster!

I say in response, I'm sick of the bull! Years before President Turnbull's administration our leaders and leaders around the world worked to prepare the citizenry for this time

When I was Vice President we worked side by side to prepare this country. The only thing we didn't do was hog tie you and spoon feed you the truth that the world was serious trouble and if you wanted to survive, you had to prepare.

Scientific reports that proved the danger approaching were available. Talk show host turned them into jokes. Cartoonist had a field day.

Stupid movies parroted and ridiculed. Remember the Novel that became the movie to watch? The bronze hairless muscled hero with piercing black eyes, the enormously endowed dumb blonde heroine spilling nearly everything over the top of her shimmering satin gown. Remember his piercing black eyes probing hers of shining blue as they discussed the coming disaster while sipping dirty martinis in their penthouse apartment?

Remember the movie critic who wrote he knew what was wrong with the American male when all the hero did was stare into that broad's blue eyes? He wrote the only reason he knew that was his wife told him so because he was too dang busy looking lower. Twice as busy."

The audience, loving where she was going and remembering both the novel and the resulting ridiculously funny sci-fi movie groaned, laughed, and applauded.

President Brown- Parkinson's voice became that of a news reporter. "Tickets for "Our New World" the Oscar nominated blockbuster were twenty dollars apiece. DVD's easily took fifty of your hard earned cash.

Kids were hungry, heat was shut off, but somehow, America went to the movies. Why? They wanted hope. They wanted to believe. They turned away from God to a man made mess that promised everything, delivered nothing and helped pave the way to the loss of many lives.

In spite of the hype and lies, over three million ladies convinced their husbands to believe and prepare. That those of you who did not listen and prepare survived is in itself a miracle.

To those of you who now complain the loudest and the longest, my advice is stop acting like your name is Adam and this is the Garden of Eden. Neither are you destined to wander without purpose or direction for forty years in this man made wilderness.

Face your responsibilities! Shame on you for not listening to Christian evangelist and preachers of the word! Shame on you for not reading your Bibles! Shame on you for not finding the truth and turning your lives over to the Lord!

A few seconds ago I said if you were clueless to my religious take on this disaster, you needed to find out what I was talking about. To those of you who want to learn copies of the New International Version of the Holy Bible are available in the reception area, and in every bookstore in the area.

We have not highlighted prophecy and verses that point to Christ. If you want Him, seek Him. If you want salvation and life eternal you will find the path here. If you want peace, you will find it here. In this book." (She held up her well worn red leather bound edition)--"In the words of prophets; in recorded history, and from those who walked with Jesus, and from Jesus Himself, you will find everything you need to know. And that includes but is not limited to creation of the universe. No matter what liberal free thinkers taught, the earth and the heavens were not made from nothing colliding with nothing. Human beings did not crawl out of slimy muck.

The world we live in and the universe that surrounds us are the creation of God!

A few weak boos and murmurs were silenced by a standing ovation and applause. Since she knew this praise was for God, President Brown- Parkinson let it continue.

When silence was once more almost thick enough to slice, the President continued. "The best sermon on the subject of our Triune god and His love for humanity was preached by a great man from the Lone Star State, Baptist Minister Doctor Shadrach Meshach Lockridge. He was 87 years old when he left this life for eternity with Jesus on April 4, 2000.

Since I do not have the ability to do justice to his sermon, videos and the printed version of this sermon are available next to the Bibles in the lobby."

President Brown-Parkinson was not aware she was pacing the stage or that her voice took on the timber and cadence of the famous pastor. In the few minutes she used to quote Doctor Lock ridge, her audience said it was like they were hearing the voice of the long deceased pastor

"Pastor Lockridge spoke about the wonder of Jesus. He couldn't stop talking. But every now and then, he'd pause and ask "Do you know him? I wish I could describe him to you."

When he spoke of our Lord and Savior, he said, "His goodness is limitless. His mercy is everlasting. His love never changes. His yoke is easy and his burden is light. His grace is sufficient." And once again, he paused and said, "I wish I could describe Him to you."

As when the sermon was first heard and in every replaying, ripples of laughter surfaced.

When they ended, President Brown- Parkinson continued. "Reading from Psalm 19, I will add. His laws are true and fair and more desirable than gold. They are sweeter than honey AND a great reward for those who obey them.

In the New Testament our Savior tells the Apostle Paul-- who three times asked for a thorn to be removed from his side--, "My Grace is sufficient. My strength is made perfect in weakness."

Interpretation? Theologians debate the meaning of this thorn. Was it guilt over his earlier zeal to persecute Christians? Did he remember standing guard over the cloaks of those who stoned to death the martyr Stephen as Stephen looked up into Heaven and said he saw the Savior seated at the right hand of His Father? Or was his thorn something physical? Did his experience with The Light bring on terrible headaches and near blindness? We don't know.

But this we do know. When the Lord Jesus told this obedient man "My Grace is sufficient for thee, my strength is made perfect in weakness," he meant whatever the challenge He was at the apostle's side. And this believer's response then should be our response today. He said "When I am weak, then am I strong."

Brothers and Sisters, we've never been weaker. But the Grace of God is sufficient for us today, whatever our weakness, whatever our challenge, those who believe know more than ever it is as it was in Paul's day. HIS GRACE IS SUFFICENT! HIS STRENGTH IS MADE PERFECT IN WEAKNESS!"

Paul was strong because he knew God's grace was enough. We are strong, and will gain strength and wisdom become because God's grace is with us, and because it is enough!"

President Brown- Parkinson was silent for three minutes. Those who had joined the crowd and began walking away, those who squirmed in their seats, and those who had always said they didn't have no time for preaching had been mesmerized by her voice. Inroads of truth were etched on faces and hope shone in eyes once dulled by shock and grief.

A silent subdued nation waited.

Her voice broke the stillness. "If you did not know before, know now that Jesus is the hope of the world. Accept, or reject Him, as you will accept or reject my message.

Now if some of you ladies and gentlemen would bless me with a few Amen's, I'll stop preaching and go back to Presidential business."

From the gathered crowd at the Library of Congress, the response was a solid wave of emotion followed by a standing ovation. Millions watching at home, in churches theaters and stores voiced their "Amen," and joined the ovation.

*   *   *   *   *

President Inez Brown-Parkinson gripped the podium and waited them out. When she spoke again, her voice was factual and purpose driven. "We have survived one of the most devastating times in recorded history.

Therefore, because our future as a nation is in the hands of every man woman and child, I will speak bluntly. Because other areas of security demand attention and action, and I cannot continue to make this address, copies will be available.

The question you must all answer is this: Will we grow, or dissolve into chaos?

While warnings were ignored by a nation weary, bored, and satiated with pleasures of the mind and flesh, the administration worked with representatives from every region, climatologist and scientist to devise a to ensure the continuation of, and growth of our nation. Let us review the proposed plans as outlined in the handouts you should have received at the door. We will start with Safe Living areas. Please follow along as I read.

1.   SAFE LIVING AREAS:

To ensure our survival for the next few years Americans are advised to live a nomadic life. We will be constantly on the move, avoiding areas where natural disasters threaten lives. Our safest path is to remain nomadic and when hurricane, tornado, floods and blizzards are the norm, move to safer ground.

We are aware some of you will not follow this plan. Be warned! We will not force you to do so any more than we could force you to live underground. Now as then, the choice is yours. Because we do not have means or material to engage in rescue efforts, if you decide to return to areas prone to natural disasters, you do so at your own peril.

I stress for those of you that weren't listening the first ten times, that we cannot, we will not support rescues of those who hold to the false belief they can live in areas prone to natural disasters and escape unscathed!

One good example is the gulf coast areas during hurricane season. Those choosing to stick with the storms; or, to ignore safety warnings will be responsible for their own safety. The depleted staffing of Red Cross and National Guard cannot provide rescue efforts. We do not want a repeat of the New Orleans/Mississippi disaster of the last century.

Natives of the gulf coast area and in Hurricane Alley know the seasons and the signs and must be prepared and obey them.

As previously stated, California and areas along the San Andreas Fault are considered dangerous for human habitation at all times.

We no longer have the weather channel to advise you to take cover when clouds boil green and the air is tense.

Use your common sense. For your own sakes, learn to read the weather and the sky. For those who have not learned to do so, my son and I has concocted a short bit of nonsense. Bear with me. You might learn something.

On screen, dancing figures appeared under a cloudy sky. Near a burbling brook, graceful young men gathered arms full of daffodil and presented them to blushing maidens wearing white diaphanous gowns.

Freeze frame. President Brown-Parkinson's voice. "Ah yes, springtime, when Tom, a young man fancies Nancy. It's a good thing unless Nancy fancies Bill. Then troubles mount up like lemon drops and rain pours from the sky.

It does not matter boys and girls if all the grass and leaves are green. It does not matter if daffodil are in blossom.

What matters is Tom is so intent on getting what he wants that he pays no attention to the storm clouds gathering.

Video resumed as a scowling Nancy threw the flowers in Tom's face. Thunder boomed, lightning flashed and they were trapped.

Will Tom survive?

Will Nancy be happy ever after?

Will they learn to read the signs?

Will Bill get his act together?

*　　*　　*　　*　　*

From the audience "Will the pres and Randy win an Oscar?"

Laughter was a good thing.

President Brown-Parkinson continued: "As a reminder, in the springtime, if you do venture outdoors under a rain filled sky and are not prepared, you will get soaking wet. Be sure to take your umbrellas and wear raincoats."

The president grinned. "Same thing's true for summer only there may be a bit more lightening. That's the white and gold flashes that come when too many toasters, coffee pots, waffle irons and shavers are plugged into outlets and positive and negative electrical charges get together. I forget. Does that happen before or after the bowling balls strike the pens?

Pause

Heartbeat.

From the audience. "Hey pres don't give up your day job."

This time her laughter led the applause.

She continued. "I know you're like me in loving the fluffy white cumulus clouds running like little lambs across the May sky, but there's another type of cumulus that, while being beautiful and powerful, should only serve to warn us of imminent danger. These are called." She paused, looked down at her notes and slowly pronounced--- cumu lo nimbus" Then quickly, "Do not ask me to say that again. No telling what I'd come up with."

Before crowd reaction, lights dimmed and large screens displayed a wall of dark brooding clouds. The audience could feel tension in the air.

Since these were shot within the past year near Topeka, Kansas, I'm sure some of you saw them on the Weather Channel. These clouds, especially those with the anvil shaped heads have enough power to destroy everything in sight. Fortunately, they dissipated before damage occurred, but, as you look at the screen, the next pictures will serve as a warning. This is what tornadoes can do."

Only silence filled the room as images of destroyed homes and weeping survivors filled the screen. There a tossed battered doll, there cars and trucks twisted into unrecognizable shapes. And always the faces of people; tear streaked, shocked, their arms reaching out for what was not.

"These are land locked storms. The sea can be just as destructive. When waves are high, don't think you can escape. When hurricane season comes, don't stand in the wind taking pictures, get out. Seek shelter. Rules of thumb to remember: In Hurricane season go up. Find higher ground. In tornadoes, go down. Get in basements, underground shelters.

If you dare to stand up to a 90 mph wind," She took a deep breath, stared intently into the cameras, and said, "Be sure to wave when you fly by."

Groans and laughter as pages turned.

Blizzards and Ice storms? Stay home. Play checkers. In all cases have food, water and medical supplies available.

Now let's see how many stayed awake. Help me out here people.

How do you protect your lives during Hurricane season?"

A few voices…" Head to the hills?"

"I can't hear you. Tell me again. She cupped both hands to her ears and the questions flashed on the screen.

"Hurricanes"

"Head for the hills. High ground, get away from the coast!" Answers filled the air

"Tornadoes?"

"Down baby down! A young vice yelled in response and others picked it up.

"Wind storms?"

"Hide, stay indoors away from windows"

"Blizzards? Ice storms?"

From one side a young male voice "Stay home and make love?"

From the front "She didn't say that, but it's not a bad idea!"

President Brown- Parkinson marveled at the ability of a mourning population to find humor and laughter in a time of world wide disaster. Marveled, and was thankful for the resiliency of the human spirit. She enjoyed the laughter but did not waver from her intended purpose.

"I did not mention flooding. This happens any time anywhere all over the country. Resulting mud and rock slides destroy homes and lives. Don't live on a bluff above or near a river, don't attempt to cross swollen streams. Know your terrain and be prepared.

I've told you about a dozen times, but it won't hurt you to hear it again. The country is in no shape to rescue people who choose to ignore safety warnings. If you walk into the face of any storm, know your lives are in your own hands. We do not have men, material or means to work rescues."

General discussion lasted fifteen minutes before President Parkinson, after conferring with technicians, returned to the stage.

"As looters and sexual predators are wrecking havoc around major cities this is not the time to become city dwellers. If you choose to do so, consider your choice twins to other dangerous areas.

We are fortunate to have electrical cables secure underground. However, by necessity electrical usage must be diminished. By doing this we will be able to maintain houses of Worship, law enforcement agencies, water departments, and hospitals. Temperatures will be controlled in museums and libraries.

Public schools, private schools, colleges and universities will be in session from April through September, and electrical usage must be monitored.

Our focus will be on critical areas, not empty buildings. In your homes, you must plan on electricity and heat in main rooms only. In the winter, thermostats are to be set at 65 degrees. If you're cold, layer up. Remember: Bathrooms yes. Bedrooms no. Kitchens yes, dens no."

Ignoring the moans and groans she went down the list. In summer, there will be no air conditioning. Open windows however are 100 percent permissible.

In cities like New York and Chicago, Dallas and Topeka, Saint Louis and Seattle, in fact, in all large cities; within a few years major buildings will become unlivable and hazardous and will be demolished. All useable materials will be salvaged. For example, in costal and lake side areas, some material will be used to shore up the sea walls and dikes. The land left behind will be cleared for vegetable gardens and orchards."

The president pointed toward a large monitor: "Notice the activity on the screen. As I speak, looters in cities across America are being rounded up and given uniforms of sanitation workers. They made the messes. They get to clean them up. Supervision, as you can tell on the screen, is available." The camera focused on khaki clad military men and women issuing uniforms and attaching ankle bracelets.

She continued. "The looters have no choice. The good news is they get off easy.

The flip side of the good news bad news coin concerns drug dealers, murderers and sexual predators. For these unfortunates, THERE WILL BE NO LAWYERS OFFERING PLEA DEALS. JUSTICE WILL BE SERVED AND THE INNOCENT PROTECTED. GOD'S LAW IS THE LAW OF THE LAND.

Silence stretched as her intent penetrated each mind. Then, applause and roars of approval filled the auditorium and bounced from sea to shining sea.

Voices rose in agreement and, as usual in public meetings, disagreement.

"Hey Inez I'd be glad to hang the bastards that raped my sister."

"I'll help, but first we're gonna do a little carving. In public."

"With rusty razor blades!"

"Mercy, not justice!"

"Due Process. Due process." This from a suited brief case carrying lawyer who was booed down.

"Hanging's too good for those creeps" a grey haired grandmother shouted. Those around her cheered.

President Brown-Parkinson stood patiently as voices rose in a tumult of agreement and disagreement. Once again, her voice served to quiet the crowd.

"I did not say execution. I did not say hanging. I did not say we would become vigilantes."

As Christ has forgiven our sins, so too will He forgive theirs. Those who do not repent will meet God's justice. He said He would repay. He's working on it now."

Questions, garbled voices filled the area. She heard: "Who? Doing what? God's too busy now."

We can get the bastards?"

"Shut up Charlie and let her talk!"

She waited. Charlie sat down and clamped his lips. The cigar he started to light was snatched and stamped out.

The cold strength of the president's voice stopped more complaints before they were more than thoughts. All eyes were on her.

"When I first saw scenes such as we will all soon witness, I thought they were scripted. Believe me, they are not. What we will watch in a few moments is real. It is reality TV such as none of us has seen before. These are real people. Not actors.

For the past two days Christian TV has traveled across the country and sent me scenes identical to what everyone watching (including myself) will see for the first time today. This is a live telecast of people choosing between heaven and hell. I have not seen these films before, but having watched others, I know to tell you to watch faces. You might even recognize someone you know.

Of special interest to the homeland security group is one man wearing a gold lame body suit. Gold chains practically drape his shoulders and he wears what appears to be a cape made of diamonds and emeralds. We've seen him in every video. It's like he has a private jet or knowledge of our intent and shows up in every city. I feel confident you will see him in these live news cast.

Three big screens were alive with scenes of men and women kneeling at crosses, and baptisms. They emerged from lakeside and swimming pools and creek swimming holes looking like new people.

"Hey pres, the man in that suit ain't there."

"I prayed he would be, but did not expect him. I'm sure he'll be in other segments."

The announcer's voice came into the hushed auditorium: "What we are witnessing is rebirth. These people have been washed in the blood of the Lamb. God has forgiven their sins and welcomed them into His kingdom. Lives are starting over, fresh and clean.

As it is stated in the New Testament book of Two Corinthians Chapter

15, "Everyone who belongs to Christ has become a new person. Christ makes everything new." In case you miss the message in Corinthians look in Hebrews, and Colossians. If you're still holdouts, read the truth in the entire Bible. It's full from the get go of what God does to and for those who love, trust and obey Him.

People all over the country stared open mouthed as the scenes unfolded and the voice of the announcer filled quiet rooms.

"There are also very vivid word images of what happens to those who do not. What we will film live and show you now is happening now and it is not pretty. It should scare the pants off you. But bear in mind, these images are real. Happening now!"

The cameras moved into inner city enclaves and focused on crowds of people shooting up, popping pills, and publically engaged in acts of sexual perversion as cheering crowds watched.

A voice; "He's there, that guy she talked about see him, over to the left. He's watching. Just standing there watching. See him? How could he be smiling?"

Men and women carrying Bibles walked through the crowds, some singing, others praying. Their faces were shining. Hope filled their voices as they reached out to the unsaved and were slapped aside. Cameras juxtaposed faces: the triumphant forgiven sinners and those who refused.

"There he is again, walking toward the women with Bibles. He's doing something? Oh my God! How could he do that to the Word of God?"

Cameras focused on clear faces, then men and women in filthy clothing, their eyes bloodshot and filled with both fear and hatred.

"That's my son. My son," a woman screamed in the auditorium. As if he heard her voice, the lanky dark haired pale man turned from the edge of the crowd and looked into the camera.

"Oh Eugene come to Jesus now!" she begged. He turned in slow motion as if to run, turned again and looked into the camera. His face registered shock and surprise and said clearer than words that somehow, he had seen and heard his mother. Sobbing, he fell to his knees.

A camera focused on an overweight grey haired woman singing. Her clear soprano voice filled the Auditorium. Filled the hearts and minds of watchers everywhere:

"Just as I am, but with one plea,
That thou my God didst die for me,
And that thou bidst me come to thee,
Oh lamb Of God I come, I come."

Laughing, the bejeweled man pointed toward a group of drinking men. One looked up, moved as if mesmerized, and grabbed at the white robe of the singing woman.

"You ain't exactly a sex symbol sister but what the hell; I've got something for you too. C'mon down." He pulled her to the pavement, ripped at her clothing and in the blink of an eye, was swallowed by a smoking hole in the earth. His screams echoed as he disappeared.

A few bystanders moved to help the injured woman. A chain smoking younger woman with dirty matted once beautiful auburn hair, emptied her bottle of whiskey, crumpled her cigarette and knelt. "Oh Jesus, forgive me" she sobbed and reached to embrace her mother.

Laughing men cursing God pulled her aside. Intent on finishing the depravation, but now with "meat to go around," they reached out. They took two steps and on national television, a slightly larger hole belching more yellow sulfurous smoke swallowed them alive.

The surrounding crowd that minutes before had cheered the intended rapist froze, broke into splinter groups and ran. Some knelt. Others, afraid to move stood and stared wide eyed into the camera.

In the audience, two ladies, sisters united not by blood but by loneliness and need, watched their children, mourned their husbands and vowed somehow, in someway, to make their world better.

Lessons began when their husbands refused to build shelters and they, and their children had done it on their own. They listened to the warnings and raced for shelter and survived.

Their husbands died because they were somewhere, doing something more important than following directions given by a woman president. "No way in hell," they said, and they died.

Now these new sisters sat in the big room surrounded by others. "Did you see him?"

"See who?"

"The man who did that nasty thing to the Bible."

"No, Marge I was caught up watching that mother and daughter reunion. Made me feel good to see that girl reach out to Jesus. The look on her face said she knew she was forgiven. Just like that. In an instant. That was wonderful!"

"Yeah, but that man, the one dressed in gold and jewels redefined the meaning of fool and coward at the same time. I never seen anybody turn tail and run as fast as he did. And y'know what?"

"Well, Annie you're gonna tell me anyway, so I'll save time and not ask."

"Well, Marge, since you insist. Right at first, I looked at his clothes and that cape of diamonds and emeralds and thought that he had it made. I always wanted diamonds and emeralds. You think that was envy or lust or greed?"

"Coulda been just wishful thinking without thinking about consequences."

"Maybe, but I really had it bad. When the kids and I walked in the mall, we'd always look in jewelry store windows and I'd steer the talk to owning diamonds and emeralds because then we'd be rich. I liked the idea of having stuff. I thought our troubles would be over if we had stuff.

Then I saw that man wearing enough jewelry to fill a bank vault, and saw what he did and how he turned away and couldn't feel envy at all. All I felt was a kind of sadness. Like he'd had everything offered he would ever need and he turned it down."

"Yeah, I know what you mean. I feel like me and my kids came here with no idea about all our tomorrows, and we're gonna be leaving with everything we need, while that poor rich man is…" She left the sentence and the thought unfinished. But they both knew.

President Brown- Parkinson wiped her eyes and turned away from the now dark screens. "Any of you think you can do a better job than God, please step forward," she said.

There were no takers.

Two hours later after a luncheon break of vegetarian Sub Way sandwiches and diet Cherry flavored Doctor Pepper, or Cherrywine, the favorite soft drink of the Carolinas, the crowd reassembled. A quiet crowd. A crowd who, when seats were filled lined the walls and when they were filled, stood shoulder to shoulder in the hallways. A crowd who would never forget what they saw there.

Someone, a little man wearing a miner's cap quoting Abraham Lincoln's Gettysburg Address was joined by a thousand voices. "It is for us the living rather to be dedicated to the unfinished work which they who fought here have thus far so nobly advanced. It is rather for us here to be dedicated to the task remaining before us. That from these honored dead we take increased devotion to that cause for which they gave the last full measure of devotion. That we here highly resolve that these dead shall not have died in vain. That this nation under God shall have a new birth of freedom and that this government of the people, by the people, for the people, shall not perish from the earth."

A standing ovation welcomed President Inez Brown- Parkinson's return to the podium. She stood under the spotlight, head bowed, and hands clasped in prayer.

When the noise showed no sign of abating, President Brown- Parkinson walked to the edge of the stage and shading her eyes, peered into the crowd.

"The glory you're giving me belongs to God. You'll continue to give Him glory as you live your lives. Now if you're ready we'll finish the program."

The cheering continued, was louder, more intense.

President Brown-Parkinson shrugged her shoulders. "Well, if you'd rather, we could have a gospel sing and come back for business in a few days."

"Music first, we ain't got anywhere else to go today."

For half an hour they poured hope and faith into gospel songs and praise songs until their voices grew hoarse and dim.

President Brown-Parkinson waited for them to resume seats

"It's been a long day and we have a lot of ground still to cover. If you would, please return to the program. Where were we?"

Voices called out.

"Oh yes, NUMBER TWO. You've noticed a lot of topics here, and each is accompanied with a brief resume. We've used enough time today so your questions will be answered at a later date. Now we have enough time left to cover the basics." She paused long enough to sip from a bottle of vitamin water, and adjust the jacket of her blue suit.

"2. A. FOOD. B. CLOTHING. C. MEDICAL CARE. D. EDUCATION. E. THE FUTURE and last but not least, F. HOMELAND SECURITY:

A. Enjoy frozen foods while power grids last. Dried foods have a shelf life which were good for sales but didn't make much sense. If the food is not moldy, it's safe to eat. Canned foods will be edible as long as cans are not leaking or bulging. Dehydrated foods end the ready to eat food chain. If you haven't learned how to plant harvest and preserve by the time you get there, you're in a heap of trouble. See the pamphlets you were given. Follow directions.

B. CLOTHING: That should be obvious. Plan well. Take what you need. Use what you take.

C. MEDICAL CARE: Doctor Thaddeus Greer of the Mayo Clinic is in charge of establishing health care centers. Present plans include mobile medical and surgical units. Rest assured, medication for heart, diabetic and kidney patients will continue to be disbursed. Restarting treatment programs are a top priority. Transportation and housing for patients will be provided.

The time of medical indulgence is over. There will be no more abortions, transplants, and cosmetic surgeries, handouts of male enhancement drugs, steroids or hormones. We will live as God made us.

As most critically ill patients were caught in the dust, there will be little need for invasive surgeries.

After their sixth month of pregnancy, all expectant mothers will be quartered in local hospitals. They and their newborns will be given the best care available. As dairy herds are not yet prolific and because formulas have a limited shelf life, mothers are encouraged to breast feed their newborn.

As for diapers, maybe in a hundred years we'll run out of disposables.

We heard the moans and groans on the hill when you lined up for flu and tetanus shots. Gripe all you want to, but remember you will have a healthier winter.

D. EDUCATION: Will continue. At all levels. The three r's are not part of the curriculum, but are available as extra curricular subjects. Topping the list of required subjects are medical, construction and farming. Specific learning strategies are found in manuals thicker than the Manhattan phone book. Survival is not a given. It is a learned skill and requires our best effort.

E. THE FUTURE: She checked her list and leaned over the podium. "Out of a population in the billions, we have accounted for nearly ten million civilian survivors; most of whom were led to shelter built by ladies tired of their husbands and community leaders refusing to take this world wide threat seriously.

In America when and where women took charge and men listened to reason, shelters were built and stocked, and human and animal lives now saved."

I cannot say ladies were the saviors and men the destroyers because it would not be truth. The irrefutable truth is that women believed first. Together, men and women of logic worked to save this country.

Some of you are here because you listened and planned and believed. Others survived by accident. We have this in common; we survived for a reason we have yet to learn.

Scientist knew the disaster was approaching but could not pin point time and date That it happened so quickly and that so many met their death on July 4th is an ironic twist of fate and unexplainable."

Deep silence that had filled the room was broken by intermittent sounds of weeping. Like a great tidal wave, moans and tears reached the president. She stood head bowed. Waiting.

Then: "We lost mothers and fathers, husbands and daughters and sons. We lost dreams and dreamers, music and art. We lost those we loved more than our own lives." Her voice broke and she gave in to her own tears.

Fighting for composure, the President looked directly into the camera. "I lost half of my family that day. My husband a pediatric oncologist and our twin sons, both nurses were en-route to Children's Hospital to be with grieving families when the dust fell. There was no time to save them, and they wanted to live... They had worked with my team to save many lives but theirs were lost.

If they were here, I would tell them, as I tell you now, WOMEN AND MEN WILL WORK TOGETHER SIDE BY SIDE. LEADERSHIP WILL NOT BE BASED ON GENDER, BUT ON INTELLIGENCE, ABILITY AND ENDURANCE.

THERE WILL BE NO RACIAL PROFILING. WE ARE A MULTICULTURAL NATION. RED, YELLOW, BLACK, BROWN, WHITE AND SHADES OF EACH, WE ARE AMERICANS."

She stopped pacing the floor and stood under the unfurled American flag. Her voice lowered until they strained to hear. And they did. "We will stand united, sharing our heritage and our lives or we will fail and fall. The choice is yours."

Cheers filled the room. President Brown Parkinson waited for silence and called their attention to the program.

"E. HOMELAND SECURITY: I mentioned that before. The Joint Chiefs of Staff and Military leaders have divided the states into regions. Each region has been assigned an overall director, who in turn assigns local directors. They will distribute complete lists of your duties and responsibilities. Now in place in each area is a law keeping force made up of former police officers, and members of all branches of the military.

The commander of Homeland Security is Navy Admiral Adam Dimitry Bladgovicz. His headquarters are in Sainte Lillian's Missouri, a small town in the Missouri Ozarks near the Mississippi River.

F.B.I Specialist Donna L. Brygal is Director of the Eastern Seaboard. Doctor Claire T. Clap will take over the southern states, and James U. Venable, a former climatologist will direct operations to the west.

Applications for homeland security positions are available in the lobby. Before you sign up, be aware you will undergo rigorous training. When I say rigorous, I'm talking a few steps up from Marine Corps Boot Camp."

Hands and voices raised in the crowd. President Brown-Parkinson did not wait for applause or questions. She stepped away from the podium, motioned to her escort and walked into the crowd. She touched hands, shared tears and hugs and lost track of the times she said "I don't know, but we're working on it. Come see me. Call me. Bring your questions and your answers when you do. Remember, if all you have is complaints that entrance door is also an exit. Like I said, once before, don't let it smack you in your rear as you hurry out.

Better yet, if all you're gonna do is complain don't show up. We need workers not whiners."

TWENTY-ONE

To the observer, she was calm, collected, and very much in charge of her emotions.

She worked as directed by the President and the Department of Survivalist Training. She taught. She lectured. She demonstrated. She had answers for questions she'd never heard before and worked on solutions that six months ago would have never entered her thought process.

Just months ago she was someone else with a husband and a family and a dumb old dog. Months ago she was alive.

It was the quiet times when no one was watching that her mask fell off. She lived then in a time and place others could not see. There she was with Mark John and their kids. There old August was chasing a Frisbee and Anastasia had gravel imbedded in her knee after she fell from her two wheeler on her first solo flight. Eve iced the knee, tweezed the gravel, disinfected, and bandaged the oozing wound with Barbie Doll band-aids, and put her baby on the bike.

"Mommie, I can't" Anastasia sobbed.

"Yes we can," she said and walked the hill beside her daughter, talking all the while about bike safety and fun exploring trails and the wonderful things they would do together.

"We did it mommie! We did it!"

She smiled. She laughed. People looked at her like she was nuts but they didn't say anything. They too were busy remembering. Too busy surviving to spend more than a thought about a skinny pale woman walking alone, smiling and talking and laughing.

Her mother said "Since we're going to be here awhile, the President wants us to get busy on some survival booklets."

"Why mom?"

Well, in my opinion, I think it's to get your mind busy. She don't like the way you look like life's plum gone out on you."

"It has mom."

Suddenly she was eye to eye with her mother. "You think I don't feel their loss? You think I'm not half crazy worried about your brothers and their families? We haven't heard a word from your sister or her girls. It's been too long for us to hear nothing. Evangelina do you think you're alone in the universe?"

Mac said she needed her mother. She did. Now she was in her face as usual. Issuing orders. As usual.

Eve wiped a grimy hand across her face, rubbed her eyes, and looked into the milling crowds. Possibly, she was seeing them for the first time.

Finally, "Got anything else mom?"

"Well, she…that is, the President did say something about using our knowledge of edible wild foods to prepare booklets. In the event our food supply runs low, she wants city folks to know what is and what ain't fit to eat.

"We can do that mom."

As if Mac were whispering in Laney's ear, she said "We're not doing anything until you pay attention to your appearance. Clean yourself up for goodness sake!"

Eve vowed to never need a third reminder.

At night they roamed halls of the National Science Library refreshing long buried memories of edible grasses, weeds and wild fruits. They knew how and when to select wild asparagus, doc and rosemary, dandelion, burdock and thistle, lambs ear, fiddle fern, and the pungent dark green watercress. Native American Medical treatments were a treasure trove of information.

Eve and Laney found hundreds of cookbooks and common sense pamphlets from the Smokey Mountains. These and others were copied and piled for distribution. Laney said although she didn't in particular like the idea, it was best to include recipes for alcoholic beverages as they were a dang sure fire way to preserve fruit and corn.

They copied almost delicious sounding recipes for cattails and marsh weeds, and refreshed their memories about soothing teas made from mints, clover and daisies. "Tried it once for a spring tonic. Today I wouldn't drink Sassafras root tea if you paid me," Laney said, but the recipe went into their collection.

They tasted barks and seeds of white pine and worried over how much was too much of white acorn. Liver damage available if too much ingested. They shuttered.

As if there weren't enough protein in lake fish and wild nuts, they did papers on grubs. Eve gagged at the thought of eating worms. Her mother said "Guess we've never been that hungry."

They studied and catalogued edible natural foods for every state in the union. Eve learned more than she ever thought she would about cactus-- or was that cacti? She asked her mom, but Laney wasn't sure. They copied information, stapled and stacked booklets

To their students they said, "As we do our nomadic journey we need to recognize and make use of and preserve natural foods"

"What's that mean miss?"

It means if you're in the forest you'll know the difference between dandelion and doc, doc and poison ivy. Some things that grow wild you can eat. Some you absolutely must not.

Sometimes they listened. Some doubted they'd ever run out of food. Others said there was no way of telling, but it didn't hurt to learn.

Their best lesson was a student discovering a pretty vine in the national park and bringing it to class. He figured since 'teach' had said they'd have to be careful in woodlands and forest, national parks didn't matter, and wove his pretty vine into a crown and wore it to class. Admiring girls delighted in sharing his find until Eve and Laney walked into class.

"Calamine lotion" Laney said.

"Better get antihistamines too," Eve said and the kids asked: "Cala what? Calla what was followed by "Why? Their answers came within three days.

Continuing education on everything wild and edible had to include mushrooms! Missouri bred born and raised, Eve had eaten practically every edible weed, tree nut, fruit and root in Missouri. Doc and Plantin and lambs ear made a fine side dish. Wild berries made delicious pies. Nuts greens and berries were part of their lives. They'd even boiled the green walnut outer shell to dye pants and shirts for the annual Civil War enactment. But, her family had never, not once in her life eaten mushrooms. The first time they made a tuna noodle casserole and used canned mushroom soup, they baked the casserole 45 minutes in a 350 degree oven and said "No wonder we don't eat mushrooms."

Then Eve married a Michigan man and heard the wonderful stories about Morels. His family said "Morels are the most beautiful, the most wonderful, the most delicious mushroom in the world," Hoping they would take the hint, she smiled, blanched, and buried her nose in a book.

In the early month of may on a beautiful damp morning when little puffy white clouds were like lambs racing across the soft blue sky, they drug her to the van and like it or not, she went mushroom hunting. "Look for little sponge like things that resemble fir trees," they said.

She walked no more than 15 feet into the forest and looked down and said "There's a bunch of them things over here." The "bunch" spread out at her feet, under the May apples and down past rotten and rotting logs. They filled peanut butter buckets and dumped them into a bushel basket and went back for more. She was the Mushroom Queen.

They "oohed" and "aahed" and cleaned and fried and force fed her her first Morel. Practically had to tie her down to do it. She broke the bonds of upbringing after the first bite. She knew Morels. The good, the bad and the ugly. But that was the only mushroom she knew, and or would admit to knowing, or eating. Those white things in the store and those big brown things sliced, diced, fried or sautéed turned her stomach. But not Morels.

Suddenly she was faced with the need to identify, classify and red line every poisonous mushroom. Once again Eve hated mushrooms. Her revenge was the pamphlet heading: DON'T BE STUPID. The pamphlet was filled with pictures and descriptive of penalties incurred for harvesting, preparing and eating these fungi.

Mushrooms out of the way, Eve decided the best part of working with the Department of Natural Nutrition; (a sub department of the Department of Survivalist Training) was building dehydrators using screen wire and sturdy slabs cut from two by four's. Left over yardsticks from lumber yards determined spaces between each eight horizontally spaced shelf.

She knew every non-root vegetable; including her favorite the green great and slimy okra, and nearly every root vegetable except white potatoes which turned black with their starch and sugars exposed to light, could be dehydrated. Okra and tomatoes took more time but to her mind, they were worth it

Her helpers in the building and preserving project were a rag tag band of hillbillies from south of the Mason Dixon Line led by a short wiry man they all called boss. They all took a shine to her in a friendly brotherly sort of way. She took a shine to them and to his dogs Pete Jr., and Repeat, and for two months they were the best of friends.

Her group feasted on their first dried squash and apple pies in early November before Laney and Eve headed home to Sainte Lillian. Their friend said he "lowed as how he'd not tasted anything better than them there pies since Peggy Sue up and"… He looked down at his pie and couldn't talk.

Laney and Eva went home to the Missouri Ozarks… Their co-workers said they had to see a man about a horse. Eve knew about men and horses and didn't ask. There had been enough of both in her life.

They said good byes before the November winds and rains blew cold. Eve and her mother each drove a loaded truck to Missouri. W.D. and the boys took ATV's and cut across to West Virginia.

There they would meet their leader, learn their mission and make ready to meet up with the rest of their crew who were on training missions in other parts of their assigned area. Since they were new to the Admiral, the president figured they needed this time alone together to check strength and weaknesses and be sure of a good fit.

One thing they figured they'd have to get used to was the number of women in all the security groups. Last they heard, Admiral Adam had more than 20 ladies in his crew alone and it was fact that more women joined every day. This kept up, they'd outnumber the men.

Not that W.D. saw anything wrong with that. He'd trained quite a few female deputies and they weren't nothing to mess with. When he compared men and women in the force, it was like men had to have a map but the ladies had eyes back of their heads and could smell trouble before the pot boiled. Considering everything, he kinda liked that.

TWENTY- TWO

Christmas came without Black Friday sales. Without Santa Clause and bargain buys at 50, 60, 70% off. Without any of the hype and expense, Christmas came.

Eve was home in Sainte Lillian, helping on the farm. Christmas came and they walked to church and sang carols. Lit candles and listened to the story of Jesus Birth as recorded in the Gospel of Luke.

Her dad played Silent Night on his guitar and they wouldn't let him play anything else. They sang it over and over and over until they were hoarse and his fingers almost bloody.

She whispered "There were shepherds abiding in the fields keeping watch over their flocks by night." And she remembered the solid good warmth of her children snuggled in her arms as they sat in their own home a Christmas ago and Mark John read to them.

It was Christmas and winter and star bight nights and skeletal trees covered in diamonds of ice and full moon glory and breath outdoors so cold it looked like snowballs tossed about.

It was Christmas and New Years, and Lincoln's Birthday and Saint Patrick's Day and Valentines Day, and somehow or other in there that ground hog Puxatahominy Phill or whatever his name was in Pennsylvania a state she always wanted to visit but never did made his predictions without help and the winter drug on and she was a year older. It was Mark John's birthday and then the twins, and before she knew it seeds sprouted in the earth.

Anastasia was a year older.

Little green apples came when pink and white apple blossoms fell away and bees from the hives kept so long underground rediscovered nature's nectar. There were peaches and pears.

It was the Fourth of July.

Her life was a three ring binder notebook, never taken from the shelf. Each pristine page nice and neat and every precisely drawn blue line blank. Completely absolutely eternally blank

She walked that morning down the red gravel road sat on the dark moss covered steps of the fieldstone Presbyterian Church building and looked for the longest time at nothing. *Rembered nothing for the longest time. She drank cold clear water from the spring and looked at nothing. Leg cramps drew her up and on.*

Her long walk took her past the old country store where countless generations of men folk answered their duty and warmed the bench. They chawed Red Man tobacco and spit juice like they were playing basketball, and managed cheers every time a stream of juice hit dead center. Sometimes their conversations made it past "Yeaup!" and "Yessir by doggies!" and they talked about important stuff. Crops. Baseball. Women. (But nothing disrespectful was said about women. They knew which side of the bread the butter was on.) They had time then. Not now.

After she crossed the old high water highway bridge at Whitewater Creek, she turned right and followed a narrow one lane red gravel road across the low water bridge. Fella drowned there once. Thought that little old creek couldn't keep him from getting home to the wife. Water hit him full bore with the force of a rouge railroad engine. Got him smack dab in the driver's door, turned him ever whichaways. Didn't hardly have time to holler help but nobody'd heard him anyways. Took them two days to find him and the truck and they was both smashed up pretty bad.

"Lucky man," she said, and walked.

Past the foundation of Fadler's old homestead. Nothing left there but a wire fence and a gate that creaked on rusty hinges as it swung back and forth in the wind. Creaky creepy sound in the stillness. She closed the gate, braided triple strands of fresh green rye grass together and locked it shut. Top, middle, and bottom. Good for a season she guessed, and walked on.

There on a pleasant rise the white country church and the cemetery where so many she had loved were. A slow walk to the grave of her best girlhood friend. Dead at 14. With Jesus on earth and forever with Jesus in Heaven.

"Missed all the excitement Mil" she said, and felt a soft breeze on her cheek. Felt in her heart the answer.

"Excitement? C'mon Eve. You know better than that. Heaven has more excitement and pure wonder than you could ever dream. Remember when we used to visit grandma's grave on spring evenings and bring her lilacs and mock orange and watch the sunset? Remember how we felt so good here in this beautiful valley and all our talk about heaven?"

She heard Mil's laughter again, teasing her about calling the valley ringed by beautiful green hills a perfect salad bowl.

Tears streaked her face. She remembered. She remembered bringing Anastasia here when she was a month old and placing her on a blanket above the body of her namesake. She remembered the peace she felt then as if Mil were caressing her baby. Loving her. And knew that somewhere, somehow in that great big wonder called heaven her family had found Millicent Anastasia Jones and together at that very moment they were sitting at the feet of Jesus.

Most of the river folk disappeared that Fourth of July as did a bunch of revivalist at tent meetings, Democrats up in arms at the VFW about a President that wouldn't shut up, and shoe factory workers hoping to get double time for the family vacation. Folks up and disappeared all over the place, and this was not a time for a census. Guesses were dime a dozen

After Eve and her mother came back from D.C. with a brand new Ford truck and wood burning cook stoves, quite a crowd gathered at the courthouse square.

"Land sakes, what else they givin' away? Reckon we'll go get ours," they said after she told them everything.

Half of what she said they heard, a third of that they remembered, and a third of that slice left in the pie plate they had a time working on believing.

Good new is, they would. Not that they had a choice because by the time Spring came and traveling time resumed. Admiral Adam Dimitri Bladgovicz and his Homeland Security Crew was set up and something resembling order with a purpose other than individual community was taking hold.

Overall they were safe in and around Sainte Lillian. Town, county, and rural route, they adjusted to this new world like farmers adjust suspenders to hold up loose work pants.

Take a tuck where needed, plant more of this, less of that, Always be alert. They did what they had to do. The steady drum beat of a farming community went on. Changes and chores and duty made different demands but they responded well as they always did in Sainte Lillian and in very farming community.

Admiral Adam, as he was called by locals, was more like a hometown boy seein' as how he'd married into the Owen family. But there was some kind of wall there. Other than paying his respects at Noah's Ark, and making suggestions for disbursement of farm animals to other parts of his area of supervision, he was all business.

"Laney did you tell him any family news, anything at all." Noah asked as they relaxed on the porch swing. His long tough muscled arm cradled her as if she were a newborn. Her callused hand caressed his as it lay over her shoulder.

"Tried to half a dozen times, He'd get that lost look in his eyes that nearly broke my heart and turn away. Kept staring at pictures of the girls on the mantle and looking at photo albums, but he wouldn't listen to tapes or watch DVD's or home movies. He shook his head once when I asked about Zoe and Cheyenne and Esther but didn't say anything. Just that head shake. It's like he's got this closed door and won't let any light in."

"So he doesn't know about Eve?"

"Noah Owen! How many times do I have to tell you I can't get through to him? You want me to bake a cake and write it in the icing? He plum shuts me out."

I remember last time them fellas now part of his crew were here there was a downright mean looking bunch. Now it's like they got religion all over again or found a reason for living y'know what I mean."

"Noah I'm thinking you done it again," Laney said as she patted his work worn callused hands.

"Done what Laney? You know I don't touch the liquor or hard cider even. My thoughts are as straight as a ten penny nail. Whatcha talking about?"

"Just hush and listen honey bun," she said and kissed him right there in front of God and every body.

Noah kinda liked that. He decided to hush and listen.

"What you did Noah was hit that nail smack on the head. They all got religion sure as shootin' and working under Adam they've found a reason all right."

Noah lapped up her praise like a hungry hound lapped fresh water. He couldn't help grinning all over his lined sunburnt face.

She snuggled comfortable like, and before Noah could do more than give her a hug, she was off and running. "Remember how downright rebellious that group was last year?"

He said "Yeaup".

"First chance I got, I took W.D. aside and got him to talking. Seems they lit outa here bound and determined to get some answers and everything else they wanted.

He said right at first they wanted things they'd never had. Said it was easier getting Rolex Watches and Pink Cadillac's like that old time singer Elvis Presley used to have than it was skipping rocks across the creek

For awhile it was kinda like living high on the hog, but it didn't feel right somehow. Said he got to thinking about his pretty little wife Peggy Sue and their three girls and three boys and the way they was bringing them up. Said they all believed in Jesus and he just couldn't go on helping himself to stuff that didn't matter no more. Especially when there was so many people walking around like lost sheep.

Said they saw so many lost and helpless people on their way to D. C. they stopped being mad and started helping out. Said he put on his sheriff's badge and brought a little bit of order into every town they went through. Said it made him feel like he was doing what the Lord wanted when he'd go into churches and talk about God's love and forgiveness of sins and the chance to live better lives.

By and by, they made it to Washington D.C., and first thing they knew there was this group of nice looking folks inviting them to the White house where lo and behold, they met up with the President." She nudged him in the ribs. "You know, the one you insist on calling by her first name only? Inez. it is. I asked her about that and she had a good laugh and said she'd preciate it if I would do the same. She took one good look at my face and said "Well Laney at least try." So I did, but I always refer to her as our president. Seems right somehow.

"Now Laney I done told you I didn't make that up." He got that far

Noah didn't you listen? I had a talk with her myself and could tell you a thing or two if ever you want to hear everything," she said, and he stared open mouthed.

"Laney you do beat all," he said

"Noah let me finish. Now where was I? Oh yeah, Inez (she laughed at the expression on his face) "Inez said she'd been hearing about him and the boys and their good works and if they was interested she had a job for them right down here close to where most of them was from.

W.D. said that's where they up and met Eve but she don't remember them at all. Asked her about them I did and she just gave me a blank look. "Mom" she says "we worked with a lot of folks there. I do remember something about two dogs and they had the funniest names. Oh yeah. one wore a blue collar with a blue bow tie and the other had pink ribbons in her hair. But mom I don't remember the men. Said she was sorry, and went on about whatever she was doing in the barn. Getting animals ready to take to Eden, I think it was." She paused and took a deep breath

"Laney, I," Noah said and knew to close his lips when she opened hers.

"So anyway, I asked him what kind of training and he said most of it was survival stuff. Wound up he had to teach a bunch of newly deputized men and women how to shoot and clean their rifles and stuff cause lots of them were city folks and didn't know much about anything except 9 millimeters and they ain't no good for jungle warfare," he said. What do you think he meant by that Noah?"

Noah scratched his head said "Well, I reckon," and that's as far as he got.

"Land sakes Noah if you'd been there and seen what God was doing to people breaking his laws you'd think it was Old Testament times and them that lied to God or broke his laws was getting what come to them. It was on the T and V and all. You can't mean to tell me you didn't see it. Seeing that and all makes me downright curious about this here jungle warfare stuff. Seems like it wouldn't be needed."

"Pray it won't be, but it helps to be prepared" he said.

And when she said nothing, Noah got a few more words in edgewise. "Laney I was out in the fields. Or was it the wood lot? Anyway, one or the other. I heard about it though. I'm thinking about the Old Testament stories about the people watching what God did to evil doers.

Seems as soon as they got over snake bite, or them holes opening in the ground and swallowing them and whatever else happened, it didn't take them long to get all selfish and mean again.

I guess if you were waiting on proof we haven't had the Rapture, this has to be it because there's still a mixture of saints and sinners and the devil is fighting the Lord just like he used to. And that just might be the reason for all this gun stuff. But like I said, it don't hurt to pray we won't need it."

Now he took a deep breath and a deeper drink of clear cold spring water.

"Why Noah Owen, you do beat all" Laney said. She found her place on the previous page and Noah listened like a good husband.

"So anyways, after he told me about all this military type training and what they went through with the city boys, the President sent them to West Virginia. They was supposed to meet their boss up there. Only they didn't know anything cept he was an Admiral.

He was supposed to be in this log cabin getting ready for them and they were gonna get serious plans wrote about this here region of the country. I think he said they cover Missiouri, Illinois, Kentucky, Tennessee, and about half of Ohio and Kansas. Maybe bits and pieces of a few other states that sorta reached down close to Missouri, and they're headquartered here but don't stick around much as they're always on the road like supervisors or some such. Managers maybe?

Sometimes W.D. acted like he wasn't sure he was supposed to be talking to me but I had him in a corner and was feeding him apple pie so he talked. Home made ice cream helped too.

He said they drove their four by fours to West Virginia and parked in the big barn out back and got to the house before the winds started hollering and the rains got so dad blamed cold.

Him and the fellers had just enough time to cut a lot of firewood. They filled a shed and seein' as how there was a downstairs bedroom they filled that and the front and back porch. They said that great big two sided fireplace with the indoor chimney kept the place nice and warm.

Said they looked into the bedrooms. Two was fixed up real pretty for little girls and there was a nursery like it was waiting, and a huge master bedroom with its own fireplace, but they didn't do nothing but close doors and walk away quiet like. Like it hurt. Y'know?"

Noah hugged her. He knew.

"Anyways, they cooked over the fireplace like they was camping out and said it was the first time since July they'd had time to do nothing and they caught up. Said the cabin was stocked with food and home canned vegetables, and the freezer full of meat. He got a funny look on his face when he said he found one kitchen cabinet full or Hershey Bars, Graham crackers and marshmallows.

He couldn't talk for a few seconds after that, and I couldn't say anything either. I got real busy pouring us coffee and trying not to show I knew he was talking about Zoe and Adam's place, and the babies stash of S'mores. Almost broke down, but I waited him out.

He said after about a week, ten days they got serious worries about their boss and one dark and stormy night his dogs Pete Jr., and Repeat got to fussing so about going outdoors, even though it was stormy, he let them go. It was them that set up such a howling, and that's how they saved Adam.

Course they thought he was nearly dead, blue and cold as he was and all, and had all sorts of ways to warm him up, but all of a sudden when W.D. was talking about dried apple pie, he started stirring and calling out names.

By the time Doctor Greer got there the next morning Adam was up and dressed, but had such a bad cough the doc wouldn't let him leave. Seeing as how Doc Greer didn't have no x-ray unit, he listened real good to Adam's chest and said it was the closest he'd ever heard to double pneumonia without calling it that and he wasn't about to let them leave till Adam's fever was down and his chest was clear. Set up an IV with antibiotics.

Wouldn't you know they didn't have an inkling Adam was allergic to half the stuff he was getting. They had to fight that off. Seems like he got some kind of rash and got all puffy. Doc wrote down he was never to have anything related to penicillin ever again. Ordered him some special bracelet to wear. Adam said he wouldn't. Doc Greer asked if he needed a presidential order to do the smart thing. Said Adam groaned and held out his arm. Like he'd done business with her before and don't want no more Presidential orders.

Anyway, it took over two weeks to have Adam up and around and another week or so to get their plans made. They made it to D.C., before the blizzard hit in December and spent the entire Christmas holiday and the next couple months in the white House.

Said he'd never forget that."

"Honey bun, did W.D., tell you any more about the rifles and 9 millimeters and that Para- military stuff?

"Why Noah, now that you mention it, I don't think he did. But he surely did fill me with stories about the National Cathedral at Christmas time and the pure beauty of our Nation's Capital all white and filled with snow. He said it looked like a thousand Christmas cards all at once, seeing the stone angels, and Arlington Cemetery and all the historic buildings decorated just by the hand of God."

"He's a good man for the job" Noah said, and Laney stood looking at him, her mouth forming a big round O.

"Gonna bake that boy another pie and sit him down for another talk," she said, and Noah laughed. He knew she'd get the whole story.

In the meantime, there was the mystery surrounding his son- in- law but he didn't have time to ponder the predicament cause just then a gentleman driving a brand new black shining like it's just been waxed and polished till it was set to be wrapped and tied up pretty with a ribbon Cadillac pulled up in the driveway.

The recorder enjoyed this conversion so much it was all copied.

Soon as Noah got out a friendly greeting: "Hi howyedoin, kin I hep you? The fat got in the fire so to speak.

The good lookin' young fella said he was a ministuh and on his way from Bastan and wanted to know where he could pak his cah. Said he was unduh odors to offer assistunce. ..

Noah, a natural born curious man if there ever was one, said "Do whut?"

One of the new fellas, records indicate he was from one of them Carolinas, North or South, record keeper wasn't sure, but he was now making his home in Sainte Lillian said "Well, I'll be et fer a tater if he don't talk funny."

The ministuh fella from Havad said "Pawdon me?'

Laney walked up to offer help. "Hold your horses young fella. We'll get it figgered out. Whut exactly is it you was wanting?"

By that time the young ministuh was looking awful flustered. "Mam?" he said and cleared his throat, and looked at his shining black car like maybe he'd been mis-directed.

He said: "Help."

Iffin that's your destination, you took a wrong turn and kain't get there from here but iffin you're lookin' for a cuppa tea I can fix you right up."

Tex ambled up. "Oil well round chere?"

"Would you have some chowdah to accompanyh the tea?"

"Food and drink Laney. Food and drink." Noah offered his best answer.

Laney took charge. "As for chowdah, I ain't too sure what that is but we got some potato soup and fresh outa the oven biscuits and cornbread that'll fill you right up."

She walked right up to the ministuh and gave him a big hug and said "Since you're under odors we'll get the horse hitched up right cause we sure want that dog to hunt."

"Yes, mam!" he said, and grinned and returned her hug.

Skinny as a rail tobacco chewing balder than a chrome dome Alabama scratched his head. "Y'all listen up now. We'uns is gonna have to have usns some of them elloqutions lessons, or we won't be unnerstandin nuthin."

The ministuh from Bastan said "Amen to that brother."

Everyone understood that one word plain as day and a round of many different accents sent "Amen" heavenward.

TWENTY-THREE

Because Admiral Adam kept himself and his crew very busy, folks didn't learn much about their business. Word leaked out about his responsibilities and that explained a lot to more than curious people in Saint Lillian.

One story was the planners in D.C. spread out a great big map of the habitable United States and then treated it like a great big pizza. They cut long vertical slices of most of it and the rest didn't look all that different.

Mostly, who was in charge of what and how much depended on what was produced in those states and who was left to do the job.

On the map, the pizza slice for Admiral Adam's crew was cut straight down from International Falls, Minnesota, through Iowa, Missouri, and the eastern part of Kansas. It went through, Oklahoma, and Texas. From Galveston, they went past Lake Charles, then north through Baton Rogue Louisiana, up past Meridian, and Tupelo, Mississippi, and Memphis Tennessee. They gave a nod to Saint Louis, Missouri and went into Springfield Illinois. They passed Danville and Fort Wayne Indiana with a brief stop near Sturgis, Michigan before back tracking into Chicago up through Wisconsin to tie again with International Falls and start all over again. Each trip they went into different towns, visited different people, and explained as best they could the reunification plan.

Each trip Admiral Adam assigned a district security group of men and women. More women than men. Men in the communities didn't like it. Their wives and daughters did. To say the least, it was interesting, especially the first time in each area when a man dared tell a woman to shut her mouth and let men take over.

One of many similar examples: When Big Bad Tom's wife said "There are some parts of your plan that require modification for our particular area,

Big Bad Tom hitched up his suspenders and told her to "Shut up and let men handle it."

It is documented that she said," All through recorded history; you men have had your chance. War after war, you've had your chance. Financial mess after financial mess, you've had your chance and women aren't taking any more. Now it's your turn to shut up and set down".

Resenting being embarrassed by his usual meek and compliant wife, he reached for her and found himself on the floor groaning in agony.

"Oh dear, excuse me, did I forget to say please?" she asked sweetly.

Typically male, he counter attacked and learned the hard way. (Took him two days to walk like a man.)

Richard White said, "That's what we get for giving them the vote."

His twin took one good look at a row of angry women and slunk deeper into his chair. "Dang good thing you're a bachelor."

When Richard looked like he had more to say, Bill thought it prudent to move. Fast.

Laughter started, but faded as other women stood and surrounded the security force.

"All in favor of Sister Ellen's motion say "aye"

Never in recorded history have so few women paid back so many men with one decisive movement, or owed so much to one pair of size seven steel toed boots.

W. D. saved the day when he took the mike and told the crowd Ellen reminded him so much of his beloved Peggy Sue.

He turned to Ellen. "Tiny thing, just like you, but she managed our farm and raised six of the best kids in the county. Her word was law and even though I was sheriff, we was smart enough to listen up.

W. D. held he audience spellbound as he described his life, his wife, his family and their dreams. "Dreams a lot like yours," he said.

W. D. blew his nose on a red bandana and wiped his eyes. "Me and Peggy Sue we agreed we was a team. We had a goal to raise Christian Kids in a Christian community and we worked together for it. Neither of us was the boss. But God sure was...

Now in my opinion any man that thinks he needs to rough house a woman just to prove he's smarter is smart alright, but not where it counts." He turned his back to the crowd and spoke over his shoulder. "Get my point?"

The ladies were first to laughter. Slowly at first but catching speed, laughter eased the room once filled with tension.

"There are things I am sure women would like to do to abusive men but, considering our circumstances, now is not the time or the place. We saw today, a woman who had been pushed too far. She reacted to violence with violence, and feels perfectly justified. Good for her. Good for all of you who won't take pushing around."

He pointed to Ellen's rough looking overweight and definitely hurting husband. "I'm saying from the looks of that that there man, he probably deserved more than he got and I'm hoping he's smart enough to know it and change his ways. The only way we're gonna make this work is all of us pulling together. When women turn out smarter than some of us men, we should have enough sense to listen."

Big Bad Tom proved he was smarter than he looked by leading applause that filled the room.

Admiral Adam shared the video with regional directors, and with presidential approval they appointed ladies as local directors, and department heads in all areas. From the Atlantic coastline to what was left of the Pacific, a new era began. Slowly at first but it spread like a good warm fire. .

Adam no longer thought of cities, but of regions. Not of people but of their needs and the needs of a nation. He knew the farm belt would eventually play a major role in their survival and that industry would resume. It would start with a type of cottage industry but it would branch out hopefully in his lifetime to feed and nurture a recovering country and economy.

Economy. Guns and butter. Guns or butter. That was one of the major problems. One of their main jobs was to convince the population progress was not tied to paychecks. Because they didn't have paychecks. They would come later. Progress in one sense was almost communistic, but in the main completely Biblical because as he said in very town meeting, "We must all work together for the common good. "We are entering a new era, the era of Christian Democracy."

Adam quickly identified populations so angry with God they threatened his life. More than once, he escaped in the quiet hours of night. More than once he was followed and hounded by angry men intent on causing even more trouble. More than once, ladies came to his rescue and his duties continued.

President Brown-Parkinson responded by adding additional female members to his security force.

In a memo to Admiral Adam and other commanders, she stated that in some communities they could be the only representatives of Jesus these lost souls would see. She stated their best plan was to continue community prayer meetings, cut short sermonizing, and model the behavior of the Lord.

She wrote, "Adam you're accustomed to giving orders and having them followed. We're dealing with a population recovering from a major disaster and to say some of them hold on to anger is an understatement. I propose you start each town meeting with the Doctor Shadrack Meshach Abednego Lockridge video.

You have musical men and women in your crew that play guitars and sing, use them. Get the people to sing along. Have a friendly time, not a forced time. They offer you beer or wine drink it. Eat what they eat. Talk with them. Work with them.

Your area directors (smart plan Adam) will tell you of needs. Give when they do. Heal when you can. Help build and plan and prepare. Work with the people. Show them how American can rebuild by working as a unit. We must transport and trade and share what we have with one another. In this new nation it is imperative we live as the constitution states, with freedom and justice for all."

"Damm, she sure can cut to the chase!" W.D. said.

"Amen!" Stephanie Reynolds said.

Adam rested his heels on the porch railing and looked into the starlit night. His mind was a hodgepodge quilt of images: The one area behind a steel door lined with Kryptonite was the thought of his in-laws and reports of a red headed woman who looked like his wife. He knew that had to be Zoe's twin, Eve. She was the woman beginning to fill his heart and mind until he met Zoe.

He'd heard enough to know she survived but his brother-in-law and the kids had not. She was alive. Her husband and kids didn't make it. Zoe and his girls were gone. He survived. He didn't want to go down that winding road.

Adam forced his thoughts back to his job. He alone coordinated the breadbasket of America, from the Great Plains to Montana, wheat, corn, oats, soybeans, rice, and fisheries in Maine and on the Atlantic seaboard.

Once again, they were trading with Canada. It was, you give, we give pound for pound, need for need. The need for imported goods had trickled to a slowly drying stream and finally that evaporated. Made in America supported the economy more than goods from abroad.

Adam thought of medical research stilled in its tracks, on medical needs barely met by a remnant of dedicated doctors and nurses with their skills stretched to the limit, of schools of nursing, dentistry and all fields of medicine training at hyper speed.

He thought of the bond growing between himself and the young Thaddeus Greer. If ever there was a genius born and bred and 100% American it was that young man. Once Inez gave him the nod, he established medical schools in every state. Usually they were staffed with one nurse and one doctor but with his instructions cut to common sense and holistic medicines, his success rate was phenomenal.

One student said once politics was out of the way, medical care was a lot easier than building cars in Detroit; and the human body a much more interesting machine than anything Ford or GMC ever offered. "Especially the heart and lungs" said one and another "Yeah, but look at the brain," said another asked. What good are hearts and brains without eyes?" "All of these are great, but what about musculature?" asked another. Questions and discussions filled lecture halls.

Doctor Thaddeus Greer and his colleagues recognized the potential, grasped it, and developed it.

TWENTY- FOUR

Eve settled into routine. It took a little longer for her to admit routine was no longer the cornerstone of her existence.

Once again horses roamed the pasture land of her Great Aunt Samantha Lynn's farm. Cows gave birth, milk overfilled pails, butter was rich and creamy. Pigs produced. Chickens laid eggs and made more chickens.

Trading flourished

Three of the eight students that traveled with her from Noah's Ark decided to live at the farm. Two girls, one lean silent young man who worked sunup to sundown just as she did. Always looking like he saw someone she couldn't see, heard music she couldn't hear. Or cries? He worked, he ate. He slept. He existed. She tried but he wouldn't talk. As if he were mute he pointed to his lips and throat and smiled and went on working. Odd though. He could sing, but he would not (or could not) speak.

Every evening they read from the Bible and prayed. Eve and the girls talked about God. The silent young man listened. "God has a purpose and plan for us," she read, and closed the Bible. This night her mind filled with memories of a white envelope and her excitement that John Mark would walk again. She would have been with them had she not wasted time in the basement. Was it part of God's plan that she endure this loneliness? She could not talk.

Lorna Doone who said she was named after her momma's favorite cookie said she "kinda wondered sometimes but being out of the city and away from the drugs and bums that hung around when her mother came down with AIDS after her blood transfusion during gallbladder surgery, maybe she was in the best place."

"You mean you think God got you to the farm to keep you alive?"

"Well, in a way. But when the pastor came by and told mom about Noah's

Ark, she said it wouldn't hurt. She knew she was dying. She knew Noah's Ark was the only way to get me out, because there'd be no help when she was gone. She said she loved me enough to let me go when we could remember the good times and she wouldn't have to worry about me. She made me promise. She made me come." Lorna Doone was crying. Again. Great sobs that shook her frame and robbed her breath. Knowing she had to release, they waited.

"Two weeks after I got there, Ma and Pa Owen got the word mom was killed in a shoot out and the house was burned to the ground. We didn't have a funeral because she was all burnt up. The Owens held a memorial service for her at the church and was there I decided to honor my promise to mom and lead a good life. I'm learning every day about Jesus and God and the Holy Spirit. But I can't help wondering where God came from, and how about these other religions and their gods?

"I don't know. Never thought about it."

Eve spoke... "How does the sun rise, how did it get up there in just the right place?"

"Same answer Eve."

How about the moon and stars, the water we couldn't live without, and grass and snow, and hearts that beat and minds that remember and dreams we dream and work we do?"

"What am I supposed to be some sort of philosophical scientific genius? I don't know!"

"Yet we are surrounded by proof there is a creator, a creation and life in abundance. You live knowing these things exist. This knowing, this acceptance is called faith Lorna Doone. Yet we must worship the creator Lorna Doone and not the creation."

"Was that a question or an answer? Because I still want to know where God came from?

"Look at it this way Lorna Doone. If we could answer the question who created God? or where He is from, would we then not have to answer who created the creator? Then in turn who created the creator's creator's creator? We could go on and on up to the trillionth power and still be asking who? Where? Why?

The silent young man leaned forward, listening intently.

Lorna Doone unable to sit quietly, hummed as she braided her long blond hair.

Astrid, until then the quiet member of the quartet opened her Bible and read from Genesis "In the beginning, God created the heavens and the earth." She paused.

Lorna Doone's voice barely masking her irritation; "That brings me right back to my question."

Astrid understood the young girl's wonder. Her voice was assuring. "This is from the New Testament, Gospel of John, Chapter One, Verse One and Two. "In the beginning was the Word, and the Word was with God, and the Word was God. He was with God in the beginning. Through Him all things were made; without him nothing was made that has been made. In Him was life, and that life was the light of men. The light shines in the darkness, but the darkness has not understood it."

Lorna Doone looked up and for the first time noticed Astrid had not been reading but speaking from memory.

What are you, some kind of a preacher?"

"Nope, some kind of a nun," Astrid said and the silent man jumped as if shot.

Astrid continued. The first time God spoke, he created everything we see and don't see, what is known, was known and will be known. The second time He spoke...The second time God THE WORD spoke, He created Jesus."

But Jesus is also called the Word. God is the Word. Jesus is the word? The word is something spoken right?

"But, But, But Why did God stop with Jesus?"

"Think about it this way Lorna Doone. God the creator created everything. He spoke and created everything. He gave us lessons. Us being humanity-- for centuries-- and humanity walked its own path. So God, the creator, the Word, spoke again and created Jesus.

God didn't stop speaking. His Word, His only Son, our Lord and Savior lived as a human. He knew from the bottom of his worn feet to the inner depth of his soul the yearnings of humanity.

His only Son Jesus is a part of the Triune God. While on earth he faced every temptation known to man. And more. Because Jesus is the Son of God, the evil could tempt him in ways we will never know.

This prince of the world offered the Son of God everything in the world if he would do only one thing; bow down and worship him. "Turn away from God" he said, "and I will give you everything.

I think Jesus had always known his destiny. During this time of temptation, He not only told the devil where to go, He backed his message with scripture.

It is recorded in this time of temptation the devil used scripture to convince Jesus to follow him.

I wonder sometime if Jesus laughed when he stared evil in the face and sent it away. Can't you just see the devil shrinking and slinking away when Jesus told him "Get thee behind me Satan" Here this evil thing so swollen with pride and self importance had tried to win Jesus over and Jesus sent him slinking away with five words.

It's wonderful. Five words sent the mastermind of evil running. Five words!

Think about your life Lorna Doone. Your family was poor. Your mother couldn't work. Your father deserted you. You sang and played your guitar on street corners to make money.

Mary, the blessed Mother of Jesus, and Joseph, his earthly father were poor. Joseph was a carpenter. Jesus worked by his side because every boy child in Israel carried on the tradition of their earthly father.

Because He was fully human and fully divine, Jesus was also absorbing lessons from His heavenly Father.

He knew hunger. He saw the rich walking by, the Pharisees and Sadducees in the synagogues. He knew the temptations known to every hungry child. Yet he never gave in to envy or greed. From the soles of his tired feet to the top of his sweating sunburned head, Jesus never gave up and never gave in.

His hands, the human hands that fashioned plows and benches and perhaps even crosses, were callused and work worn. These same hands in divinity reached out to touch the untouchable, to heal the sick, to bless the children, to raise the dead.

These hands did not resist the soldiers who drug him to a mock trial. They steadied his cross on His shoulders as He forced himself to walk the agonizing trail to the hill of Calvary. His hands were stretched out on a rough cross beam and nailed to it. His legs were crossed and his work worn feet were nailed to the long bar.

Nailed Lorna done. Big railroad spike nails went into his flesh.

He did not resist the soldiers. He did not curse those who beat him and those who placed a crown of thorns on His head. Without tears or complaint, He went willingly toward His death.

He willingly and silently suffered lashing and laughter and torment. He willingly died the most horrible death known at the time. And y'know what He said when He looked down at the soldiers and mockers watching him die? Y'know what Jesus said then Lorna Doone when He could have cursed them or cried out for help? He said, "Father! Forgive them for they know not what they do."

Think about this: While the Jewish leaders so afraid their lives would be ruined by this man claiming to be the Son of God had said His death could be on them and their children, Jesus wiped out that price on the cross He Said "Father Forgive Them for they know not what they do"

The true ending, about this crucifixion was Jesus forgave them. Mankind, on the other hand has not. These words uttered in the heat of passion and fear have been used to promote murder, pogroms, for the holocaust, and, for all imaginable kinds of evil against a people Jesus forgave as he was dying. This was his last healing for a fractured humanity. And what did humanity do? How did we accept this grace and mercy? History should weep.

After the horrible lashing and beating and mocking, after the horror of crucifixion, Jesus died of shock, blood loss and suffocation. Soldiers ordered to break the bones of their victims and speed their dying, reported He was already dead. But to be sure, they pierced his side with a spear. Water and blood came from the wound. Just like it was predicted long years before that dark glorious day on Calvary. Jesus died.

But Lorna Doone the story does not end there. Rather it begins. On the third day, Jesus rose from the dead. He conquered death.

Now in His resurrected body, Jesus lives eternally with His Father God. God, is alive, His words are in the Bible.

Lorna done still looked puzzled.

Astrid chuckled. "Think about it this way girl, after God created Jesus, he didn't need to "say" anything else."

Light illuminated the corner where Lorna Doone sat in silent wonder.

And the silent young man who had not spoken in three years began to sing.

"Amazing Grace, How Sweet the Sound
That saved a wretch like me.
I once was lost, but now am found
Was blind but now I see"

Before he could continue, Astrid asked "And you?"

"Juilliard, and private lessons, training for the Metropolitan Opera."

Eve and Astrid stuttered. Astrid was quicker. "We've got Eve a farm manager, me, a Nun, Lorna Doone the best cook in the county,"....

"Excuse me, not cook. I was just about a full fledged chef. You should let me get to work with fish heads sometime. There's not much I can't do."

"Fish heads!"

Lorna Doone waited through minutes of more than mixed reactions before jumping into open air. "Yeah, fish heads. Ox tails too."

Since the room remained silent, Lorna Doone finished her bragging and turned the topic to music. "I know a lot about food but not much about that high faluting music. I heard about that opera though. It's in New York right?"

He had time to nod.

"We had the Municipal Opera in Saint Louis and believe me, I snuck in every chance I got. To me the music and dancing especially in Brigadoon was another world. But what I really want to know is can you play any musical instrument?

"Do you prefer string, brass, or keyboards?"

"How about a boot stomping boogie on a guitar? Me and mom, we were partial to those. I bought me a guitar at Sears, and found a fiddle out back at the Muni. Figured nobody wanted the old thing. Some kind of fancy scrollwork on the inside Stradi something or other."

"You… ah, that is… you say you… found it?" His voice was strained, his expression a mixture of disbelief and discovery.

"Yeah, I didn't steal it or anything. People were in a room talking and laughing, and cases were piled up against the wall like they were being taken out. I snuck by the room and went out the back door and found this old case down by a dumpster. Just laying there on the ground like it'd been trashed. That old leather case looked worn out and sickly and I felt…well, y'know, sort of a kinship . I figured it was like me and needed somebody to care. So I just took it home to mom. She could make that fiddle sing."

"I assume you still have the—er-- ah fiddle in your possession?"

"What's the matter with you anyway! The best memories of my last months with my mom are tied into that fiddle… Y'think I'd have left it behind? It's at Noah's ark. Now I know you can play we'll get it." She detailed plans while eyes of Astrid and Eve went first to her face then to those of the confessed musician.

"Was the case brown leather with shining clasp like gold, and the inside a crushed blue velvet?"

"How did you know that? Oh gosh, was it yours? I didn't mean to steal it or anything, just give it a home. Honest!"

"Would that it were mine," he said, and sank back against the piano. He remembered the front page headlines about the disappearing Stradivarius. In its old and almost equally valuable case supposedly a disguise for the priceless instrument, it was placed against a dressing room door in line to be moved to the securely guarded waiting van.

Lorna done said she found it down the alley by a dumpster. Puzzle pieces clicked together. Lorna Doone completed her unexpected exit. High heels in fast abrupt sharp staccato alarmed the thief. He (or she) in panic, dropped it and ran.

He chuckled at the thought of this lovely girl and her mother playing boot stomping boogies while police around the country worked on a conspiracy theory and waited for non existent- ransom note.

Evening shadows began their silent tiptoe across the floor before Astrid found voice. She knew music. She also knew Lorna Doone's need and went back to the heart of the matter or, as she liked to think about it, the matter of the heart. "Lorna Doone, you asked about other religions and other gods?"

"Yeah, Astrid. Or should I call you Sister Astrid? I never talked to no nun before. I thought you people wore long black robes and funny hats and carried pretty beads in your hands and walked around with your eyes down. Here you are wearing blue jeans and work boots and mucking barns and slopping the hogs and working just like real people. In fact when you smacked your thumb with the hammer on Saturday you said words I never ever would have connected to a Nun. As I recall, you said."

She paused, laughed at herself. "Not that I mean you nuns aren't real people. Don't get me wrong. It's just like I said."

Astrid's laughter stopped Lorna Doone's tongue twisting monologue. "We are real people little sister and you can call me whatever you want as long as you don't miss calling me to breakfast lunch and supper.

Once again warm laughter filled the room.

But, since you asked and if Eve and" she looked at the singer. paused "We've called you Silent for such a long time, now that you have recovered your speech, we'd like to know your name."

The tall dark haired young man stood, came to a formal attention and bowed. "Ladies, I apologize. Allow me to introduce myself. He bowed again. I am Georges Luis Pavarotti," and I echo what Astrid said about mealtime."

"Eve gasped, Astrid stared open mouthed and Lorna Doone said "I can't remember all that. How about we call you Looie?"

"Done," he said.

"Pavarotti! As in?" Eve questioned and he nodded.

Lorna Doone said "Can we please get back to the subject. Pretty please."

"Yes, please," said the newly named Looie. There was no mistaking the yearning in his voice.

Lorna Doone meant music but Looie meant Jesus and Looie won.

Lorna Doone we'll talk about Looie's past and that fiddle later, let's finish our first discussion," Astrid said and smiled at Lorna Doone who sighed, smiled, and settled down. All eyes were on Astrid.

"Earlier you asked about the other religions and the other gods. I'll give you the short story tonight and to get us started, we'll take a side trip into movie land and look at the entertainment your grandparents and great grandparents enjoyed; "Y'ready?"

"As my great grammy used to say, Sock it to us teach." Lorna Doone settled on the braided rug, her attention and the attention of others devoted entirely to Astrid. Night sounds, some new but none seeming threatening floated through the open windows. Perfume of roses and lilies and evening blooming four O'clocks filled the room as a light breeze blew curtains aside at the open windows.

"Well, I'm sure Mickey Mouse; the flying hero is as good a start as any. Kids believed he was real. And it wasn't long before the invincible Dick Tracy was replaced by Superman. He came to save the day and the world as long as kryptonite wasn't around. The bat duo always responded to the bat signal, often leaving lavish parties at Stately Wayne Manor to rescue the helpless. Superwoman and Wonder Woman got their sound bites. Star Wars, and Spiderman, Harry Potter and the Transformers followed as fast as Hollywood could find a gullible audience… These a evolved into animated games, the so called virtual reality, the vampires and werewolves, the shows, songs and videos that promote sexuality and bestiality and so much more to capture a mind. With all these good guys fighting evil what happened? If it was real, why didn't the lessons sink in?

"Yeah, I knew people who acted like they thought it was. They spent a lot of money on movie heroes and action figures and other stuff. Even underwear."

"What do you think?"

"Honestly, I think it was made up to entertain the so called masses and make the rich richer. It also did something else, it created a fantasy world. People didn't have to face reality if they could loose themselves in all the pretense movies and videos poured into their heads

But aintcha off the subject? What's that got to with other religions and other gods?"

"You've answered part of your question Lorna Doone. People who didn't know about The Triune God could look around and realize they weren't responsible for life or disease or death, or sunrise and sunset, the weather, changing seasons, crop failures or abundance, floods or natural disasters. They needed someone to thank and or someone to appease, so they created their own gods and goddesses."

"You mean they got an idea and made them up?" Just like all that junk?

"Exactly! And where did that junk take us?"

Lorna Doone thought of her mother shot killed and burned to ashes because of drugs and greed. She thought of empty eyed children in the projects, of wasted lives and empty minds. Tears washed her pale cheeks.

They knew her tears were answers.

Astrid continued. "Way back in the beginning, some religions sacrificed slaves and prisoners of war and killed their first born children to appease their gods."

"Sacrificed? What do you mean sacrificed? Like killed them? How? Why?"

"Why first: "To keep their gods happy. Because people thought when their gods were happy, they always had enough to eat and won their battles against others who sacrificed to their weaker gods."

"Yuck. Doesn't make sense."

"My point exactly. Do you still want to know how? Do you think with abortion on demand and euthanasia these past generations were that different?"

"Don't tell me. I couldn't handle it. Maybe someday, I'll read those parts of the Bible. Old Testament stuff. Right?"

"Right! I'll give you references later. Now we'll peek at the so called gods of these religions. None of them were real. None of them fulfilled prophecy. None of them healed the sick, raised the dead, or gave a path to follow and promise of eternal life with the real and only God. None of them died and came back to life.

They were the exact opposite of Jesus who fulfilled every prophecy and loved humanity so much he gave His life as the final sacrifice and died forgiving us for our sins.

I know you're going to ask me how a God who loved us so much could let all the horrible things happen. Don't just look at what this world has been through, that man made dust that killed nearly everything that took breath. Look at the history of mankind.

Start with Adam and Eve and Cain and Able. Follow the scriptures written history. Read from the library in this house what man has done to man and then you tell me how much was from man while God who gave us choices between right and wrong warned us and waited. You tell me Lorna Doone. You tell me."

Outdoor noises intensified.

Dogs barked.

A single rifle shot louder to their hearing than cannon filled the air.

Eve jumped to action. "Well troops, we've been talking what if something like this happened. Time to put our plan in action.

Looie get your trumpet.

Astrid are you sure you want to do this?"

Astrid, a major player in their defense, laughed aloud.

TWENTY- FIVE

After a great deal of soul searching, W. D. had not only bottled his wonder but capped it and put it back there in the cave with what was left of his pa's bones. Probably not much considering the last time he'd been there, all he saw was a boot with a gnawed tibia and a few other bones critters hadn't gnawed.

Sometimes he felt a tinge of sorrow for the old man but times of sorrow were getting to be fewer and farther apart. His mind and memories were more on Peggy Sue and their kids and all the dreams they had. "Some dreams!" he said and looked off somewhere listening for the sound of their laughter, the soft whisper of her voice as they prayed over the kids each night.

Maybe the other fellas in the group felt the same way about their past. At least they were willing to talk about what was and wonder what could have been. That old Cajun boy Jean (pronounced John) La Fayette Le Fever from Port Allen Louisiana had more wonder what's than a room full of fifth graders. At least they kept him sane and kept him busy.

W.D. thought it was like his friend was planning to go home any day now and find them waiting, He wanted to be ready. He always found little souvenirs for his kids, and carted them around in his suitcase and duffel bag. Ball caps, and stones, and globes, things like that.

Then there was Tex…that's what he said his name was, and what he wanted to be called. Bowlegged horse back riding, cattle roping six gun shooting tall tale teller: Put Le Fever and Tex together and one would talk your right ear off whilst the other worked on the left. Kinda like they were afraid to keep quiet.

W. D. had all but memorized books on grief and coping mechanisms and never once seen a chapter titled "talk all the time itis." Course the psychologist and psychiatrist and grief counselors who wrote all them books only dealt with death on a one-to-one basis. How would they handle a whole world bawling its eyes out? Well, not exactly a whole world, but what was left of it after the dust settled.

Last he heard, President Inez Brown-Parkinson had another million or so accounted for in the U. S. of A. Considering the population before, there weren't that many people left. Every year she did her best to keep survivors safe by stopping migration when winter storms began. She wanted people where they could be reached and work together. Mostly, it seemed to be working.

When he asked Admiral Adam about survivors, the only answer he got was stragglers kept upping the ante. Maybe some of them holdouts were desperate and it took others awhile to believe there was a future.

He didn't want to guess how many lost souls wandered around. For dang sure he was tired of crowds too dad blamed dumb to help out. Complaining they was good at. Working to make life better was like pulling hens teeth.

His mind compartmentalized his thoughts about the talkers and brought it front and center again! Maybe it wasn't that they talked, and the complainers complained but what they talked and complained about.

Yeah, that was it. Le Fever never quit talking about his family. What they ate. What they wore… where they worshipped. How much fun it was flat boatin' on the bayou. When he talked about his mother's crawdad gumbo, a body was ready to pull up a chair, grab a bowl and dig in.

"Mon, momma be up early cookin' dat gumbo. Just gotta get the herbs and spices in right and let it simmer all day long. Not quarter a day or half a day, but the whole dadgum day and long about the time sun she start sinking, momma she ring dat dinner bell and we be there, scrubbed clean and thanking the good Lord for what our momma she done cooked.

My sister Diane, in the Navy at the time, brought one of her Wave friends home for a long weekend. Skinny thing. Didn't tink she'd eat much a'tall but onct she tasted dat gumbo she couldn't stop.

Momma made us some of dat home made root beer too, and, that poor Navy child just kept on eatin' and drinkin.' Told my momma that was the best food she ever tasted and tried to pologize for eating so much but momma wouldn't have none of it. Said it made her heart proud to see a Yankee enjoying real food. Come morning 'she didn't have no trouble with grits either.

We took the ferry across de big lake. Watched the big ships unload, took a horse drawn carriage through Baton Rogue. Bought momma some baguettes and pastries and coffee she fancies."

At the same time, Tex was filling his other ear. He was halfway through the roundup before the dust fell. The squall of calves as branding irons seared the BART brand into tender hide, his riding across country after strays, the night in the arroyo, finding the calf stuck in a cave, the rescue and his exiting, calf over his shoulder into a changed world.

Maybe their talking all the time was like people eating everything in sight at funeral dinners. They talked because they were alive. People ate because they knew the dead could not and eating equaled existence.

He wondered: "They eat, they talk. They're alive. Is that why I think all the time? Like that old guy said, I think therefore I am. Maybe in that way Admiral Adam and I are a lot alike." He snorted. Then defensively, "Well we don't talk all that much and we're always thinking and working. But me, be like him! He's about the smartest fella I've run across and sharper than a tack. Nothing he can't work out He shook his head and walked toward the SUV garage.

As he waited on Admiral Adam W.D. checked each SUV, got the clean up crew to washing and waxing, then made sure his gear was packed. He tried to focus on nothing. He couldn't.

Peggy Sue was always there with the kids. Close enough to see in a soft moon glow kind of way, but not ever close enough to touch. She always used to say "God is just a prayer away, all they had to do was talk to Him, reach out to Him and He was there."

Once he questioned "Doesn't God ever start a conversation?"

"Look around at earth and sky and family, at how God has blessed us," Peggy Sue said. That was her answer.

He wondered; Peggy Sue and the kids being with God, could he just reach out to them with his heart and mind and find them there, just a breath away?

Wouldn't that be something? The soft breeze on his face was Peggy Sue's lips and the rustling leaves the footfalls of his kids running to him. He tucked the thought into the secret pocket of his heart, and went back to business.

Soon they'd be headed back to Operations Headquarters at Sainte Lillian, Missouri. It was a long trip ahead with major stops along the way. Major stops and major problems.

Concerns were no longer settled communities where people worked together for the common good; but the isolated areas where survivors kept to themselves. How to reach them? How to unite a fractured country and a monetarily strangled economy?

Admiral Adam had some ideas on that. He said while money was not the root of the problem, it was the love of what money could buy that caused problems.

In W.D.'s mind, Admiral Adam would have been a good musketeer back in the days when they rode horses and flashed swords and their motto was "All for one, one for all."

"Novel idea," he said, and laughed at himself.

Communism and socialism, free love and liberalism, and the great big have an open mind lifestyle didn't work either. What was the answer?

He knew Christianity and education combined was the key… But how? True, President Brown-Parkinson's plan of on going schooling worked. But was it fast enough considering some of the students had to be taught to read?

To get everyone on the same page (so to speak), their primer was the Bible. The King James Version stayed on the shelves while the Children's Bible, the Student Bible and editions of the NIV each with detailed explanations missing in the King James were widely read and discussed.

Admiral Adam and his crew were silent observers at one of the first on line classes for young adults.

As they read detailed accounts about human reactions to adversity and change, students in the classroom and around the country quickly agreed there was little new under the sun.. One student said "That King David wasn't any different than any man looking at a babe."

Imagery, metaphor and parables were discussed, dissected, slowly understood and applied to everyday situations.

"The Prodigal son could be any one of us coming to Jesus" said one. And another "The lost coin didn't have to mean money," and another "Who the heck would hide a light under a bushel? Wait a minute, could it be that's not a literal light t like a candle or flashlight, but something else, something we can do and share to help others?"

What I don't get is Jesus saying He is the Bread of Life. What's He talking about; Jesus being bread?" Explain that teach."

"No problem," she said.

Anticipating research assignments, they said one word that combined relief and wonder. They said "Huh?"

"To start this discussion, let us agree we are discussing food. Now, draw a line down the center of your paper. On one side your title should be Physical and the other Spiritual. Under your physical heading, write "food to sustain the body." Under your Spiritual heading write "The only food that guarantees life eternal."

When they finished, she set a timer and said, "In two minutes on the physical side, list everything you love to eat."

"Hey teach, I ain't done" was echoed as the timer buzzed but groans dissolved into laughter when she asked those who had written Okra and Brussel Sprouts to raise their hands.

Before students snickered at the thought of eating such stuff, Adam and W.D's hands were up. Both men sheepishly lowered their hands.

She waited for laughter to settle.

"Let's look at the physical side. Our point here is we eat and drink to stay alive. As we digest food and drink our bodies become performing engines. Muscle and brain use the fuel we provide.

Remember what you had for lunch three days ago? Of course not! You have a vague memory of eating and drinking. Five or six hours after lunch your gut growled and your brain wanted more fuel. If you refused or could not provide this need, your brain would nag worse than teachers do when papers are late. If your hunger strike continues, you will die. Death takes over. Both physical and spiritual death takes over, unless…"

She waited.

Finally, one voice: "Unless what teach?"

Never one to give an immediate answer, she used opportunity to expand their knowledge by making them think… "Let's review. At the top of the page your title is food. On the left side, under the sub heading of physical, you have a long list of things you like to eat and drink.

On the right side of the page under the sub heading Spiritual, all you have written is…say it with me class." Voices joined: "The only food that guarantees life eternal. And write the reference John, Chapter Six, Verses 35… and add those little dots that mean keep on reading."

We will fill this side of the page as we continue to read the scriptures and apply them to our lives. There are some parts in the Bible you'll be tempted to treat like sprouts and Okra. You'll read, but you won't like reading about personal accountability for sin, or forgiveness, or sharing.

However, Spiritual Food feeds our hearts and minds in a different way. The more we ingest the stronger we become spiritually, and the more we want. Physical food leaves us. Spiritual food, when ingested by a hungry soul willing to follow the Lord, never will.

Sometimes, it seems to wait, like it's locked in a storehouse, but when we need the strength this food gives us, it is there. There will come a time in your spiritual journey when you discover you love the Okra and Sprouts because they are truth and truth is what sets us free from sin and despair."

A subdued saddened voice "Jesus being the bread of life and all, how you explain the…you know…, what happened to so many people??"

"I can't tell you why the dust fell. I can't tell you why we survived. But I can tell you Jesus didn't do it, and with all my heart I believe Jesus is the Bread of Eternal Life."

Logan raised his hand. "I found where He's saying it teach. Can I read it?"

"You always read. It's Luke's turn." His sister Leah handed the Bible to Luke and pointed to the passage in the Gospel of John, Chapter Six.

"Where?"

Luke, cleared his throat, placed his right hand over his heart and in a solemn voice read, "Then Jesus declared, "I am the bread of life. He who comes to me will never go hungry and he who believes me will never go thirsty."

"There's more teach. You want me to keep on reading?"

"Thanks Luke. You may finish later. In fact you should all read the entire chapter so we can discuss it at length tomorrow."

Groans with varying degree of intensity filled the room.

"Stay with me on this: Ingesting food fuels our bodies. When we read the Bible and believe what we read and accept the words of Jesus, we're ingesting food for out eternal souls. Our need for more of this spiritual food is met when we go to Jesus.

Unlike a peanut butter sandwich, which sticks with us for awhile, the Bread of Life never leaves. And, get this, like the food we consume, our souls long for more spiritual food.

If we deny this great soul hunger, our eternal life will be in far worse shape than any of us can imagine.

Jesus said he was the bread of life because He is. He is the bread of eternal life. Are you ready for me to repeat?"

Silence filled the room. Eyes focused on the slight grey haired teacher as she wheeled her chair front and center. Her voice filled the waiting room and hungry hearts. "What we ingest of the Word of the Lord never leaves us. His word is a light to our path. His Word is the bread of life. When we believe and live our belief, The Holy Spirit indwells us, our spirits are filled and we have eternal life".

"One voice " Yeah, but!"

Another. " What! Didn't you listen?We ain't talking about knife and fork food; we're talking about the Word of God becoming a permanent part of our lives. We're talking about His mercy

And love offered, and our accepting and living like we have accepted this great gift. I believe only a real God could love us so much. God's mercy offers this gift and unless we're blind, dumb and stupid we'd better reach out in faith and take it in."

Silence. A room full of silence. Silence so thick it seemed to grow and spread and overflow the confines of the small room. All eyes were on the unkempt speaker who suddenly reached in his jeans pocket for a comb and began working on his tangled mass of dark hair. "Sorry, I didn't mean to preach so much, but this makes sense and I want Jesus in my life."

There was a small chorus of "Amen," applause, nods of acceptance, and different looks of wonder on each face.

"Mrs. Pringle broke the silence. "Class this Friday, we'll celebrate Holy Communion. Pastors and priest will be here to explain the stand of their denominations. You will note differences, and similarities, but overall what all Christian denominations have in common is acknowledging the death and resurrection of our Lord and Savior.

As we have less than 30 minutes remaining of class time, please read Chapter Six in the Gospel of John, take notes and be prepared to discuss it tomorrow.

Before we leave remember our focus on the Holy Scriptures is your guide book for everything else you learn. As you study, you will see the connection between faith and practical living. Math and science and industry, poetry and adventure, love and life and plans for wholesome living are in the Bible.

You carpenters know about plumb lines? You bakers know about yeast? You Parents confused about raising children in what well could be a pre- apoplectic world, need all the help you can get. Read the Bible. You like love stories? Read the Bible. You like bigger than life heroes? Read the Bible. You have worries about tomorrow and life after death? Read the Bible. Any more questions? Read the Bible!"

As the students left, Admiral Adam and his crew gathered around the retired elementary teacher. It was his request that brought her out of the hills and into the threatening maelstrom. He felt it to be one of his wisest choices.

Their reunion not for what was said, but for what was understood, was deep, emotional, and in its way, very wonderful

Traveling the country and reading reports from other sections, W.D had not only seen the people but had a good handle on the overall mood. In a nutshell, those who believed knew hope. Those who did not, did not. Fear and unrest was an undercurrent sitting like a fused keg of dynamite.

Was it possible the President's plans and classes would convince people who had lost nearly everything that what God said was best actually was?

Early on, still mourning Peggy Sue and the kids, he'd asked her that question. Her answer was a warm hug and a whispered "Read the Bible.

Years had passed without revolution. Was this the end of the beginning or the beginning of the end? And if it was the end, what was ending? Was it despair and depression? Was it hope?

Admiral Adam called his name three times before he heard. Four before he responded.

TWENTY- SIX

Admiral Adam's plans for swift return to base H.Q. was sidetracked by bulletins from the White House. Each began with "President Inez Brown-Parkinson not hurt in assassination attempt."

In an impromptu speech minutes after the shots were fired, she said, "President Abraham Lincoln was shot by a man who thought he was doing the country a favor. James Garfield, William McKinley and J.F.K were killed by nut cases.

As for attempted assassinations, I now join the ranks of Both Presidents Roosevelt, President Truman and yes, President Kennedy who was the target of more than one attempted assassination. Attempts were also made on Presidents Nixon, Ford, Carter, Regan, George Herbert Walter and G.W. Bush, and Clinton.

However, even as I join the ranks of my distinguished predecessors, I do have the distinction of being the first female President to be so targeted. I do not know why this attempt was made. I am grateful for the swift action of the Secret Service that saved my life.

As to those of you who wonder why, perhaps it is my heritage. Remember, I am African American who dared to step out of the mold. I am an ordained Baptist Minister, and hold doctorates in Economics and foreign language from Harvard.

My twin sons, both nurses and my husband, a pediatric Oncologist, died when the dust fell. We were… no, I misspoke: as our sons and husband live in my heart. Issac and I are parents of five bi-racial children. My three surviving children are studying medicine.

Among other things, I have been called Socialist, Nazi, Communist, and a few filthy names not worthy of repeating. They are words, not facts. Undoubtedly, I will hear them again.

I said this at my inauguration and will repeat as many times as circumstances allow. I am a Christian. I am an American. I supported my predecessors in their plans, and we continue to work together for the common good.

To set the record straight politically, my credentials for the bulls eye include: my service as Secretary of State for four years, and Vice President for eight years. Now I am the first female black Baptist married to a Jewish doctor to be President of the United States.

If that is not enough fuel, I (a black Baptist woman) am serving as leader of what's left of the free world in an era where we don't know what is coming tomorrow.

Yet we continue to dare. We continue to dream. We continue to meet obstacles head on, pool our resources and grow as a united country. One example is our weather and climate controlled migration. For two years hurricanes tornadoes and floods took only the lives of those who dared to challenge the inevitable. This year, there have been no casualties.

Don't think this attempt on my life will change our course. We must look fear in the face. We will continue to flourish. Our schools and fast paced training centers are turning out engineers, electricians and workers that keep our country flourishing.

We have come a long way down a toilsome road but we are Americans. We have faced adversity throughout our history and have always grown stronger and more compassionate.

The dying took guilty and innocent alike and let guilty and innocent survive. Yet, in these years of facing challenges, our country is relying more on the God of our forefathers than it has done before.

Yes, sin still flourishes.

But grace and mercy flourish even more.

The poor soul who blames me for loss of all he held dear, held nothing of value in his hands or in his heart. Yet I do not rejoice at his death or at the death of those who could have come to Jesus.

I can only echo the words of Martin Luther King Jr. "I have a dream." A dream for a better freer Christ oriented America where all men and women are treated equally, and can freely worship the Lord. Is that why this man wanted to kill me?

Lord have mercy people! This is still America. Study your history. Every time a president engages in activities for our betterment, some nut case comes along and tries to end the work. I think you should be asking what took him so long."

She turned away from the microphones, and was stopped by a secret service agent who pointed into the crowd.

She returned to the stage. "In case you're wondering, at this time, indicators are my would-be assassin acted on his own. The note in his pocket blames me for the death of his family and the end of his empire. I invite you all to join me in prayer for his soul. "

Heads bowed and she prayed, and America wept.

Had anyone noticed, throughout the busy room and on street corners and in buildings across the country, some men and women were silent observers of the crowds. Watching, as they had been watching that morning when the clean shaven man walked to an area within fifty feet of the president. Watching when he pulled the 9mm and watching as he fell.

President Brown-Parkinson turned again to the phalanx of microphones and eager reporters and was stopped mid-stride by a cordon of agents.

"I want," she said

The lead agent said "Madam President, with all due respect, we have work to do. We'll escort you into the White House and whether you like it or not, double our guard, and reinforce security areas. At this time your security is top priority Mam."

"Don't you see that your actions isolating me from the people will fuel his spark of resentment and rebellion?"

"Madam President! That you tripped and sprained your ankle while entering the Oval Office will be explained. Cameras will follow your recovery."

"I did what?" She looked into the coldest grey eyes she'd ever seen. A squared jaw and tight lips told her she had met her match.

"Oh, my ankle," she cried and agents rushed to offer assistance. Her fall was caught on camera.

"At least bring me the note," she ordered. She read and looked at the surrounding Secret Service men and women. "He blamed me," she muttered. "In spite of everything President Turnbull and I did to save lives, he blamed me."

*　　*　　*　　*　　*

One-half-hour later a bulletin from the White house stated a full investigation into the assassination attempt was under way and President Brown-Parkinson would address the nation within the week.

"Under doctors orders" for complete bed rest, President Brown-Parkinson cancelled all public appearances and visitors but managed to continue her daily TV and radio broadcast.

The knee length cast on her right leg was always visible to TV watchers.

Feeding radio listeners need to know she waxed long and eloquently about the onset of almost unbearable cast itch.

The next day she was swamped with so many long handled three pronged plastic scratchers she threatened to sign each one and auction them off. Rather than stop the flow, as she intended, it increased.

Each day after her broadcast, she was locked in her study reading top secret documents.

The attempt on her life was on a Tuesday morning. By Friday evening, she was ready and went on the air.

Cameras panned every presidential memorial in the Nations capital, resting at last on the etched face of Abraham Lincoln, and moving slowly across familiar territory. Pausing sometime: There, a study of the Korean and World War Two and Vietnam and Iran-Afghanistan memorials, there the Washington Monument. There Arlington and the eternal flame The camera panned miles of almost empty streets before pausing as uniformed police officers opened the doors of Ford's Theater. Row by row the camera advanced until the small figure on the dark stage was identified. President Brown- Parkinson, her right leg propped up on a folding chair, sat in an old hand made rocker behind a simple wooden desk.

She looked intently into the cameras and motioned to her left. An aide hurried across the bare wood floor and handed her a single sheet of paper. She nodded thanks and without preamble, spoke.

"On Tuesday, I promised this nation we would investigate and deliver to you all information we have on the attempted assassination.

This is not going to be a John Wilkes Booth Manhunt, or a John Fitzgerald Kennedy Cover up, or a jelly bean Regan tale, or media frenzies such as followed attempts made on Presidents Tanner, Eastman and Burlock. It would be a waste of time.

I have in my hand one of the most beautiful examples of calligraphy I have ever seen. It is written on exclusively expensive paper found only in universities like Harvard or Yale, or in corporate offices of leading CEO's, or In Las Vegas.

I was so curious about the paper itself my research revealed that at one time an individual sheet would cost over ten dollars. Trivia out of the way, I will now read the suicide note of my would be assassin.

It begins "Cowards of America. I have waited three years for someone to assassinate the person responsible for the disaster that wiped out most of our country and all of my family and my lucrative business.

For years I have offered millions to the person brave enough to do what must be done.Cowards. All of you are cowards!

She must die. America must be free to pursue its own interest.

You are cowards. Every week kneed one of you is more interested in following this Jesus she talks about than revenge for losing the life style we valued.

When will you realize this massive killing was her fault?

Revenge is the answer. When she is dead, America will be free." The video paused.

President Brown Parkinson looked down at the single sheet of expensive paper and held up to the camera. She pointed to the signature and a few handwritten sentences. "Vulgarity is readable. The rest is gibberish."

One fact stands out above all others and does more to encourage me than anyone could imagine. I reference his statement: "For years I have offered millions to anyone who would do what must be done."

President Inez Brown Parkinson's voice was filled with emotion. "He said years. Every since the dust fell he tried to hire an assassin. And for years, his job offer was not accepted. If this is not an indicator of a true rebirth of this nation, I'd like to know what it is.

Also, my sincere gratitude is extended to the entire population. Your refusal while driving him further into madness, served to save my life and to prove America is on the right path. I shall forever be grateful and proud of each of you. From the bottom of my heart, I thank you."

President Brown-Parkinson bowed her head and reached for a tissue and was completely taken aback by the round of cheers and applause that filled the theater. It was several minutes before her sense of order took control.

With a catch in her voice, she returned to her prepared speech. " My would be assassin was 38 year old John Smith, the second of three children born to a working class family near Las Vegas. John possessed a keen intellect, and left home when he was 12 to work the clubs. Bacchus-King Midas became his chosen name and the name recognized in many circles as a leading casino owner and strip club entrepreneur. His signature is written in what appears to be gold and is sprinkled with diamond dust."

She returned the note to its file and spoke again "The video you are about to see was found in his briefcase."

She signaled to technicians, and large screens descended from the ceiling. Now the slurred voice was accompanied by a larger than life video that played to a watching nation.

"The only reason you're watching this is my plan to kill that so called great and innovative president didn't work and I am dead.

Knowing how she pries into private lives, I'd be willing to stake my fortune she knows my identity and told you I didn't use my given name. I haven't used it for years. John smith was too common for a man of my ambition. It bored me. And I never found a name I liked better than Bacchus-

King Midas. Bacchus, the god of wine; King Midas the man who turned everything he touched to gold.

That's what I did. Everything I touched turned into gold and expensive homes, and luxury resorts. We, my family and my followers, had everything we wanted. Look at my world. Look at my beautiful girls living in the lap of luxury."

The video showed hundreds of dancing girls in strip clubs across the country. Bare chested tanned muscle men were everywhere. Doing everything. Champagne flowed. Slot and blackjack dealers raked in and spit out fortunes.

Nude men and women with tanned ripped bodies played at life in the Bahamas, and raced through the French Rivera's aquamarine waters. They were perfect. Their smiles were perfect. Their bodies were perfect. Their search for attention and media spotlight was perfection. Luxury homes, planes, yachts, designer clothing and jewelry were theirs. What money could buy was theirs, and true to themselves and their own desires only, they bought everything they wanted.

The film centered on a drunken crowd cheering as two blond haired men embraced before jumping from the balcony of a 30 story penthouse.

It closed in on Families watching white tigers and lions wearing diamond and emerald collars kill and devour their prey. Little girls peeped from behind their mother's knees and young boys pounded on the glass enclosure, pointing to a deer hidden in a small copse of trees.

The slurred voice continued. "This was my world. We worshipped our own gods; the gods that are a part of everyone who enjoys my lifestyle. Some fools called it greed. We didn't. How could greed give so much pleasure?

We were free and my leadership pandered to the selfish nature inherent in every man woman and child in this country. We had everything. We had luxury. We had pleasure. And thanks to your beloved president, we lost it all.

She knew this death was coming. She could have sent the National Guard in to round us up and protect us. All she did was talk, talk, talk and tell us what to do to save our own lives. If we were that valuable to her why didn't she save us?

Why didn't her loving God save us?

I've watched and waited and seen my dreams turned into ashes and people who could have been part of my world living without what my life style could provide.

Yeah, I'm dead. I'd rather be in hell than spend any more time in this mockery of a progressive free thinking country. I did my best to save you. It wasn't good enough. I gladly sacrifice my life for the freedom of people who were denied the best life has to offer."

President Brown-Parkinson sighed, signaled and the video ended. In its place, copies of her speeches and the speeches of her predecessor filled the screens. Once again, people heard the warnings. These played for ten minutes before she signaled again and her voice took over.

"Before we review the history of the dust, I must comment on what Mr. John Smith alias Bacchus–King Midas said about the god in each of us. He worshipped himself. His god was sex, pleasure, and the useless trifles money could buy.

We must never forget these idols they worshipped were more important than our triune God. Not only in our life time, but for thousands of years, greed for these worthless things controlled the heart and imaginations of millions. They took the place of truth and justice. They led to war and death and eternity without love. They led to the death of our families and friends. The God that indwells those who believe in Jesus Christ is the Holy Spirit, the gift of our triune God to believers.

The Holy Spirit will never lead you down the path this deranged man described. If at any time you feel yourselves more interested in possessions and pleasures than in serving God, you must test the spirit, deny the temptation, and turn or return wholeheartedly to our one true and Triune God.

Trusting in scripture, we can be assured the soul of John Smith alias Bacchus-King Midas has found its eternal home. I cannot help but feel sadness for him and for those who turned away from the true God to worship these false idols, for now they are all in eternal torment.

What this self proclaimed king and those of his persuasion didn't acknowledge is while they turned away from God, God never stopped loving them. Even now, as they suffer torment in hell, he loves them. I hope they know it. I hope they know there is no power in earth or in heaven that can separate us from so great a love."

For fifteen seconds she was silent, staring into the cameras as if she were staring into the eyes of the watching people. Then, "I spoke from my belief and my heart the truth many of you have believed and many of you are beginning to believe. Now I will speak the historical truth of the lethal dust.

When I was Secretary of State, I dusted off top secret documents that revealed that early in the twenty first century this weapon of mass destruction was produced by every country in the world. Scientist in secret designed rockets that were to take it into outer space and explode, thereby eliminating the threat of world wide destruction.

As we know now, their technology was not as advanced as they hoped.

In this century the satellites began a slow orbit of earth. Every decade or so, intelligence indicated the satellites were weakening and nearing our atmosphere.

World leaders conferred. Presidents knew, but they were always busy with economic crises, and war.

Top secret meetings turned the problem over to nuclear scientist and weapons experts. Give them credit. They tried. Their final advice to world leaders was to remain silent and let the people live until they died. They saw no other solution.

I shared this knowledge with influential ladies around the world, and we, known by many as the "Gentler Sex," decided to fight. Wise military leaders agreed to participate in our effort to save civilization. Some. Not all. Often, leading ladies worked behind the scenes.

President Roscommon and I conferred with world leaders. These top secret meetings continued under President Turnbull.

As scientific knowledge proved the deadly effectiveness of the dust was only 15 minutes, and the only sanctuary was either underground or underwater, leading ladies around the world began building underground cities, reinforcing caverns and doing their best to convince populations the threat was real and the solution workable.

The only information we could not provide was the exact date the dust would fall. We tried. As God is my witness, we tried. We tried to tell a world tired of war and hate to prepare.

I praise God so many were saved. All of us mourn those we lost. All we can do is go forward in faith.

Now we are turning again to the God of our Fathers...

My continued hope and prayer is that America and the entire world will stay on this path."

The large screen was filled with a photograph of a childhood drawing featuring a centered cross framed by flags of the free world.

* * * * *

UPDATE: Many years have passed since President Inez Brown Parkinson addressed the country after the attempted assassination.

When voters wanted to elect her president for life, she said it was against the constitution. Their response for that time and place was to rewrite the constitution. With no other choice, she accepted, and under her Christian leadership. The country flourishes...

Americans are recovering, commerce is blossoming and relations with other countries are off to a good start.

Medical centers, staffed by Osteopathic, Medical and Chiropractic and holistic physicians are in every state.

A short list of evolving life style changes is listed below.

Change Number One: Prayer and petitions to the Triune God are a part of every day life Public schools start and end the day with prayer.

Change Number Two: Women everywhere are no loner subservient. Times are changing.

Slowly.

Surely.

Definitely.

Change Number Three: Men don't like it. Wait a minute! There's nothing new about that! But it goes to show you, even in the worst of times some things stay the same.

I have used detailed records to complete this version of life after the greatest disaster to hit our planet. I am absolutely certain other stories will be written around the world. And almost as certain their stories will parallel mine because after all is said and done, human nature remains the same.

TWENTY-SEVEN

To: Tasha Maureen O'Rourke

From: Your favorite pen pal:

I just chased Randy from the computer so his love letter is on save while I reply to your latest. The good wishes and prayers of your community for my welfare are greatly appreciated. Rest assured my soon to be daughter- in- law all is well.

Concerning my recent emergency appendectonomy, I was brought to my knees by the outpouring of love from the American people. As it was after the attempted assassination, I was overwhelmed by support. The news that many denominations across the country have held services of thanksgiving supports the news our faith in Christ is growing by leaps and bounds.

However, one issue that concerns me deeply and which I'd like you (and others) to explore is a rumor that I have advocated an Amazon society. Nothing could be further from the truth.

Tell everyone to tune in a week from tonight for my address.

Randy is reading over my shoulder and urging me to hurry.

More later

Your loving pen pal and soon to be Mother-in-Law,

Inez

PRESIDENT INEZ BROWN PARKINSON'S ADDRESS

(Author's note) Be aware my recording of the President's address was blurred in places. I am confident what I am putting in print is accurate.

"My fellow citizens. Not only do I extend to you my deepest appreciation for sharing your concern and your prayers for my welfare, but also for tuning in tonight. Your support and work is what keeps this country growing and great.

This is why I must bring to the forefront issues of concern to our population. These rumors based on the muddled and slightly vaudevillian events near the Homeland Security's Headquarters in Saint Lillian, Missouri, and grievous events in the southwest are nothing more than rumor.

That these events occurred is true. However, the rumors surrounding them contain not one iota of truth. Yet, as it is with rumors, they remain rampant.

They cause dissention and threaten the structure of our country. Each rumor will come face to face with truth and will be discussed, dissected, and dismissed after we review the happenings mentioned earlier.

Before we journey into the darkness that enveloped many families in the southwest, and before the end of my address we'll revisit events near Headquarters in Sainte Lillian, Missouri.

Both stories show clearly the roads some people choose to take after the dust fell. Of the two, the Sainte Lillian story is a mixture of sadness and humor.

The southwestern region, however, has little humor. Its saving grace --is saving grace-- and shows clearly how from the most desperate and horrifying circumstances, hope can blossom and grow. I am reminded of a scratched in the wall message found in a concentration camp at the end of World War Two. It reads "If in this place of darkness, death and gloom, the sun can shine and flowers bloom. So too will I. I will not die."

I do not know if the young person survived that horror. History has not answered that question. But this I know Hope lived in her heart and hope lives today

To give perfect examples of the present upsurge of hope in our country, we will now review the tragedy/comedy that came from near our Homeland Security Headquarters in Sainte Lillian, Missouri.

After Sainte Lillian's story, we'll review events that unfolded in the southwest. Both contain stories of grief and confusion and pain. But overall, hope and faith shines through and points the way.

THE SAINTE LILLIAN STORY

Perhaps others at the farm home known as Eden recorded events of that evening but only two records were in my grandmother's files. The first was written by Lorna Doone. Following that will be the testimony of the gang leader. We are given two perspectives each equally informative and telling.

LORNA DOONE'S ACCOUNT

"It was a dark summer night. The breeze was nice and we were relaxing after a busy work day. The silent guy didn't talk, he sat and watched us seeming to take in everything we said and store it away.

Just the four of us, me, Eva, the silent guy, and Astrid enjoying a quiet evening at home, and completely unaware of what was just minutes away. Not unprepared, just unaware.

Astrid had just bomb shelled us with news she was a nun.

Then the guy who never once had said a word turned Astrid's news into a speck of dust when he started talking. He said his name was Jean Luis Pavarotti. We knew he was a musician, but that's all we knew because he never talked to us.

He would sing and play the violin and piano and trumpet, but he never talked. Oh, I've said that. Now, he was Mr. News.

Somehow or other, I managed to tell him about the fiddle I found out back of the Muny in Saint Louis and he acted really funny. Got all choked up and everything.

Anyway, everyone knew his name meant a connection to the music world. I sorta did, but didn't care. I figured his name and five dollars and ninety five cents could buy us a Starbucks coffee (if we had a coupon), and a place to buy it. I said we'd just call him Looie and he liked that. He said I could call him anything I liked as long as I called him to lunch and supper.

We were talking about God and religion when all hell broke loose.

We heard the dogs barking.

Next we heard a gunshot.

Eve said we knew what to do and we got busy doing it.

Looie got his trumpet.

Astrid was laughing like a little kid as we raced upstairs.

I helped her into her angel uniform, which was a white sheet Eve had made into a robe with wide sleeves that looked like wings when Astrid raised her arms.

Astrid got situated on the ladder and I handed her the silver sword we'd made out of plaster board wrapped in foil. It looked good.

I took my position by the moat control panel while Looie made sure we were wearing our black Ninja robes and that our faces and hands were camouflaged. We wanted to be as invisible as possible.

Looie went to the sound effects control panel.

Eva was at the lights.

Noises came out of the darkness.

When Eva finished her backwards 10 count, we were more than ready. I was so ready I could hear my heart beating.

Eve said "Bingo" which she wasn't supposed to say, but it made me grin and relax.

Then the darkness surrounding the farmhouse and outbuildings disappeared as flashing strobe lights lit the barns, chicken coops and fields. What a show! Everywhere; red, green, brilliantly white lights blinding in their intensity!

We weren't expecting divine intervention but got it anyway. Wow! God gave us a thunder and lightening show that made hairs stand up on our heads. . . and we were indoors. Except for Astrid. We heard her cheering though so we knew she was all right.

Thunder just didn't rumble, it exploded almost like cannon fire.

Lightening flashed jagged silver and gold spear points across woodland and pastureland. Donkeys brayed. In field and forest, lions, tigers and bears roared.

Lions? Tigers? Bears?

(Gimme a break, I'm just copying the report.)

Then silence. Thunder and lightening ceased. Donkeys and roaring beast quieted. Strobe lights replaced by searchlights swept the fields.

From the rafters of the farmhouse a bugle sounded the centuries old call to arms. Suddenly, everyone heard the sound of hoof beats. They were faint at first, like knuckles on a board but within seconds they were louder and stronger. Like cavalry was coming to the rescue.

Another pause.

One white spotlight focused on the fireplace chimney. It crept upward like a caterpillar in a hurry. Finally, it reached our angel.

Then Astrid went to work. Suspended six feet above the house a tall blond Angel with a long silver sword in her right hand and measuring scales in her left stood upright and waved the sword... Slowly, the sword seemed to move on it's own toward the field nearest the house. The sword swung low, cutting a wide swatch of air. Piercing screams of mortal agony came after each wide cut.

Our welcome to the marauders was perfect. Lions tigers and bears roaring, donkeys braying, thunder and lightening, howling wind, hoof beats pounding, bugle playing charge and a tall angel wielding a sword that took on a life of its own. And those blood curling screams! Scared even me, and I was in on it.

From field and pasture land over twenty men armed with all kinds of weapons including bows and arrows and clubs, dropped them and ran in surrender toward the white farm house.

I was ready. When they were so close they couldn't stop if they wanted to, I pulled levers and pushed buttons and the sides of our pit dropped in. Running blindly, the men took one giant step and fell into our muddy hole.

Naturally we had provided sound effects. I've never heard an alligator growl, but Looie came up with something he said was genuine. Snake skins and bat wings lined the walls. Screams came from the pit.

Blindfolds were dropped in the pit. A gravely voice from the depths of the earth ordered the men to blindfold one another. One by one they were pulled up and gagged, and because each one of these would be thieves had messed their clothing in ways too stinking to describe, they were told to strip. Then they were hosed down, and given bright pink jail uniforms. Each man was chained hand and foot before being led away.

They never saw us. They never knew three women and one man captured them and held them prisoner. Other than basic orders from the gravely voiced man they did not hear other voices until interrogations began

Thanks to Astrid and Looies talent with voices, each 'prisoner' swore their interrogators were a group of Chinese, Russian, American Indian and Bostonians. Eve could do that Cling Eastwood "Make my Day" thing and did it each time a bound and gagged prisoner was led into interrogation. She'd kick open a door, drag them to a stool and whisper "Prisoner number" –such and such—"now it's your turn to Make My Day"

These big bad men were so terrified; they never knew my instruments of torture came from the spice rack in the kitchen. I was really good with black pepper and homemade limburger cheese.

Roaring lions kept them docile.

The best part is other than our theatrics designed solely to keep them compliant, they were probably treated better, had excellent medical care and were fed more nourishing food than they'd had in years.

They did not see daylight until two days after Homeland Security carted them away.

We learned later that each man, even the one called Longshanks was rehabilitated and serves the country. They say Longshanks took the longest to get it right.

INTRO TO RINGLEADER'S ACCOUNT
WRITTEN BY LORNA DOONE

"I found this man to be almost a kindred spirit. He was definitely from South Saint Louis, probably the same home area as mine, but a lot older. He had a look about him that was secretive yet open, like he was a little boy finally caught in mischief and wanting so much to tell why. But, at the same time, he was a hardened man. A man who had seen so much and hurt so much he didn't know whether to reveal everything, share half truths, lie, or remain silent.

As far as looks go, he was about six feet, underweight, yet with a muscled medium frame. I'd say nothing remarkable; all around average except for his very aquiline nose. His eyebrows were deep blond and straight. His hair while close cropped was curly around the neck. I'd loved to have seen his eyes, but as blindfolds were never removed, I'm judging by his fair skin that they were blue; deep blue, with some kind of secret depth.

For some reason, he made me think of my mom. Maybe it was the eyebrows and fair skin. I've wondered if we were related, but never went into it. Mom told me that when she was 15 she was raped by a big blond giant. Her baby was a boy. She saw him once, and remembered the strawberry birthmark on his right shoulder. Then her mom took him away. She was told he died an hour later and she never saw him again.

Fifteen years later mom married my dad and three years after that I was born. She said when she saw the strawberry birthmark on my shoulder she thought she was seeing her baby son again.

This man is at least 18 years older than me. I've seen a strawberry birthmark on his right shoulder. His voice tells me he's from South Saint Louis.

I know he could be my brother.

I guess this is one lonely question among billions of lonely unanswered questions that will never be answered.

As you read his story, pray with me that he'll take this opportunity to find his real life work.

This is what he wrote:

RINGLEADERS STORY

"Where I'm from, they didn't have real names for kids like me. When I was a kid, the woman who said she was my mother said I could never tell my story. Not ever, because the people would take me away.

She said they were moving into the tenement and carried boxes to the alley when she heard a baby crying.

That was newborn me, Not even washed or diapered, just wrapped in an old towel and put in and tossed in a garbage can.

Her and the man I learned to love as a father couldn't get a kid of their own and they didn't see anything wrong with wanting me since it was pretty clear nobody else did.

Lucky me. Don't get me wrong, we had a good life.

Even though their last name was Williams, mom named me Bill.

She said it was the only name that fit because they felt like they'd found a million dollar bill in that cardboard box. My middle initial was M. No name, just an initial. We never told anyone what it stood for.

My birth certificate lists my birth as home delivery the cold day in March they moved into our apartment. On record for the world to see the names of my parents Leah and Wilhelm Williams, both age 30.

Health Department doctors checked me out, made sure the folks had formula, set up appointments for my check ups, and that was that far as the health department and bureau of records was concerned. They said with my blond hair and blue eyes I was the image of my mother.

M y dad nicknamed me Double Bill.

Mom said "That's just ducky," and somehow, that nickname stuck.

Kids called me Ducky Bill.

I started to quack and waddle just like a duck after we saw a bunch of them down by the river. Ducky Bill made people laugh and that was good. Way back then, I liked to make people laugh.

I did o.k., in school, especially baseball. Coach said if I kept it up, I'd be a shoe in for the Cardinals.

It was my dream to get rich playing ball and get my folks a nice big house and a farm in the country. Mom always fancied the Sainte Lillian area near the river with the terrain full of rolling hills and peaceful valleys.

You know what they say about dreams.

My crash and burn started when I graduated from high school and joined the Army.

I figured playing on the Army team would get me noticed by big shots. According to my plans, in no time our address would be easy street.

Our team won every tournament. My pitching and batting skills were front page on the sports section at home and across the state. Me and my ball and bat were front page the Stars and Stripes, the official U. S. Army newspaper.

The folks were so proud of their son the Airborne Ranger, top notch player in the all Army league, and geared for a great future that they did what all proud parents do. They bragged.

The night they died, they'd watched my team whip the socks off the Navy Blues conference All American Team. On their home turf no less, good old Pensacola, Fla.

I called home from the locker room. They were cheering and laughing. Dad got the phone and was kidding me about my celebratory duck walk waddle after I brought in the winning run. Mom said she'd be back for more as soon as she answered the door. I heard the phone connect with her maple end table

She greeted the callers by name.

I heard voices demanding money.

Mom screamed. I heard a long drawn out Oh nooooo."

Then, gunshots.

Dad yelled their names clear as day. His voice was loud enough for my teammates to hear. He had time to ask "Why?"

Then more shots.

They saw his hand clutching the phone as he fell and cursed one another.

I testified at their trial. Told the judge and jury everything I heard.

Clean shaven, well dressed, the picture of well brought up young men, they sat quietly at the trial. Tears streaked their faces as they viewed the prosecution display color pictures of my dead parents.

Their mothers swore they were at a family party.

The families agreed.

Their parish priest testified on their behalf. Friends and neighbors lined up to praise their good deeds, community involvement and clean habits. Their alibi was air tight.

With only my testimony about what I heard over a phone 700 miles away accusing them; with no witnesses, evidence, or confession, they were free.

As they left the courtroom, they walked past me with their right hands in their pockets. They smiled, nodded, and looked down. Really quick, just a passing look so only I could see.

South Saint Louis bred and born, and living where neighborhood gangs ran rampant, I knew what that meant.

Late at night two week later, I'd closed the apartment and was packing to leave when I heard footsteps on the stairs. Something about the sound made me look up. I'd been sitting for hours going through photo albums, remembering the good years and bawling.

There was mom, smiling at me, all the love in the world on her face. There we were as a family going to sunrise service on Easter Morning. Their faces seemed to be shining with joy. I was between them, looking up at the sunrise.

Turn a page, and there was dad, holding me up to blow out birthday candles.

There they were at every little league game, at my graduations, when I made that first jump at Fort Benning, Georgia, when I made the All American baseball team.

There they were, together, alive and smiling. Loving one another, loving the

Lord and making sure I grew up as a Christian. In every picture they were doing everything they could to keep hard times and hurt away from out door.

They were the best parents any kid could have.

The one picture that would never be in any book because it didn't need to be was forever embedded in my mind, the cold blue look of them, together in death as they had been in life, but not together. Mom was on one cold slab in the morgue, dad on another. Blue white. Cold. Dead.

I'd heard footsteps, but engrossed in memories, I paid little attention. Footsteps were always on the stairs. Always marching solid and strong up 14 flights. People came home late every night. Then a thought penetrated my grief. Our apartment was the only one occupied on the east wing, and footsteps were coming closer.

Something-- some inner voice made me move. I put the last photo album in my luggage, zipped it shut, and was in back of the door in less than five seconds. The same door where mom and dad always stood to welcome me home. The same door they used permanent ink to mark my growth spurts.

The pole light above the couch made a bright spot in the suddenly darkened room.

A keening wind through the open window blew mom's sheer curtains out. Caught in the light, they looked like shapes. Maybe like mom and dad. I stood behind the door. Waiting.

Footsteps came closer. Heavy and solid. Laughter, Drunken voices. I heard beer cans open and whispers as these good clean young man drank more courage.

Then the only sound was my heart. Loud in my ears. Loud like they could hear it. I forced myself to breathe slow and easy, to think clearly, and to wait.

My breathing.

My beating heart.

Sensing my mom and dad in the room.

Empty beer cans hitting the tile floor.

Then the unmistakable sound of the front door being jimmied. They were good. Very good.

The bastards called "Ducky Ducky, see what we've got for you," and started shooting.

I let them get off a few rounds and, then like a true duck quacked loud enough for them to turn. My home run was a double header that went out of the park.

I called the police.

Good clean boys with the same guns in their hands that killed my parents survived as little more than vegetables.

My baseball career and brilliant future went from promising to hold after newspapers spread my picture and the story across the country.

This time, the good clean boys could not lie out of it. There was no escape. Forensic evidence validated my story.

Yet the legal work took forever before I was cleared of all charges brought by the outraged families of the good clean cut all American boys.

The baseball commission said I could return to training camp, take it easy, wait a year, and recover.

I wanted to. I wanted to make my parents proud. But every time I picked up a bat, every time I threw a ball, I looked for them in the stands.

I couldn't function in or out of the ball park. It was like my reason for living was under white slabs in twin mounds on a little hill at Jefferson Barracks, the National Cemetery on bluffs above the Mississippi River.

I left Baseball.

I left the Army. .

I left life. At least the sane caring part of me did.

For years, everything was a fog.

I don't remember. I wish to God I could remember.

Somewhere in the Smokey Mountains of Tennessee a group of men live like hermits in hillside caves. I remember that, because I was one of them.

Old John, the guy in the cave next to mine, found me wandering the hills one day and took me to his cool dark cave home.

He didn't so much as talk, he rambled. He knew everything. He could quote the Bible and discourse about Einstein and his approach to light and time. Then, in the same breath, he'd start a critique on Charles Darwin's "On the Origin of Species by means of Natural Selection, or the Preservation of Favored Races in the Struggle for Life." He said the book, first published in 1859, didn't sell much till they shortened the title to Origin of the Species.

Maybe he thought I would laugh.

I didn't. I just watched him.

He cooked.

I ate.

He talked.

I listened.

Not that I had a choice.

Every day, old John watched me for reactions.

One day- I don't know how long I'd been there, I knew I'd put on a few pounds and was sleeping without headaches and nightmares-- but one day he made a comment about a football player making a home run. Maybe it was the way he said it, the way he acted out the football player grabbing the ball and running around bases. I don't remember that either, but whatever he said and did made me laugh. Next came tears, and after them, the dam broke. Everything spilled out.

He listened for two days, and didn't say ten words.

He cooked,

We ate.

I talked.

Old John was my teacher, my pastor, my advocate, and my best friend. We walked the hills together. Hunted together, scavenged together.

Dressed in our coveralls with one strap down and red underwear for a shirt, we'd work the old grist mills. Dressed in coveralls, carrying old brown jugs (full of spring water), suckin on corn cob pipes, our beards down to our rib cages, we made a fortune posing for pictures. Old John, so loquacious at the cave, never said more than "By doggies, that's a good un, yessir!"

I never talked a'tall. Like a true shy mountain man amongst them city folks, I just grinned a shy smile like I was plum amazed all them thar tourist folks wanted a picture of usuns.

We was just honest hill folks. When we got smart and added long rifles to our get up, the money really poured in.

We had more meat than we could eat. Bear, venison, rabbit, squirrel, turkey, fish from the rivers. Old John made elderberry and blackberry wine. He dried berries and wild apples he scavenged from what had been homesteads before the Government took control of the smokies. .

I learned more about survival from that old man than I ever did from the Army.

Other stuff too. Old John spoke every American Indian dialect and more'n half a dozen foreign languages. I never got fluent in any of them but he made dang sure I could get by. He said my slightly southern accent French was downright musical but my German wasn't guttural enough. I had to eat, sleep and dream in German, Russian and Polish. Funny thing about the Polish. I could translate Polish into English as long as it was written. But the spoken Polish! Oh Vey! Which is to say my Yiddish wasn't bad either.

When Old John took a break I taught him about baseball. The fella that could argue Einstein and make sense out of Darwin and speak a hundred languages, had trouble with the all American language of sports. He never did get into stats and RBI's, but he did learn the difference between touchdowns and home runs. I made sure of that.

About the only day of the week we noted was Sunday. There were times Sunday was such a blessing, Sunday followed Sunday followed Sunday.

We did, however count seasons. We were into my seventh season genuine Smokey Mountain summer when all the hills and earth is green, when fog kisses the morning and sunrise and sunset are glory on earth. It was hot and humid and close. Cool air a premium to breathe.

One of my bad headaches snuck up on me that morning. Old John said he knew just the roots to brew and fix me up. He set me up way back in a cool dark part of the cave, closed the doors to keep light and sound out, and lit out of there around 8 or 9.

For a coupla days, I puttered around the cave, and waited for old John. He never came back.

Reckon it was the quiet that got to me. There was nothing to call noise or sound except the rain which nearly washed out the hillside that first morning. It was just me and the wind and roaring waterfalls.

I never noticed how much noise rushing water made until it wasn't in competition with rafting kids and all the forest critters. Some of it was like tinkling piano music as it ran lazily over rocks. Other places it roared and churned like thunder coming over the smokies.

O.k., that brings me to where I've been the years since that July. What I've done. How I ran into this gang of footloose men. How we decided to roam at will and help ourselves.

You need to understand that living in the caves, me and old John we didn't know much about what was going on in the world. We didn't want or need news. We were content and knew whether we cared or not, the world wouldn't change. We had no communication with the world outside.

Sure we saw the tourist but remember what I said about them. They saw us as mountain men. If any of them thought to talk about world politics, wars, rumors of wars and the fast track to hell in a hand basket our civilization was on, the thought never left their brains.

Because they were on vacation, names and faces changed every few days.

They wanted to fish, sneak a few drinks, take our pictures and forget-- if only for a few days, what they left behind.

Why not?

All of us who lived in the caves had wiped our slates clean.

If I ever thought about it, I guess I thought our lives would go on forever the way we liked them.

When I got sick with that headache and Old John lit out for herbs, I figured he'd be back in a day or so. But he never showed. Eventually, I got better on my own and I looked for Old John and the others for a few days. Then, still not knowing what happened, I walked through the silent hills and forest to the nearest grist mill.

Empty cars, campers, trucks and busses filed the parking lot.

In the shaded area near the hitching post I stumbled over an empty twin baby stroller. All that was on the seats was empty diapers and sun suits.

The parking lot was lined with empty jeans, shorts, shirts, shoes, sandals, billfolds loaded with money and credit cards, and those big multi colored beach bag purses women carry filled with lotions, snack food, cameras, photo albums, and cell phones.

I picked up a total of 18 cell phones, each set on speed dial. Hundreds of numbers rang across the country. Answering machines picked up. People didn't.

When I got over that, I raided the general store, packed the biggest Winnebago camper in the lot with whatever I wanted including candy bars and RC Cola, and lit out.

Those were lonely quiet roads to Sevierville and on to Nashville.

Nashville became Memphis.

Memphis became Texas.

I found Thomas in Waco. Or maybe he found me because I sure wasn't looking for him. Thomas "Never call me Tom, or Tommy. My name is Thomas." is the fat bald headed buck toothed one that don't talk much. He jumped in the bago when I stopped at a Piggly Wiggley. I said "If you're planning to ride along, you'd best get gear."

He didn't say nothing, so I tried all them languages old John taught. Finally came to me maybe he was deaf. I took him into the store and pointed. He understood that well enough. We got what clothes and gear we needed at Sears and J.C. Penney's, a couple ham radios at Home depot, and treated ourselves to T Bone steak at the Long Horn Saloon. Thomas looked me in the eye, picked his teeth with a gold toothpick and said "Good eats."

Hearing a voice other than my own was such a shock I jumped three feet. "Talk much," I says, and he says "When I need to."

Then he didn't need to for awhile.

After Thomas in Waco, there was Ralph and Oscar, the twins in Tupelo (that's in Mississippi) and don't ask me which is Ralph and which is Oscar because I don't think they're sure. They were born fair to middlin' ugly and not quite as smart and stayed that way.

Other men came along for the ride gradual like. Time came for more room so we helped ourselves to one of them de-luxe air conditioned Greyhound tour busses... We went wherever we wanted, took what we needed and didn't cause trouble. Think about it, as long as we stayed on back roads and stuck to country towns, how could we cause trouble?

NOTE FROM LORNA DOONE

At least ten more single spaced pages in this same conversational manner put me to sleep. I mean there was nothing there except we did and he said, and we saw until I wanted to scream.

I took a few days off for yard work and gardening to clear my mind and deciding to omit the run of the mill reporting.

Then, because it was necessary, I sifted through everything I'd decided to ignore because in those pages he introduced the other members of his so called family, and very slowly worked his way into their activities. I'll do my best to condense his writing.

According to the ringleader, these men were true representatives of the American Melting Pot; every size, shape, and nationality, true American wild west types and patriots to the core.

Wild west in that they were of one mind and one purpose. That was living their way with no regard for the law. Except their own; it had to be one of those musketeer things.

"Family members", their origins, ages and area of expertise, are listed below:

Sven. Anglo Saxon. Age 45, Minnesota farmer. Big guy. Loves the earth.

Adolphus and Henri, American Indians. age 60, Michigan Elementary school teachers. They were lost without a textbook, rulebook and roomful of kids.

Jorge, Mexican. Age 29. Distiller. It was said he could make vodka from cucumbers.

Bill. American Eskimo. age 36. CEO of chain store corporation HQ Nevada. Never got his hands dirty.

Pete. Jewish. Age 40. Colorado native. Owned gas stations across mid west.

Claudio. Italian age 41, University of Michigan Language professor.

Thomas. African Emigree, Age 28. Biology teacher at Baptist Theological Seminary.

Delvin. Welsh age 65, janitor at small college.

George. Pennsylavania Dutch. Age 40. Windber Pa., 747 pilot.

Dennis. French. Age 40. Cape Giradeau, Missouri. Banker.

Barry Michael. Scotch Irish, Age 39. Chief of Police, Boston, Mass.

Harry, Moe, and Curly, no age given, no history. Bums from the bowery.

Rob. French Indian Acadian, Age 23 Mechanic.

Eric, English. Seattle, Washington, age 43. Divorce Lawyer.

Rollo. Bowling Green, Kentucky. Age 33. Dental Hygenist.

Fat Tony, Italian. Pawtucket, Rhode Island, and Brunswick, Maine, Age 44 Chef and Lobster fisherman.

Skinny Franklin (aka Longshanks). English, Followed tourist. Home state not recorded. Age 55. Pastry chef, card shark, instigator. Prison record.

From the testimony:

"Main thing we had in common was we lost everything and everyone we loved. No families to come home to, no jobs. What we had was a lot of nothing and yesterday to hang it on.

Put together, all our talents and interest and abilities didn't amount to anything. We couldn't do what we did, and didn't know what to do with what we knew or how much time we had left.

We agreed on a few things, like mistakes and all we were the only family we had. The rule about families is families stuck together. No matter what happened, we weren't going to be bossed around by big brother or big government. We were our own world.

Since I ran the show whichever day of the week I said was Sunday, we parked and held worship services. Sometimes we talked about the meaning of life and death the whole day long and tried to figure out why we were alive. Had a lot of theories, but...

All of us except Longshanks were kinda philosophical, trying to find the part in our minds and lives where yesterday ended and tomorrow began.

Longshanks never said or did much on Sunday. He'd sit still, knees drawn up to his chin, staring off into space with tears just a washing his face. Longshanks let us have our quiet times, but he wanted action and noise. He came alive only when he started trouble. More than once, we turned a deaf ear when he took what he wanted. You name it he helped himself.

I'm not saying I supported him. Fact is I did my best to curb him in but my best wasn't good enough. Don't think he ever killed anybody. I'll never know for sure.

We figured he was a nut case. When his dark moods come over him, we'd let him be.

I decided we needed a permanent home and remembered visiting the Sainte Lillian area with my folks when we were looking for a farm. We scouted the area, and watched you people for over a week.

Longshanks had his eye on the little blonde gal. He said the two men and three little women wouldn't put up a fight and we could scare them off. Anyway, that's what he said. I didn't know he had a gun until that night.

When he fired that first shot and started screaming, I knew our plans had to change. Thomas and Delvin got to him first and knocked him down. Thomas broke the gun against that big old gum tree out by the barn. Longshanks started cursing and fighting and the rest of us just made a racket and lit out for the house. If you want the truth, I think we were running from Longshanks.

He ran hell bent for leather right after us

You've got 23 men to talk to. Their stories won't be much different. If any of them confess to crimes against other people I'd say they need to be punished.

Longshanks in particular needs a lot of help. Good luck getting him to talk.

My diary notes places we left in a hurry. I'd advise whoever is in charge of this world to check for any criminal activity on those dates.

The Bowery boys are harmless long as they're fed and around folks and kept away from booze.

Even when they're drunk, they're harmless they just ain't as pretty when they get drunked up."

(The description of the Bowery Boys when sober: short, under five six, fat, bald, and snaggle toothed, makes me wonder how alcohol could have made them worse.)

END OF REPORT

After our interviews, Admiral Adam and his crew showed up to haul them away. Their blindfolds never came off while we were around and I'm pretty sure the Homeland Security men never talked about us.

Admiral Adam checked in very week. He spent a lot of time with Eve. She blushed so much when teased that we let up a little. I figured nature would work its magic.

Eve wouldn't talk about Adam, But she did say the men were doing well in rehab. Even Longshanks was starting to turn his life around.

TWENTY-EIGHT

THE COMPLETE SOUTHWEST NARRATIVE BEGINS WITH THIS LETTER.

Dear Favorite Pen Pal Mrs. President,

Although we've been pen pals for years and are now in a family relationship, I couldn't resist greeting you the original way. You will understand as you read this report.

As I wrote previously, rumors of nomads in the desert persist. Occasionally we see smoke rising above the far mountains but our search parties have found no one. As you suggested, we wait for contact.

They will be welcomed. We are in agreement with your policy, and like you we cannot advocate beliefs that are against Christ.

I didn't understand those parameters until mom pointed out what Jesus said about our enemies. Christians or not, they are our neighbors. We can provide sustenance and show love.

Just a few weeks ago, what mom said really hit home.

Our community had an experience of another kind which I must relate to you in detail.

Sociologist note a catch phrase of a former century was, "I've got good news and bad news.' You my dear future mother- in law get the good news first. You're going to need to reference it, and remind yourself there is always a silver lining as you read through the heart breaking gut wrenching almost unbelievable report that follows.

Yes, I am stalling, but once again, I must write about the wedding. Your son, my fiancé (I love writing my fiancé!) Randy and I have finally agreed to the pressure combined moms have exerted (did we have a choice? I mean really, when four want to be mothers-in-law get together, brides and grooms might as well give up!). We will happily participate in the Washington Cathedral wedding of the century.

When I gave in to the wedding plans, Randy agreed to wear cowboy boots and jeans. (Just kidding) He'll wear his dad's tuxedo and I my mother's wedding gown. As for the parties and all that stuff, we'll do the reception any way you want…BUT, for the rehearsal dinner brides and grooms insist on a picnic on the South Lawn. The girls and I are planning the menu.

And get this, even though hot dog and sausage aren't on the market, we'll bring them. Our friend Clyde Oberly's great great grandparents were sausage makers in Germany and brought the recipes here. Clyde says for this wedding, he'll sacrifice his rations of pork and beef, and make sausages to remember. Spicy, smoked or plain, we'll bring two coolers full. We'll feast just like all those innocent years ago. Now if someway, somehow, somewhere we can find our favorite gourmet mustard! Do hope that's not impossible.

Now that you're smiling, do you remember when I helped daddy grill hot dogs and burgers on the south lawn? Do you remember my looking up when Randy walked in to give you a hug and I just stood there, forgetting everything. Everything that is except the way I felt when his eyes found mine. .I think, even though he's so much older (well four years is a lot), we were both instantly in love. Now that I've written that, I cringe at the thought of writing events that changed our world

But I must.

You must admit I'm good at procrastination!

However as you need the report for Homeland Security I can't put it off any longer. What follows is so heart breaking and horrible I know without our Christian faith my community could not have lived thru these events and emerged sane.

I think it only proper to separate the report from this family letter.

TO: Inez Brown Parkinson, President of the United States and Admiral Adam Dimitri Bladgovicz, Homeland Security CO

FROM: Southwestern Regional reporter Tasha Maureen O'Rourke

SUBJ: Cult from Nowhere

1. Personal narrative.

One early morning nearly a month ago I'd swept the west porch free of the night winds gift of grit and sand and turned east in time to catch sunrise. When my eyes adjusted to that great brightness they focused on what had to be the poorest excuse for a human being on the planet.

Even the gun he had aimed at my chest was a sorry looking sight, what with it being all dirty and the barrels full of dirt and sand.

I looked from the gun to this...thing...standing in front of me and recoiled. I stood staring with my mouth wide open and nothing coming out (that's seldom happened).

I knew this wasn't a woman, but I wasn't sure of much else. Man? Boy? Beast from the dark lagoon? Zombie? It was that frightening. This thing was at first glance, bone skinny. His torn and filthy clothing fit tightly enough, so I knew there was flesh somewhere. It was his long claw like fingers, protruding shoulder bones and skeletal face that threw me for a loop. His jeans and blue plaid shirt were so smeared by sand and dirt they looked like he had rolled here from the cave side of Mount Sandy. That's like twenty or thirty miles across the dessert near the town of Nowhere.

Yes, you read the name correctly. History says the little town was named Nowhere in the 1880's because there was nowhere else to go except the desert.

Once upon a time before the dust fell, Nowhere was a thriving town. Shoe factories and dude ranches kept the population very busy. Nowhere was also known for a commune run successful produce market. They shipped vegetables and exotic cactus based preserves across our region.

After the dust fell, Nowhere became a ghost town.

Now to tie in Nowhere and our uninvited guest: What was left of his red hair was matted, and because it was going in all directions, I could clearly see scaly patches of flesh. The more I stared, the more I saw open sores. Dried yellow puss patched his face. His eyes were so swollen, it was a wonder he could see me well enough to point the old double barrel shot gun in my direction.

People in our region are familiar with firepower. Not a family around here that don't own guns. Rifles, pistols, shot guns, you name it. We've grown up with guns.

I couldn't figure this guy out. He had to be from around here, but did he have to be so stupid as to point a rusty shotgun with both barrels full of sand and dirt at me? I knew we'd be in for big trouble if he pulled the trigger.

Since I'd taken those few seconds to recoil and then recover, I was in a talking mood. I didn't hesitate to point out that very important information. Tempted as I was, I didn't call him stupid, I just said "Excuse me, but you're handling an unsafe weapon."

Instead of responding politely, he began cursing me for speaking without his permission.

When I pointed at the barrels, he looked down.

With his eyes off me, that was the break I needed. My old straw broom smacked him up the side of his head so hard he fell to his knees. The way he fell reminded me of air doing a very slow leak from a big balloon. Fortunately the gun didn't go off as he dropped it and I was able to sweep it side.

Just then, daddy came around the corner and before that boy or man (we weren't sure then) knew what happened, we had him lassoed and into the house.

Mom brought a glass of water and a basin and while I managed to get a few teaspoons of water past his swollen cracked lips, she donned gloves and did her best to wash his face. The more she washed the grime away, the paler he became. That struck me as strange, because we've got enough sunlight around here to go around all the time.

Mom cleaned his scalp with peroxide. After she wiped that off, she treated his open sores with iodine.

He used more impolite language well spied with screams to thank mom for her help. I have never heard anyone express gratitude for having their life saved with such vile language.

If my broom had been available, believe me, I'd have given him such a whack!

While my parents did what they could for him, I called Doctor Greer on the emergency phone. The treat in store for me which I'm sure Randy has told you about, was he was working with Doctor Greer and he answered the phone.

I wasn't expecting Randy. I'd no more than said "Doctor Greer?" with a question in my voice when he laughed. He said my name with the same wondering question in his and both of us started talking at once.

Momma had to remind me why I called in the first place. Anyway, I'm sure Randy told you but it was so wonderful, I just had to repeat. Polly Parrot, that's me.

Doctor Greer, head of the United State Medical Services and my soon to be brother in law and hereafter referred to as Doc Thad, told us what to do and we did it. Ghastly work. I gagged more than once.

For all his weakened state, this creature put up such a fight it took daddy and two more men to get him bathed and into fresh pajamas. Once he was tied down, daddy and the men shed their clothing very fast and disinfected. Daddy said they had to because running sores covered the body of our uninvited guest, and a horrible jagged scar crossed his abdomen oozed puss.

Also, the mystery about our guests bone skinny upper body and his tight fitting clothing was solved. Daddy said loose flaps of skin covered him from the rib cage on down like he'd lost weight so fast his skin couldn't shrink.

Not long after we switched from giving him water to soup spoons of chicken broth every ten minutes he became more coherent, and much stronger. He was so wild the men added more rope to the cot to keep him (and us) safe.

We still didn't know who or how old he was, but we new two things: he wasn't young, and he was very very sick.

Daddy said he was hysterical. Mom said hysterical or not, she wasn't going to excuse his language. She got right in his face and told him we were a Christian household and he had two seconds to shut up or he'd be gagged as well as tied down. He didn't even think about it. He cursed her.

Mom stuffed a dishtowel into his mouth. Then she pulled a chair up to the cot and read to him from Luke Chapter Eight, the story how Jesus rescued a man from a legion of demonic possession. The more she read, the madder he got. His face turned purple.

Daddy brought some oil in from the kitchen and made the sign of the cross on the man's forehead. Then he asked me to bring the Holy Water. Since we're in agreement all water is holy because it's a gift from God, I poured vinegar from the cruet into a cup, rinsed the cruet and filled it with fresh cold water. Daddy took it and began to sprinkle it over the man. Honestly, I've never seen anything like it. Every time the drops touched him he writhed... It was like his skin recoiled.

As mom was reading, his eyes were boring into hers. His look was intense like he was trying to control her.

When his thrashing and mumbling ended, mom took the dishtowel away. At first, his language was a jumble of words and half formed sentences and made no sense. It was better than his profanity, but still terribly confusing. As he took in more nourishment his words became complete sentences.

Daddy rang the alarm bell on the front porch, and in no time there was a group of men driving to Sandstone Mountain just the other side of Nowhere. Now my story gets even weirder, harder to tell and almost unbelievable.

Five hours later truckloads of women and children were at our front door. Women and teen age girls were in various stages of pregnancy. Mom looked at them cowering from the man and the very fat woman who acted like she was in charge, went outdoors to look for other men, did the math, and just made it to the bathroom before she threw up.

While three very cute dark haired little girls snuggled against their "Dearest poppa," the domineering woman stuck a very fat boy baby onto a leaking breast and began to placate our ...guest... She called him master husband and apologized for letting his insubordinate wives get out of control. She promised they would do whatever he ordered, and as senior wife, she would make his other wives obey. She begged his divine forgiveness for being too lax with discipline.

It didn't take daddy ten minutes to tell senior wife what was what. She thanked him by slapping him so hard his head hit the wall. Then our day became even more interesting.

Until that moment, I'd never seen my mom act in a rage. Now she turned on this woman and used unchristian language. When she wound down she proceeded to teach this so called senior wife what a good slapping could do. Then mom and three of her friends gave the want to be dictator the water, pajama, dish towel in mouth and tie down treatment.

A group of women and young boys and girls that didn't look so good stood back watching, and said nothing. Tears streaked their dusty faces. The way they acted made me think of abused animals huddling together for warmth and protection.

Daddy said he didn't know what was going on, but he wasn't about to allow any kind of abuse or mind control in his house. He sent half a dozen men after their wives who practically had to drag the women and kids away. The women moaned "Master husband will beat us if we stay. Master husband will kill us if we leave."

When everyone pointed out this so called master was tied down and wasn't going anywhere, they quieted, and with no backward looks allowed themselves to be led away.

Master and senior wife... didn't say a thing. Master and senior wife didn't do a thing. Except glare.

I had the feeling the group tasted freedom as soon as they turned their backs.

We were left with two tied down whatever they were, three fat little girls and a squalling baby boy.

When the little girls tried to give us orders, momma told them they had two choices. Choice number one was to hush. They didn't. She pointed at their parents, looked at me and my sister and said "Two."

Soon the little curly haired blue eyed cherubs were spanking clean (and I do mean spanking), and very docile.

Gosh, they were cute.

Before we could do more than think, a young woman covered with welts and bruises ran into the room. She spat in the faces of our prisoners, and pulled the nursing baby from the breast of the fat woman; the woman we had naturally assumed was his mother. "This is my baby" the bruised woman said.

The fat woman started screaming at her husband. In essence she turned on him heaping scorn and accusations on his head. His denial, his assurance the miracle he told her of was truth, was as loud as her screams.

All I can say about that is quiet sure was nice while we had it.

Before I could voice my questions, my sister Martha the psychologist said it was her opinion the group behavior was definitely indicative of the Stockholm syndrome. She surmised their present state of terrified submission evolved slowly.

To make a long story short, she said he gained trust first, took control second, and then became all powerful. Verbal abuse started and eventually evolved into the physical including whippings, beatings, starvation diets, and sexual.

After the dust fell, and they lost everything, the women and children passed fear and moved on into terrified submission. In their defense, they followed orders to stay alive.

My idea to ask the women why they continued to live under such abusive control abated when I learned they'd been held captive on the mountain since the dust fell. My questions began to focus on the man as in how could he, or, for that matter, any human be so controlling and abusive.

Mom's answer was that he was a bully and a coward. That seemed to fit, but something was lacking.

Daddy said in his opinion the man was evil; pure unadulterated evil. That still wasn't good enough.

It was Martha's turn. She said he was the perfect example of a man who had grown up in an abusive environment. His self esteem was so low he was afraid to break the pattern. To insure he'd never be hurt again, he needed to be in control of everyone and everything.

The belief he and his wife held, and therefore the rule was simply this. If anyone was hurt, unhappy, or rebellious, it was because they refused to acknowledge his authority. His

Rules, Martha said, were subject to change without notice. Therefore, there was always trouble. He was always in control, and the Stockholm syndrome behavior pyramid ruled.

So much for my family and their opinions, which at this time were really missing my imput. So I told them that in my opinion, one answer alone didn't fit the couple that they were all right.

Naturally we were so loud trying to diagnose, the couple stopped yelling and stared at us.

Also, while we were trying to make sense of the mess, the man (we'd learned by then his name was Ganson North and his ' senior wife' was Alorisa) ordered his wife to order us to set him free. She tried. That didn't happen.

Daddy and three other men carried Ganson -cot and all- to our jail isolation cell. Other than providing food, water and medical care, and keeping him locked up, we didn't know what else to do.

Ever so grateful for having his life saved, on the second day in isolation he plugged the toilet and then yelled he couldn't live in a toilet.

Mom pushed a plunger, soap and rags through the bars and wished him good luck. He didn't do anything until the men aimed the fire hose at him.

What we needed and didn't have was a police force, psychiatrist, family counselor and family court judge. We knew enough to know the family was dangerous and Ganson belonged where he was.

The town council decided to keep 'senior wife' and the three little girls under twenty-four hour guard in a small house across town.

Each day armed guards escorted them to the jail. Their basket of food and jug of tea was inspected.

They didn't know it but everything they said and did was recorded.

They sat in a circle. He spread his cloak on the floor for his three daughters. They would sing and play, have lunch, and then the girls would nap on his cloak.

As they slept, Ganson ranted about his place in heaven. He knew glory waited. He promised Alorisa she and the girls would reign with him. His rants were 100% egotistical, misguided and definitely not from God. Worse, there was no way to silence him.

Every day he checked the food basket and begged Alorisa to bring his favorite recipe. Every day she refused. Every day the little girls begged him to stop upsetting their mother. "Mommy cries," they said. He said "if mommy makes enough cookies for all of us, she won't cry any more." Mommy said no. Daddy begged. Little girls cried.

For all that they spent time together and prayed and feasted, and sang, the one thing their daily time together was not was definitely not happy.

By the end the first week, the women chose a spokesperson. Her statement word for word, is next. Favorite pen pal it would be a good idea for you to ask the Lord for compassion and endurance as you read, because her story seems to unlock a hell on earth. Had she not omitted specific mistreatments and abuse, it would be too terrible to comprehend.

STATEMENT OF MAUDE SMYTHE SPOKESWOMAN OF LADIES FROM NOWHERE

"My name is Maude Smythe. I am 38 years old and worked as a surgical nurse.

To begin at our beginning, Alorisa and I were next door neighbors on a pleasant shaded street leading out of Nowhere. Neither of us had sisters so we adopted one another. She lived with her family, I with mine, and we avoided a lot of that common infighting.

From the time we were toddlers, we did everything together; we dreamed the same dreams and had plans about a happy future serving Christ, and making the world a better place. We were in love with love and universal peace.

Ganson grew up across town in the worst possible environment. Abuse, drugs, everything that could misshape him was there, but he escaped. Kids at school laughed at him, but me and Alorisa liked him a lot. He had the most upbeat outlook and just never let anything get him down.

In high school Alorisa and Ganson became a secret couple and I dated my Kenneth, the wonderful man who would become my husband and father of our four boys. Our youngest survived that terrible day because he was too young to join the shopping trip.

Alorisa and Ganson, Kenneth and I always talked about serving Jesus.

We went to college on scholarships.

Long before our heroes finished training, Alorisa and I shared a one room apartment and were busy in our chosen careers. She taught special needs kid and I worked six days a week at Mercy Hospital.

Because we had our future ministry planned, we pinched every penny we could two or three times. We dressed like grand dames in twenty five cent bargains from garage sales. We cut our own hair, ignored make up and ate so much peanut butter and ramen noodles I still can't stand the sight of either.

But our Spartan lifestyle was worth it. When Ganson and Kenneth finished training, we were ready to put our plans into motion. They were so charismatic, people flocked to them like flies to honey. Families stood in line to join our loving church.

It took a few years, but eventually, thirty growing families settled in perfectly beautiful homes in our commune on farmland on the outskirts of Nowhere.

With the exception of Ganson and Alorisa who lived in a mansion complete with a community swimming pool and gym used for ceremonies and Sabbath services, we lived two families to a large house.

We considered ourselves related in word and deed. All our material goods and money were shared by the family. Ganson and Alorisa were in charge of finances and distribution. We learned to look to them for everything. Ganson arbitrated disputes.

His decisions benefited the commune family as a whole, and it wasn't long before we thought of him as a holy man.

We were on a first name basis with townspeople who were always welcome to our services. The curious and those without a religious background were easy to win over.

We had wonderful pot luck dinners, went to rodeos and street fairs, worked in the homeless shelter, and spread the word about our life of service and joy.

It seemed right to elevated Ganson and Alorisa to places of honor. One Sabbath eve under Kenneth's guidance, our husbands worked overnight to build a platform on which we placed two thrones carved from oak and padded with red velvet cushions. A red velvet curtain separated their thrones from the congregation. We were so proud. They were so humbled.

We insisted they wear special purple robes on Sabbath days. The original family members approved wholeheartedly their reigning like the royalty we knew them to be.

However, participation from the community slowed to a trickle after Ganson gave sermons on his special revelations. Some said he was too strict and domineering. Yet he never lost their respect as they saw the good we were doing in the community...

Kenneth, as Ganson's right hand man, refused a place of honor and worked our farms and markets with the others. Our produce was shipped across the southwest. Our commune was known for our wonderful family style restaurants, home made preserves, hand made quilts and hand carved souvenirs.

While Kenneth and I had three peas in the pod sons one after the other, Alorisa remained barren. Our prayer meetings began to center around their desire for children. When our prayers were answered, we celebrated.

We were overjoyed when her first ultrasound showed triplets. As her pregnancy advanced, Alorisa wasn't allowed to lift a finger. When she protested we said it was our pleasure to serve because she was bringing special lives into our family. By her seventh month, Alorisa was a walking talking dark chocolate eating blimp. We gave her everything her appetite ordered. It was fun.

Ganson not only approved our devoted service, each Sabbath he praised and blessed different women for service to their queen. We lived for that praise.

Alorisa's almost pain free and speedy delivery of three perfectly beautiful dark haired plump daughters was the talk of the hospital. She pushed once and they popped out so fast she didn't manage one grunt.

However, Ganson said labor and delivery had weakened his precious wife. For the safety of his precious wife and our queen he advised us to continue our service. The babies were so beautiful, we didn't mind. We delighted in caring for them.

Frankly I felt Alorisa could do more for herself and her daughters, but I kept a smile on my face and did my shift. Usually, she sat in a queen sized recliner nursing babies and eating candy and chips. Her favorite meals were fried, sauced, and loaded with sodium. Her thighs were dimpled and as big around as buckets. When she complained of weight gain, I stopped trying to talk her into a sensible meal plan and hid her snacks. She didn't speak to me for ten days.

It didn't take Ganson long to decide nursing three babies was sapping Alorisa's strength.

His solution was not formula, but other nursing mothers. They, he said, could take turns nursing his babies. If other babies were hungry for a time, it was good and right that as infants they were learning to sacrifice.

When nursing mothers disagreed (mildly of course), and reminded him of formula available at all stores, he was not pleased. He reminded them of their sworn duty to serve their darling daughters. Ganson and Alorisa's responsibility was to humbly accept the sacrifice.

It was also the responsibility of nursing mothers to nourish their own and they did. This was the first time we kept secrets, but for the sake of the children we knew what Ganson and Alorisa didn't know didn't hurt them-- or their plump babies.

Changes in our relationship were not a sudden explosion, but more like whispers on the wind. The nursing is the first good example.

As the triplets grew, they continued to get everything they wanted. Let one tear roll down a rosy cheek, or rosebud lips pout and our children's toys became theirs. They were taught to not share. Ganson told his daughters other children weren't holy enough to have toys. His daughters believed. Mothers did not. This was another ripple on Ganson's smooth lake.

When Ganson took their toys and the boys and girls complained, Ganson came up with special punishment. Sometimes they went without food for a day. Sometime he locked them in closets. Sometimes he had the older children sleep alone outdoors. He would visit them in the night and when the children screamed or cried, Ganson told us he was exorcising their evil spirits.

Those who believed their children's tears went to the police. When the police who enjoyed Ganson's BBQ's informed him of inspection dates, Ganson and Alorisa made sure the complainers were working out of state, and the rest of us were ready with the best show on earth.

Police cars with sirens blazing pulled in to the main driveway just as Alorisa was rehearsing the children's choir for Memorial Day Services. Sweet innocent voices harmonized on God Bless America. Happy families worked gardens. Master Chef Ganson worked three outdoor grills.

Loyal commune sisters were laughing and talking as they carried bowls of everything edible to picnic tables. Fortunately, there was food enough for five thousand (sarcasm intended).

Blue uniformed investigators practical lived with us for over a week. They checked tax records, videoed our family lives and work, talked to the kids. The commune, along with Alorisa and Ganson played roles to perfection.

The complainers were not supported by others. We told investigators how much we loved them and how we forgave them for spreading rumors.

At that week long love fest our commune family was so content I've always wondered why the police didn't suspect something. But no! They enjoyed the food and bought our happy valley commune lifestyle hook, line and sinker

Ganson's official response to the complaint that brought police and press is quoted here, "With a world full of animosity and anger, I cannot bring myself to speak harshly of misguided commune members. I will not press charges."

As soon as the good citizenry of Somewhere found something else to talk about, Ganson acted. He called a special prayer meeting and excommunicated the four complaining families. Of course his voice was soft and loving as he did so.

Fed up with Ganson, their leader told Ganson where to shove his bbq forks and exactly how high. It didn't take them long to leave. According to Ganson, they were angry and jealous of his leadership.

We believed. What else could we do? He was always right. He told us to pray for them.

Focus of our worship services changed from worshipping God to worshipping his servant Ganson. Every Sabbath Ganson spoke on God's love and his wrath when believers disobeyed. He used every chance to remind us God had appointed him our leader. His sermons, he said, came directly from God. It was, he said, his job to interpret the scriptures. Interpretations continued to support his decisions and counsel, but did nothing to bring new members.

When Alorisa spoke in tongues he was the only one holy enough to interpret. Her trances were beautiful, her voice musically clear and uplifting. According to Ganson, her messages were direct from God- or the angel Michael. They helped guide us through whispers of doubt.

The god Ganson worshipped told him older girls should dress in biblical garb. Long flowing blue virginal gowns covered them from head to toe. Three of the more spiritually advanced and physically mature girls were chosen to move into the big house with Ganson and Alorisa. Their accelerated training consisted of a vow of silence, isolation from their families, with breaks on Sunday for community worship and fellowship, and, complete unquestioned obedience to Ganson and Alorisa. Ganson said the fortunate chosen three were being prepared for places of honor.

When the girls gained weight, parents questioned Ganson. He blamed it on Alorisa's spaghetti and lasagna and promised to cut back on ice cream rewards. No matter what parents said, he had smooth laughter and considerate answers. He, our leader and spiritual advisor, would take care of our girls.

Shortly after the parent meeting that came come close to a confrontation, Alorisa, Ganson, and the overweight spaghetti, lasagna, ice cream loving girls moved into our mountain retreat caves for the ultimate purification ceremony. Their parents stayed at the big house to care for the triplets.

With Alorisa and Ganson out of sight and hearing, we used community meeting time to debate pros and cons of our commune lifestyle changes. One meeting we voiced doubt and unease. The next we assured ourselves, because after all Ganson and Alorisa were our leaders.

I spoke of Kenneth's and my life long friendship with them. Kenneth questioned, but at the same time supported Ganson.

As a community, we decided to be vigilant, and continue to trust their leadership. We chastised ourselves for lack of faith and turned our thoughts away from any possibility of their harm

After four - nearly five months in our retreat caves, the girls, Ganson and Alorisa came home. We didn't know what to expect, but the pale shadows that were once laughing and carefree daughters were foreign to us. They remained obedient to Ganson and Alorisa, but the haunted look in their eyes wouldn't leave.

Of course Ganson and Alorisa had answers that soothed our hearts. The girls were simply overjoyed, in a state of ecstasy. In the time of silence and study, the girls had had communed with angels and experienced unique revelations.

One of the trio, a frail 15 year old fainted when Ganson hugged her. Alorisa explained she'd been doing that a lot because she was overcome with awe and emotion.

It was not until Ganson left us that we learned after that… "disrespectful act"…, Ganson and Alorisa's methods of discipline changed from verbal to physical abuse. It was slowly done, carefully done. Bruises were never visible. When one girl broke the vow of silence to scream, the other two witnessing her beating stopped resisting Ganson.

When the girls were not allowed to return to their parents, Ganson browbeat concerned mothers into submission. He was the spiritual leader. His wife was the queen. We were their servants. It was the duty of commune members to serve them, to obey them, and to give our lives for them if he thought it necessary.

Over and over, he worked to convince us sacrifices were essential for commune health. It was our duty to ensure our daughters and sons knew, believed, and were willing to comply.

It got worse. I will omit details because I must remain sane.

What you will read next, is a copy from police files of Ganson and Alorisa's sworn testimony about the death of Bill and Sally Bruin. This is included to show once again how manipulative and devious they were.

Alorisa's letter which she gave me their last day will follow. She spared few details.

Bur first, the sworn testimony from Ganson North and his wife Alorisa concerning the sudden and violent death of Bill and Sally Bruin:

*   *   *   *   *

"Bill and Sally Bruin, our newest commune members, requested marriage counseling. She said Bill was too controlling. He wanted her to do things in the marriage bed she found repulsive. He said she was too weak and an unwilling partner.

My advice after two joint meetings was for them to seek sexual help outside the community.

They begged me to complete our sessions, and against my better judgment, I agreed.

It was mid-day after our third session. Alorisa and I were carting food from the kitchen to our picnic area. We were laughing about the kid's excitement over birthday parties as we cut across the main hall.

I was Pushing a cart of steaks, dogs and brots. Alorisa was carrying bbq forks and tongs. Busy as we were fine tuning our schedule, we weren't aware Bill and Sally were in the hall.

Suddenly, Alorisa pointed to a far corner where Bill and Sally were arguing. I saw Bill's arm rise and fall, and heard Sally screaming.

I remember we were too dumbfounded to drop anything. I continued pushing the cart of meat Alorisa ran ahead of me yelling at Bill. Our first thought was to stop the horrible beating and rescue Sally. I'd no sooner got between them when Bill turned the poker he had used to beat Sally on me.

Blows struck my head and shoulders. Sally's blood covered my arms as I shielded her.

Next thing I knew, I was staring into eyes so full of hate it was like he was demon possessed.

Bill kept striking and jabbing at me with the poker.

I backed up against the wall.

Alorisa to my side was praying and calling to the Lord for help. She screamed at Bill to stop. He laughed and sneered and raised the poker as if to hit her.

I stepped in front of my wife and grabbed the bbq forks. I don't know why. Maybe I was divinely directed to do so. I don't remember anything except knowing there had to be some way for me to save Alorisa and help Sally.

I held the forks out like they were swords and ordered Bill to stop. He laughed and lunged forward and… then…and then, before my eyes, he was impaled. The blood stained poker clattered to the floor at Alorisa's feet.

Bill gasped. His hands went to his chest. He gave a strange garbled cry and fell to his knees. Dying he looked up at me with clear eyes and said my name. He looked at Alorisa and two times said 'forgive'. Then right at my feet, he collapsed onto the forks and was suspended on them while blood bubbled from his mouth.

We heard Sally moaning. Alorisa was screaming for help. Before family members came rushing in, we tried to save Sally. Calling for her husband, she died in my arms."

END OF STATEMENT

*　　*　　*　　*　　*

Below is the letter Alorisa pushed into my hands the day they died.

She wrote, "The only truth in Ganson's testimony was our preparations for the picnic-birthday celebration.

Bill and Sally Bruin were trouble and we both knew it. We didn't know what to do however, because they were too smart for Ganson's usual schemes.

Ganson worked to convince them part of their problem was resentment towards him. He said it was clear Sally was intent on becoming a faithful member. He said he sensed deep resentment and mistrust from Bill.

Sally sat looking adoringly at Ganson. Bill sat watching Sally, and it was clear he did not like what he saw. Ganson jumped in and offered free counseling.

Unfortunately, they accepted, and their first sessions paved the way for mutual trust and respect. They delved into the commune lifestyle, need for leadership and cooperation, and the plans and orders Ganson decreed.

Basically, he was the spiritual advisor and commune leader. Our commune family style relationship was wonderful. Ganson's spiritual and economic leadership was superior and the commune thrived in all areas.

That Ganson spoke truth about our life style was evident everywhere, in our homes, our industry, our community service, and the commune members love for him and Alorisa.

Bill and Sally admitted they had heard negative rumors, but considering the diverse makeup of the commune population, felt Ganson was doing his best to lead a spiritual self sufficient commune.

As for their confessed martial problems, Ganson advised individual sessions so each partner could speak without fear of contradiction. They talked it over and agreed.

The day they died, Ganson and I were preparing for the party.

Sally came into the hall and said they'd talked to members who had left the commune, and had changed their minds. They were leaving that day and they were talking to the media.

I knew what Ganson would do next and couldn't bear to watch. I was hurrying away when he grabbed Sally and pushed her to the floor.

Sally was not his normal brain washed scared to death teenage victim. She fought. She spat hateful words in his face.

As she turned to run, Ganson grabbed her, hit her so hard she nearly fainted, and tore at her blouse. Bill impatient to get on the road and tired of the long wait came into the room just as Sally screamed.

Ganson grabbed the poker and struck out. His first blow hit Sally in the skull as she was stumbling toward Bill. Bill grabbed the poker away and attacked Ganson. I couldn't bear it. All I wanted to do was get out of there, to get away.

Ganson stopped me and grabbed the bbq forks. When Bill hit him again, he stabbed Bill in the chest. Hard. I heard the solid sound of it as Bill was impaled. Blood. Blood everywhere.

Ganson also lied about Bills last words. All Bill did was turn and try to crawl toward Sally but movement brought him to his knees.

My screams brought people running. We heard footsteps and doors opening. Ganson grabbed the poker and crushed Sally's skull seconds before family members rushed into the room. Ganson had time enough to drop the poker and collapsed at my feet.

I bent over him, cradling him in my arms as he whispered if I wanted to save our lives, I had to obey. He said all I needed to do was scream and act hysterical.

Act? That's a laugh. I was hysterical. I had just witnessed my husband destroy everything we had planned and worked for. I watched him commit a double murder and he wanted me to act!

I didn't see there was much of a choice. After all, Sally and Bill were dead because she didn't obey, and she had shown total disrespect toward my husband.

I could never forget the look on Bill's face when he attacked my husband. Ganson did act in self defense.

By the time help reached us, I'd made up my mind. Bottom line, Sally and Bill were gone. They couldn't testify. We were covered in blood. We had a life style to save. Believe me, I was hysterical. It took me two days to calm down. Ganson, weak as he was, spent his time caring for me.

My testimony backed Ganson. DNA evidence supported Ganson. Remembering what the commune had experienced months earlier and considering our community involvement and untarnished reputation, the Investigation was quick. We were exonerated. Silence settled. Families united. Peace seemed restored."

*　　*　　*　　*　　*

On the last day of their lives, I walked with Alorisa and the girls from their house to the jail. The girls were happy because their momma had cooked special food. We talked and laughed as we once did and reminisced about our years together. As we neared the jail door, *she hugged me the old way. The way we hugged in the beginning when we loved and trusted one another. With tears in her eyes, she said "forgive me," and before I could stammer, she pulled the envelope containing the above confession from her apron, pushed it into my hands and walked into the room with her girls.*

*　　*　　*　　*　　*

I pounded on the door. She turned and mouthed "You need to know the truth." Then she called out "Husband I hope you have a good appetite today.

I spiced the soup the way you like it and brought your favorite cookies and tea." He opened his arms and embraced her."

I had been with them from the beginnings, but did not know the horrible secret of their special food. However, before their story ends, I must tell you what happened after Bill and Sally's funeral.

*   *   *   *   *

Weak as he was, Ganson led the memorial service. We prayed for our lost family members as individuals, and as a unit prayed for their soul salvation. In the community of Nowhere, Ganson and Alorisa were looked on with awe. He gloried in it while Alorisa walked humbly by his side.

After six- months of peaceful co-existence, Ganson and Alorisa decided it was time for our yearly commune retreat. Glad to earn extra money and groceries, citizens of Nowhere, took over the stores, restaurant and farms as they always did.

Our provisions were moved to the retreat caves. Cut deep into the mountain, they had solar powered generators for light and heat, sleeping quarters with thick bullet proof doors, and few of the comforts of home. However, exactly like the commune, Garson, Alorisa and the girls lived like royalty.

For the first time, relaxation, and games weren't part of a retreat. This retreat according to Ganson and Alorisa was for our bodily purification and soul salvation. To achieve these goals we fasted, worked, studied Ganson's pamphlets and books on purification and obedience, and took long overnight hikes into the desert. Large bonfires illuminated our campsites as we studied, chanted, and prayed. All night long. Night after night.

On our overnight hikes, our only food was bread and water. At the caves, it wasn't much better because Alorisa, in charge of food and supply distribution was not generous. Families of six were given enough food for families of four. Our diet of Ramen noodles, powdered milk, dried fruit, saltine crackers and peanut butter was designed for our purification on the road to holiness.

When the wonderful aroma of Ganson's grilling steaks perfumed our campsites, we felt anything but holy.

I had long since reached the end of my blind obedience and urged Kenneth to pull us away. He talked with other men. Their decision the last week of June was to leave after the Fourth of July celebration. As a group, they informed Ganson the families were taking a week off.

Wisely, Alorisa and Ganson declared a holiday and lavished each family with a generous supply of steaks, junk food and everything else we craved.

Once again, Ganson worked the grills. Once again Alorisa worked with the children.

The difference this time was we let them. They did it all.

We watched.

They waited.

As if he knew the disaster was coming, Ganson assigned our men and all teenage boys a massive shopping trip to Nowhere.

They left our caves with bundles of bills and shopping list guaranteed to empty shelves. Their wives, daughters and sisters were asked to clean and prepare. "Prepare for what?" one asked. Alorisa said "The biggest surprise in your life special food and drink, a real party to die for." She laughed with the questioner until she achieved a cheerful compliance.

Ganson ordered the shoppers to return July Fourth exactly at 10:15 a.m. Obedient to the end, men and boys were unloading truck loads of whiskey, drugs, imported foods and expensive clothing when the dust fell.

A silence only experienced in the desert when the wind is calm alerted Ganson. Alorisa's screams alerted everyone and brought us from work in the caves.

All we saw was empty clothing climbing the hillside, dropped bags of food and supplies, scattered bits and pieces of what was. All we heard was our own screams echoing off the hills.

Ganson disappeared with one of the jeeps and a week later returned with the news we were the only people left alive. Ganson (who actually spent a week in a luxury hotel) reported finding no survivors in a three state area. He said he had used every medium possible to find signs of life. All he encountered was the deathly silence. There was nothing but silence.

We mourned our husbands and sons. We mourned uncounted numbers of dead. With mementoes of our loved ones clutched to our hearts, we gathered at the base of Sandstone Mountain for a two day fast and memorial service.

Ganson in full regalia sobbed, mourned, and poured his heart out to his god. Sunset, the second day, Ganson said a piercing shaft entered his soul and voices told him his soul purpose in life. His divine mission was to take multiple wives and become the new patriarch of the human race.

He didn't waste time. The next night in a candlelight ceremony, every girl over the age of 15 and every woman of childbearing age became his bride. They didn't say a word. He did it all.

We lived in hell. Now, more than ever, we were slaves. We reached the point where we didn't talk to one another. Why? Because if we talked we were beaten.

We set up an infirmary and maternity cave when Alorisa became pregnant.

She and two others were in labor the same day. Ganson stayed with Alorisa, and I rushed from labor to delivery room as babies came.

Alorisa delivered a deformed son before midnight. His brain was exposed, his organs protruding; everything horribly imaginable was on the body of their son. Yet he lived. Not long, but he was born alive. While I cared for her, Ganson took the baby away. Before she could ask for their son, he was back with a crying squiring infant. I didn't need to ask. I recognized the newborn. I'd delivered him at 10 p.m.

I knew what Ganson had done and said nothing. After all, he was the father. Perhaps he'd done the other woman a favor. He told Alorisa their son was stillborn but he had held the infant up to the stars and prayed for a miracle. Proof it was granted was the crying infant in his arms. Alorisa believed.

One night a month later, as Ganson walked through the preen-teen girl camp sizing up potential wives he tripped over sharp rocks and fell face first down a steep incline. The gash on his head wasn't as serious as the open wound on his belly that would refuse to heal.

I was in charge of his care. I can close my eyes and still see flaps of filleted flesh and rolls of yellow fat stretched across his belly. Yellow like chicken fat. Rolls and rolls of yellow fat; all of it embedded with dirt, gravel, and sand.

As his fall was face forward, across a 60 foot path of sharp shale, Gansons belly arms and sides were raw slabs. It was like looking at bloody hamburger. Dirt and sand blocked most of the bleeding. As I cleansed and sutured his wounds, his screams pierced the evening air.

Alorisa, still under the allusion she was in control, told me I was responsible for the life of my master and she would personally see I suffered an agonizing death if he didn't get well.

For the first time in my years in the commune, I told her to shut up and keep out of my way. When she went for her whip, I grabbed it, broke the handle and threw it in her face. Then I started giving orders. That was one of the most liberating times in my life. Fortunately or unfortunately as the case may be, she became meek as a lamb and followed my instructions.

Ganson screamed like a woman in labor when I touched him, Screamed and blubbered when I cleaned the wounds. He screamed until every woman crowded into the infirmary. Alorisa ordered them out. It didn't work.

The watching women pointed at Ganson's fat and laughed at his screams. Three of the young women, the same three that spat in his face the day we were rescued, asked him if he remembered how they screamed when he sacrificed their babies in the fire

That which had not been talked about was suddenly in the open. For the first time mothers believed their daughters weight gain had not been the direct result of lasagna, spaghetti, and ice cream rewards.

He ordered silence. He screamed curses and threatened. But tied down as he was, Ganson couldn't stop the truth from coming out.

Nurse that I am, my duty was to save his life. If that duty included removing rolls of fat and washing the open wounds with iodine, I did it. I worked all night while he fought blood loss, delirium and fever.

I had no choice but to suture veins and remove his torn and shredded fat. Fat filled a wash basin at my feet. My closing of his horrible wounds was done with darning needles and plain white cotton thread so laced with iodine not one germ could survive.

I had performed the most impossible surgery under extremely primitive conditions, and felt not one measure of pity as I worked over his thrashing body. It may sound cruel, but his screams and moans were like music to my ears. When I finally closed, I knew the scar stretched across his fat abdomen would make the record books of ugly.

As Ganson fought death, if I didn't move fast enough, or treat him with enough respect, or kiss his royal ass, he found enough strength and hatred to curse me for my stupidity and clumsiness. He did that with every breath. The times I'd groveled and begged for his benevolent mercy flashed in my mind. That time was over. His curses bounced back in his face.

I refused to be his servant. When he cursed me I told him to shut up. When he threatened me with beatings, I laughed. When he begged for pain meds, I stuck to my schedule.

Alorisa's pleas to relieve her of nursing duties didn't faze me. When she tried for sympathy saying she couldn't nurse him because his suffering made her physically ill, I gave her two words of sympathy which will not be repeated. Fainting or not, Alorisa had to change his foul diapers, bathe his stinking body, and clean his vomit.

Ganson vomited. No matter what she fed him, most of it came up. Green. Sour. Foul.

Diarrhea was a constant threat. His excessive body weight disappeared almost overnight. Pus filled sores covered his body. He screamed he was burning inside, and blamed his suffering on my inept care.

The few times he slept, I watched his eyes move as if her were dreaming, and wondered if then he remembered the hopes and dreams we had at the beginning.

When his darling daughters heard their precious poppa cursing me, they kicked me. Once. Their reward was the first solid spanking of their fat spoiled lives.

Gradually Ganson found enough strength to sit up, then walk, then to issue orders. Which were ignored. Best of all, Alorisa couldn't do a thing about it.

One morning after I returned to my family, Alorisa's screams woke the camp. He was gone.

Three weeks later, we were brought here.

*   *   *   *   *

Now back to the end of Ganson and Aalorisa's story.

Yesterday his wife and daughters brought his favorite spiced soup, cookies and their special tea. I'd always thought about that special tea. Alorisa had promised that for our party. What was so special about it, and the soup and the cookies? Why did Ganson want special food when it was the same old stuff?

The tea was a herbal brand sweetened with honey, the soup home made chicken noodle, seasoned lavishly with poultry seasoning. We all loved it. And the cookies were her own recipe of some kind of no bake chocolate peanut butter loaded with protein and spices. The guard tested the food a few times and got tired of same- old- same old- and did little more than make sure that's all she brought in. As long as Alorisa had no guns or knives, they didn't much care.

That beautiful morning, we all smiled as the little girls laughed and skipped because their mommy had made their daddy so happy.

They enjoyed a lengthy lunch. The little girls as usual, were pushing cookies one after another into their mouth.

They played awhile and then, like sleepy kittens, crawled into their mother's arms

Alorisa and Ganson cradled them and sang as their daughters fell asleep in their arms.

I watched this before turning away to read the letter she had pushed into my hands. I was left with more questions than answers. What was I supposed to do? Why did she confess to me? I went back determined to get answers, but they were all napping and didn't wake when I pounded on the door.

I chatted with the guards and gave their watch captain the letter.

He read it three times, and questioned me four before he reacted. It was like he'd been given an electric shock. They were too late.

The guards recording played the morning; the happy family reunion; the girls dancing, eating, napping. All seemed normal. A variation was Ganson and Alorisa continuing to sing to the girls as they remained in the sleep that took them to death.

Seen as strange after the fact was after Ganson and Alorisa downed glassfuls of their special tea . . .

MY HEART JUST SKIPPED A BEAT!

OH MY GOD! IS THIS WHAT BOTHERED ME? ALORISA HAD PROMISED US A MEAL TO DIE FOR! WERE THEY PLANNING TO KILL ALLOF US ON THE FOURTH OF JULY? OH MY GOD! WHY DIDN'T I PUT THIS TOGETHER SOONER?

OH MY GOD!

I CAN'T THINK ABOUT THIS NOW. MUST FINISH MY REPORT.

I've got the worst case of shakes in the world but I want to get this behind me. To continue as best I can, I remember they knelt on each side of the girls and wrapped them in his cloak. They spent more than the usual amount of time singing to their sleeping daughters

Other breaks in their routine included they were not arguing and much to the relief of the guards, Ganson didn't pace the floor and shout his foolish prophesies.

This morning Ganson and Alorisa were more interested in drinking tea and singing to their sleeping daughters.

They drank tea. They sang solos. They sang duets. Their voices blended perfectly. They drank tea. Their voices weakened, but guards were not alarmed.

Alorisa's last glass of tea slipped from her fingers as Ganson finished singing "Jesus Loves the Little Children."

The recording shows the faintest glimmer of something bright as Ganson kissed Alorisa and placed her beside their daughters. Then, he lay down beside her.

The Watch captain and guards determined as Alorisa and Ganson watched their babies die and drank the tea that had enough poison to kill a draft horse, Ganson made sure they would not be revived by slitting their wrist. Alorisa lost little blood. Ganson's heart beat long enough for a small red river to run into the cloak covering their daughters.

Bodies will be disposed of tomorrow.

I feel nothing for Alorisa and Ganson. Knowing their souls are in hell neither comforts or horrifies me. Here is this heavy cold empty space near my heart when I think of them

However, my heart aches for their little girls and what could have been. My only comfort is the assurance their innocence and youth testifies for them in heaven. My prayer is they have found the love and peace they were denied on earth."

END OF STAEMENT

*   *   *   *   *

Dear Pen Pal I know you have endured so very much since the dust fell. It is enough that you know those Ganson had controlled and tormented were in charge of the outdoor cremation.

I watched smoke billowing from the cemetery and hid in my room. It was a terrible day.

Our concern is focused on the surviving commune members. Fifteen women will give birth within the next few months. Several of them want late term abortions. Some, while responding to good care and nourishing food, seem lost in grief and memories of the horror. They are vacant eyed, watching a video we can't see and probably would never understand.

What we need now is guidelines. How do we handle this? What do we do?

TWENTY- NINE

Dear Tasha Maureen O'Rourke,

My dear soon to be daughter-in-law. As you greeted me with gladness, so must I greet you. You must tell me if, after that glorious sun filled day ripe with the perfume of cheery blossoms, I should address you as Tasha Maureen O'Rourke Parkinson, or Tasha Maureen Parkinson, or Dearest Tasha.

I'd much rather ponder that these next few minutes than delve into the sorrow you presented.

However, all I can do is hold on to that promise. I know you will be bringing more happiness and joy into our lives. That hope plus my faith in He whom we worship and knowing He has a purpose and plan for these unborn children assist me as I ponder the issues.

That these women were raped is evident. That the children they carry are the product of an unholy union is true. That they do not want these children is also a given. That I mourn for their losses and weep for the untenable situation in which they are now in, is also true.

However, there is more to consider than their victimization and their desire to be free of horrible memories.

While I fully understand their consuming desire to rid themselves of reminders of the commune and the recent horror, I also understand your question about blaming the abuser instead of the abused. That understanding does not negate the fact that even after Ganson told that monstrous lie they made a choice.

Yes, they were in the grip of grief. However, they knew Ganson. They knew his methods and thirst for control. They were not mindless! They had feelings! They could question! That they allowed themselves to swallow another lie this man pushed into their faces, is their responsibility.

Charismatic Alorisa was the first victim. That she loved Ganson and followed him to hell is evidence she too was, and to the end remained under his control. She could have turned away. She could have said no. she could have been stronger. She was not.

In the end she succumbed to his hatred and control and killed her daughters, her husband, and herself. She shared his guilt. Their innocent daughters did not deserve the death he demanded.

The situation grows deeper and has life lasting implications. If these women controlled and raped by Ganson chose to destroy their unborn children, Ganson will win. They will not teach him a lesson or remove his guilt by using this NAZI rationalization that kills innocents.

That erasure typifies dictatorial thinking flourishing since the beginning of time; completely devoid of love and mercy, completely blind to the love of our Triune God. This is but one reason so many lives were lost around the world on that horrible day of sorrow.

Tasha Maureen, it has stopped.

Tell these ladies the government of the United States is based on Christian principles; not on the twisted version promoted by any type of dictatorship and in particular by Ganson and Alorisa. We are governed by the truth of God's love. Tell them their unborn babies conceived by rape are innocent, valuable, loved, and, that they have a future.

As President, I offer them and their surviving children sanctuary in D.C. Counseling, medical care, therapy, their every need and their safe future is guaranteed.

The children some carry under their hearts, while fathered by Ganson, also carry their genetic blueprints. Some have brothers and sisters. For the very young, this child is their first born.

All these unborn children are precious and loved by God.

This statement may seem harsh, but the ladies need to hear it. Please tell them it is the feeling of medical personnel they are too soon removed from evil to be emotionally capable of making permanent choices.

Their needs are rest, healing, and level headed thinking about the future of these children. Will they keep the child, or place him or her for adoption? Consideration of choices is the first step and it is good. However, we encourage them to wait until they see their child before making life changing decisions.

Regardless; to keep, to love, to nurture and raise their child, or to place it for adoption with a loving family, what these women must not do is terminate their pregnancies. These unborn children are innocent. In this time and place in our humanity, these women must respond to maternal instinct and show the world what women who love unconditionally can accomplish. It is their task to show the world that with God's help, joy comes after suffering.

With all my love Tasha Maureen O'Rourke to you and your wonderful family and community

(And know my dearest I can hardly wait to see you all again)

Your soon to be mother-in-law, Inez.

Dear Favorite Pen Pal:

Your response was so heart warming and emotional, I immediately carried it to the ladies from the other side of Nowhere. (That's what we call them) I wish you could have been here. I'll do my best to give you some highlights.

A few cried. Mable Sample who lost her husband and three teen age sons when the dust fell said you didn't know what you were talking about. You had not been on that mountain. You were safe and secure in the White House! You had not suffered the abuse, the rapes and forced pregnancy. She was so angry and full of what you had not done people turned away from her.

Before anyone else could slam you, I grabbed that microphone and told them exactly what you suffered and how with reliance on Christ you were coping and helping every one of us survive. After that, Mable didn't want to talk. She just sat there with tears streaming down her cheeks.

Honestly, I don't think any of them knew what happened in the world on July 4, because Ganson and Alorisa had them cut off from any form of communication. You have to remember they were lost in grief for their husbands and sons and also had the mind set of concentration camp survivors. Their minds were numb. When Ganson told them they were the only survivors in the world, they had no way of knowing the truth.

Not all of them were automats. Maureen Mc'Neese who had lived the hell on earth came to your defense. She said if you had been here, you'd have been too smart to fall for the crap Ganson and Alorisa handed out. She said and I quote as closely as possible, "I was born into a Christian home. I followed Christ. For reasons I'll never understand, I believed Ganson and Alorisa were sent from God. I don't know why. I don't know why my husband and sons died. I don't know why I survived that abuse. But I do know there's a child in my womb and I'll tell you what I'm going to do. Boy or girl, I'm going to keep this child and love it, and raise it as a Christian."

One of the pregnant teen agers, a skinny little undernourished thing (sorry I don't know her name, but I'll find out) said she felt like if she aborted her baby, Ganson would win. She said, "Not only did he rape me"... and paused and sobbed.

Finally after what seemed hours but probably was only a minute at most, she found the courage she needed.

"I said not only did her rape me, but I know in my heart if I, or any of us think we'll pay him back by aborting our babies, all I gotta say about that is... we're not thinking straight. We would be like him. We'd be evil. Murderers. I'm not sure what to do with my baby, but I know I won't kill it."

Shirley Brown, so big she looked like she'd swallowed two watermelons, took the microphone. In agreement with the teen, she expanded her thought. "Killing our unborn would turn us into miniatures of Ganson and Alorisa. I couldn't stop him from raping me, but I can stop him from turning me into a murderer. I'm pregnant with a baby I don't want, but I will keep this child and do my best with God's help to forgive Ganson and Alorisa and raise this child as a Christian.

If ever my child asks me about his or her father, I will tell the truth. The simple truth; he died and it hurts me too much to talk about it. Case closed far as I'm concerned."

Silence came. Thick. Weeping splinter groups evolved into muffled conversations. A few victims shouted they'd rather be labeled murderer than the mother of the devil's child.

As I was observing and absorbing this, I remembered when I was a young teen. I didn't think much about being a parent. I wasn't interested in issues like pro-life or women's rights to choose. I was a busy girl and did girl what girls do.

Mom just didn't talk about the issues

Literature at the church didn't appeal to me. Just a brief glance at the pictures of aborted babies (they were called fetuses) was enough to make me run.

But now, with most of the world's population wiped out, I had no choice. I had to come face to face with these issues and face the future. In other words, I had a lot of growing up to do and had to do it fast.

A month ago, Randy and I were planning for our ivy covered cottage and kids and all that goes with it. I knew, no, change that. Saying I knew is a negative. I positively know we will have a good clean life.

But then and there, listening to these girls and women, I was caught in this male storm (good play on words there if I do say so meself... don't sigh, This storm was caused by a male wasn't it?) I was very uncomfortable and about lost for words (who me?) as pro-choice and pro-life women worked over their ideas. They tossed some, they agreed on basics; they were pregnant, they didn't want to be pregnant, stuff like that. After an hour or so, neither side was swaying the other. Then God took over.

Shirley Brown, the watermelon swallower I mentioned earlier, groaned, and then laughed as there in front of the crowd, a mixture of blood and water stained her clothing and the floor at her feet. Wide eyed girls screamed and backed away. Shirley collapsed to the floor and before half the crowd knew what was happening, she was panting and pushing. Twenty minutes later everything changed when a newborn's first cry pierced the air.

"My baby chooses life," Shirley said, and every woman in that place--- every woman there, started acting like it was Christmas Morning. That's the best way I can describe it. Momma summed it up like this "When those who swore they would abort saw that innocent infant, their hearts of stone turned to mush. They stopped hating and started loving."

Honestly future mother-in-law, I want to talk to Randy about his plan for us to have a dozen babies. I agree, we need to repopulate the world, but I don't want to do it all. Especially after what I saw today, I'm kinda thinking we'll have separate bedrooms.

Then I think about that look of awe on Shirley's face and how the other women were so transformed, maybe not!

Momma called me away before I finished writing, and we got so busy with newborns, it's taken me three days to get back to you.

Since this is already too long, I'll give you the good news last. We have six new babies. Three of each, and every mother holds her baby and looks at it with love. Fifteen more to go.

What I don't have figured out is how we'll tell the whole kit and cabbodle they are brother and sister.

THIRTY

As you continued reading, you turned a page and found more words. As if they were there all along. You would not believe how long it took me to find courage to continue.

From my vantage point at the end of the pen (so to speak), if I were to share how much time passed since I transcribed the events in the southwest, you would scratch your heads in disbelief. So, I will spare you.

Besides, you wouldn't believe anyway. *After all you would say it was only a report. Or, you might say; well, you've let us know you documented facts. You reported facts. It's not like you went through that yourself. What kept you from the rest of your reporting?*

I hope some readers understand my feelings. I simply had to remove myself from the narrative.

It's not like I didn't try to continue. Day after day I tried.

My thoughts returned to the southwest and to the suffering women from the other side of Nowhere. I couldn't escape the nightmare existence brought about by the senseless brutality of one man. I can't believe I wrote senseless brutality. Is brutality ever sensible?

I sat for hours, staring into a void. Hours became days. Days became weeks. Time, as time does, did it's stretching.

I cried over the newborns sacrificed in fire, I cried over little girls murdered by their parents. I could see them. Thankfully, the report contained no pictures but it was so graphic, I didn't need them. I could see everything; the newborn babies, the plump curly haired triplets dancing to their death on that last morning. It was like the tortured women and frightened cowering children were in the room with me, reaching out for help.

I could feel the evil emanating from Ganson North and Alorisa.

And always, each day as I tried to write, I wondered how Tasha Maureen was able to resume her life and see her dreams fulfilled.

The bottom line is she did. The wedding uniting Tasha Maureen O'Rourke and Randolph Parkinson, the President's daughters and the loves of their lives was indeed the wedding of the century.

Tasha's notes indicate the ceremonies were overshadowed somewhat by hotdogs on the White House south lawn served with a generous amount of gourmet mustard.

Eventually she added that she and Doctor Randolph Parkinson do indeed have their vine covered cottage. To put a perfect end to their story, the vine cottage is home to Doctor and Mrs. Randolph Parkinson. Plus eight.

Update on the children born to mothers from Nowhere indicates there was one stillborn infant. A few children were adopted. Names of those who were and were not are sealed.

Mothers vowed their children would never know more truth than the one who voiced, "I will tell my child its father died and I can't talk about it because it hurts too much.

It is reported all the children are loved, healthy and thriving.

This I know, if Tasha Maureen Parkinson could go on with her life, I certainly should have no further difficulty. After all, all I am doing is compiling recorded events.

*　　*　　*　　*　　*

Now as President Brown Parkinson said, we will return to her speech which began with her addressing rumors running rampant in the country.

*　　*　　*　　*　　*

"RUMOR NUMBER ONE:

Christianity is by decree the only faith allowed in our country. After three chances to repent and conform, dissenters will be terminated.

RUMOR NUMBER TWO:

World leaders are planning a shift in power: In short in this new order as countries continue to stabilize, women will wear the suits and conduct business both nationally and internationally. The entire male population will be expected to wear aprons, stay home, and keep their mouths shut.

RUMOR NUMBER THREE:

To insure survival of the human race, military weaponry and might will increase on all continents. As it was said long long ago, the boys with the most toys wins.

RUMOR NUMBER FOUR:

Martial law.

"I'll respond to these from the bottom up. Martial law as defined in any dictionary is law enforced by military forces invoked by government in an emergency when civilian law enforcement cannot maintain law and order. It is also the law applied in occupied territory by the occupying forces.

We are not now, nor will we ever be under martial law. Though there was confusion and dissent as we began to recover, acts of God and law abiding citizenry ended the unrest. Today tomorrow and forever, the law of our land is the law of God. We will do unto others as we would have them do to us. We will love our neighbors. We will care for our widows and orphans. We will reach out to the needy. We will work for our daily bread. As we have done since the tragedy, every person regardless of ability or disability, training or lack of, skill or needing training, will keep hands to the plow, backs to the labor and brains working for the good of all people.

Whoever started this rumor and let it blow on the wind did so without knowledge of what we face and how we, as a people respond.

I wonder did this rumor start because members of Homeland Security wear military type uniforms. Ask yourselves if they would be recognizable and effective wearing jeans or business suits.

The nucleus of Homeland Security is composed of former members of all military branches and former law enforcement officers. Under the direction of Navy Admiral Adam Dimitri Bladgovicz, Homeland Security Commander-in-Chief, part of their responsibility is the recruitment and training of members from all walks of life. Primary qualification of all recruits is the desire to serve.

That desire is turned into effective and dedicated workers at training camps run by former Marines, Navy Seals and Army Special Forces. The six months of training is rigorous, and so mentally and physically challenging it makes boot camp look like summer camp. New members learn the inner workings of this country and methods and means to ensure not only its survival, but its growth as a functioning Democracy that is based on Christian principals.

Each Homeland Security member signs on for four years. When enlistment ends they either re-enlist, or return to the civilian population with their knowledge and skills intact.

I am thankful and proud to say the reputation of Americans as hedonistic self serving materialistic war mongering fools is disappearing. We will continue to thrive and survive as long as we keep to the path.

Of course, everyone has a choice. Be assured those planning to commit crimes against these laws will be brought to justice. They will be cared for.

Once again, it is my solemn oath as your president that I have not and will not invoke martial law.

$*$ $*$ $*$ $*$ $*$

RUMOR NUMBER THREE:

All countries will expand military might and eventually, the boys with the most toys wins. This is absolute nonsense. War has never done anything but destroy; people, land, ideals and ideas. War has never achieved a goal of good for all people and it never will...

We in America and citizens of other countries, do not have time for a war that kills, destroys and ruins land and people. We are engaged in another battlefield and around this planet, it does not involve weaponry of any sort.

This rumor could well be fueled by historical accounts of warring peoples and nations. War was a major occupation of all races before the dust fell. From the beginning of time, warfare and lack of same was a mixed bag.

Landowners fought landowners. Religious warfare was the norm. The Hatfield's and the McCoy's and mountain boys, slavery, servitude, ethnic cleansing, and/or countries with the best liars, most clubs, bows and arrows, spears, guns, hatred, bombs, nuclear warheads and weapons of mass destruction won. They, massacred, subjugated, ruled outright and insured other peoples lived in fear; thereby not reaching full potential.

History is replete with its military heroes overcoming evil, rebuilding, and waiting a few years for wars to start again.

My predecessor and I supported our military because it was an absolute necessity. We protected citizens of this great country while at the same time working for world peace.

Before the world as we knew it ceased to exist, submarines from our nuclear fleet and other peace seeking nations had completed top secret missions. A time of world wide peace was near. Tragically, because of centuries old military progress that created the dust of mass destruction that wiped out over three fourths of the world population, their work remained on the drawing board.

When the deadly dust fell, it erased peoples so sick and tired of war and promises of 'no more war they had turned deaf ears to warnings.

The majority of our citizenry known as "We the people" knew death was out there somewhere, waiting for the next uprising. But they didn't care because they knew war was a lesson in futility.

After the tragedy when I emphasized the history of warfare, I repeated historically documented facts. When I stressed the desire of women to not bear children that would become cannon fodder, I spoke truth.

Warfare as it ruled the world is over. Our battles now will not be fought with guns, terror, or weapons of mass destruction because they are against disease, hunger and ignorance. Abraham Lincoln said we were engaged in a great civil war. Martin Luther King Jr. had a dream. Pastors and eloquent speakers and writers of our own generations shared that dream. As do we all. That dream, our hope, and our destiny, has nothing to do with hatred or supremacy.

Our weapons are faith, work, sweat, calluses and tears. Our weapons are intelligence and a spirit of love and kindness that unites all humanity.

*　　*　　*　　*　　*

RUMOR NUMBER TWO:

Females dominant; males subordinate: The so called Amazon society

I haven't had such a good laugh in years.

Did this rumor start because I am the first female president this country has known?

Did it start because I worked with my predecessor and other women around the world to warn our populations and men would not listen because quote, "Women don't know what they're talking about." End quote.

Did it start because of happenings in Missouri and the southwest?

Did it start because women begged their husbands to build shelters and the men refused?

Did it start because over the centuries men kept women barefoot and pregnant?

Did it start because of job inequality and pay?

Did it start because of sexual harassment?

Did it start because men were louder, stronger, domineering?

Did it start because women let them get away with the caste system?

Did it start because the grass is green and the sky is blue?

Now that we are survivors and facing challenges we've never dreamed existed, it does not matter when, where, or how the rumor started. I don't know when, and don't know why, and I don't care how...

The truth of our need for growth and survival is not found in one gender dominating the other.

Male cannot dominate.

Female cannot dominate.

Now, more than ever, we must work together. If women show they are more capable in certain task, they will be in charge and men will work with them. The reverse is true. Gender will not be cause for discrimination or subordination.

For the entire history of humankind, this thinking did not work. It definitely will not work now.

As much as possible, families are composed of one male and one female united in marriage, having children and working together. Where orphaned children are concerned, adoption is the only option. We as a nation will not tolerate children living on streets without shelter, direction, nourishment, proper medical care, education and spiritual guidance.

Husbands and wives must be committed each to the other and must work together. For the good of our country, for the continued growth of our world, this cannot, this must not be any other way.

Back to aprons and hammers. Think about it people. Some ladies want to be in the work force. Some men are more comfortable on the home front. Each should use their gifts without fear of ridicule or discrimination. For your own good and the good of your community and country, let it happen.

*   *   *   *   *

RUMOR NUMBER ONE:

"Christianity by decree is the only faith allowed in the world. After three chances to repent and conform, dissenters will be terminated."

That makes about as much sense as our drinking salt water! Here we are, nearly wiped out as a humans and the rumor states we're about to kill people that don't believe in Christ!

Lord have mercy on us all people if you think this is idea is based on the teachings of Christ.

Now you folks know I'm an ordained Baptist preacher. I'm geared up, I'm prayed up, and I'm going to end this talk with a mini sermon. Time for you to listen up!

* * * * *

The following is the intact copy of President Inez Brown Parkinson's "mini" sermon.

(In my opinion this is a classic and should be taught to our children and their children)

* * * * *

"Jesus taught we were to forgive those who persecute us. We are to love our enemies.

In this day and age if we have enemies we need our hearts examined.

Jesus loved. Are we afraid to love? Do we need lessons?

We are to show kindness to our neighbors. The Biblical story about the wounded man by the roadside ignored by religious, but saved by a non-believer, is one example. If you want a better example, examine the life of Jesus.

Our neighbors are those who live next to us, and those persons far away. Their and our common bond is need. Our responsibility is the desire, the willingness and the action that assists in any way possible, through prayer or deeds to show our love.

We are neighbors to the entire world as it is to us. We are to not judge others, but examine our own lives (i.e, taking the log out of our own eyes so we can see more clearly). We are to live a life of honesty, purity, and devotion to our triune God.

From the beginning of creation, God gave humanity choices. He did not hog tie nonbelievers. People did. He did not force feed nonbelievers the Mosaic law or the Christian Creed. People did. God gave humanity choices.

In an attempt to force Christianity on other nations, crusades and misguided churchmen extolled heavy penalties of persons who did not obey man made law. The Lord God did not sanction these deeds or perform them. PEOPLE DID!

And don't think for one minute I'm saying Christians alone were guilty of these acts. Examine history. There are (or were) religions who wanted to wage so called holy wars on Christians and Jews. These wars were not to convert, but to eradicate. Tell me what Hope and Hate have in common besides being emotions that lead to actions.

Martyrs including children and the aged have been burned at the stake, sawn in two, fed to hungry beast. Christian martyrs met death in other unspeakable ways because they chose Jesus. The Lord God did not sanction these deeds or perform them. PEOPLE DID.

Did The Lord God rise up and kill the murderers? He did not need to. Those who sinned against his Holy word and did not repent sealed their own eternal fate.

When I stressed America (and other nations) had strayed far from the truth and love of Christ, I brought to the forefront what was evident in every medium across the globe. People turned hearts and minds from God to a wanton self serving hedonistic lifestyle. Television, movies and videos, what passed for music and literature, competitive sports and forms of entertainment; all were turned away from God.

Where was Jesus?

For that matter where was any other god that said I am the way, the truth and the life, No one comes to the Father but by me?

LET US EXAMINE THE BELIEF THERE ARE MANY WAYS TO GOD:

There's nothing new about this thought. (or call it a yearning if you will). People knew there was a God. When they did not know more, they created their own gods. When the Apostle Paul took Christ to the Greeks, he used the Greek's devotion to the unknown god as a springboard to introduce the truth.

In the New Testament book of Acts, Chapter 18, the Apostle Paul is in the Greek City of Athens. If you wish, turn to that story in your Bibles and follow me. For those who do not have Bibles available, I'll summarize for you.

Paul was a devout apostle of Jesus Christ. Rescued by Jesus himself from a life of rebellion against the faith, he was transformed into a vibrant leader. Educated, well spoken, able to take any situation and turn it into a story to illustrate the love of God, he did so in Athens.

He had been observing the people and one thing that caught his eye was the Athenian s delight in discourse and discussions on varied philosophies.

On this particular day, he'd walked through the city and took note of their many statues to the varied gods the Athenians worshipped.

One in particular, devoted to the unknown god, was the center of his discourse that day.

Paul said," I notice you are religious in every way. I saw many shrines as I was walking along. One of your altars has this inscription: "To the Unknown God."

Can you see yourself there listening to this learned man, mesmerized probably by his ability to make comment favorably on the city and its open minded liberalism?

They knew about the altar. They knew about their many gods. What they didn't know was what Paul would say next.

Athenians listened politely. He told them about Jesus, His Father God and the Holy Spirit. He told them their unknown god was he true and only God, creator and master of all.

He challenged them.

As it was in Paul's day, as it is today, some believed. As it was then, as it is today with overwhelming mind boggling evidence at every turn, some did not and regrettably some do not.

To some people then and today believing in 10 or 20 or 140 or 200 gods ensures they don't need to study and be proven wrong. (Besides, with this many deities to appease, how could they have time to study?)

In my opinion, it's like these people are standing on the banks of a raging river. They know they need to get to the other shore for safety, but they don't know how. Will they build a bridge? Will they find a boat? Will they have the strength to make it on their own?

They don't know, they can't decide how or when. They can't commit to one way. They spend their lifetime on the shore watching the raging river.

There is only one God.

He is the WAY through the storms of life and across the raging river.

He is the TRUTH. He is our savior.

He is the LIGHT to our path that leads to heaven and life eternal.

Once again, I ask was there another god who made this promise?

Was there another god who said the greatest commandment was to Love and serve Him, and the second was to love our neighbors as we love ourselves?

"As we love ourselves" means many things to many people but I am convinced the Lord meant as we live and walk in comfort and security, as we cherish our families and provide for them, so too should we reach out IN LOVE to those around us and on this planet..

Jesus promised us that after he ascended to be with His Father in heaven, we would be able to do more miracles than He.

Once I, like some of you today, wondered how this could be possible.

When I was a teenager, My Granny Brown saved up and sent me to a week long multi-denominational conference in the great and beautiful state of Colorado.

There, in a sermon on prayer, a great Free Methodist pastor explained this seemingly impossible happening. He explained that when Jesus was in human form on the earth he was, like all of us, limited in time and place. When He ascended to heaven after His resurrection, He sent the Holy Spirit to indwell believers. This indwelling would then reach through time and distance.

Witnesses proclaim miracles happened then, and miracles continue world wide today.

Did any other god promise this?

Have any other religious seen this fruit?

Our world has seen beliefs that advocate killing unbelievers.

There are religions that believe their god in human form is reincarnated in an infant born at the time of the reining god's death.

There are religions that worship snakes, and mythical figures.

There are gods of war and hatred.

I will not deny that misguided so called Christians have killed in the name of our God who most certainly wept as they committed these atrocities.

When persons say there is more than one way to heaven, I wonder, could they show me the proof of their so called god ever living on this earth and leading them there.

The Christian triune God; Our creator God, His son the long promised Messiah, our Savior Jesus Christ, and the Advocate, The Holy Spirit that indwells believers is the only living true God.

He and He alone gave humanity chance after chance to get life right. He is against injustice. He is against sacrilegious actions. He is against sexual immorality, addictions, ideas and deeds working to insult, denigrate and destroy His creation… His children.

He does not commit random acts of violence. He offers forgiveness to anyone, to everyone, at any time day or night. He is always waiting. Always loving, always willing to forgive and guide our steps. As we are all sinners, we must daily turn to our savior and seek forgiveness and pray for guidance. Those who do so grow. Those who refuse, rot (eventually).

Around the world at the altar of greed and sexuality, power, money and the body were worshipped. People glamorized and idolized sex, drugs, and to quote an earlier catch phrase, rock and roll.

Where was Jesus? Where were the other deities worshipped?

In this period of great shame, there was no real family life. Men and women together, lived for the moment. Fathers deserted or denied children. Women sought abortions. Children were left in gutters.

Where was Jesus? Where were the other deities worshipped?

I could speak for hours about the same stats and the same question. Where was Jesus? Where were the other deities?

Because the others were created by man, there is no answer. I do know Jesus was waiting, watching, loving and working in the minds of men and women who wanted a better world for their families.

When the deadly dust fell, many who believed in Jesus and those who had other gods were given eternal life. As they believed, so were they rewarded.

Christians and non-Christians survived. Some by supposed accident, some because they listened to Government warnings and obeyed; but all by the grace of God.

It is documented that many men did not believe the disaster was eminent and chose death for themselves and their families.

It is documented that those who followed instructions to seek or build shelters did so because women and men worked together.

It is also documented that some women worked alone because they had no choice.

As your president who has led you through these years or renewal and growth, let me make myself clear:

I have not, I do not, and I will not advocate a world order or society ruled or dominated in any way by men.

I have not, I do not, and I will not advocate a world order or society ruled or dominated in any way by women.

I have not, I do not, I will not advocate a world order or society ruled or dominated by a group of war hungry warriors.

I have not, I do not, and I will not support or advocate a world order or society ruled or dominated by materialistic self seeking degenerates. BECAUSE that is why the dust fell. That is why innocent and guilty died. That is why dreams perished. That is why faith in Christ, music and art and charity and compassion and all that is good and beautiful nearly disappeared from our humanity.

LISTEN UP PEOPLE. I have not, I do not, and I will not advocate a world order or society which orders its people to follow Christ.

After my laying it on the line, you are turning to your family or neighbor or companion and asking why? Because why covers so much territory it is one of my favorite questions.

This is my answer: History has taught us such man made mandates do not work.

On the positive side, we obey man made and governmental instituted laws because we must. As we taught our children, just laws are made for the betterment of each individual, and are to be obeyed.

Living for other deities cannot be mandated. Living for Christ cannot be mandated. Our faith is a personal choice, a personal and lifelong commitment. Those who follow other deities are free to worship as they choose, and must respect the rights of others to follow their faith. The word is MUST. Freedom to persecute on religious or any other grounds is not a given in this country.

That time when humanity persecuted, humiliated, denigrated and ostracized other people for random reasons or reasons certain groups said sounded good, is over.

We are where we are today because, even though we were afraid to say a resounding "NO!" to materialism and evil, God is giving us another chance.

I shall close by telling you--each of you- that as for me and my house, we will continue to worship the Lord God Jehovah. Your choice is personal.

Our prayers are for your well being and salvation. May God continue to work on the minds of survivors all over the world, and may He bless America, the land that we love.

As a side note, because I feel truth is for individuals to discover, answers to your questions about my references to biblical and historical truth will be found in your Bibles and local libraries.

Perhaps you will conclude as many of us have, that the human race survived not because we deserved or earned survival, but only by the grace and mercy of God. Undeserved grace. Undeserved mercy."

That was the end of her speech, and makes a fitting end to my documentation.

It is my hope this true account of rebirth, renewal and rededication to Chris will be in libraries and schools across the country.

Sincerely,
Lilly Catherine Bladgovicz, Granddaughter of Eve and Adam Bladgovicz and Lorna Doone and Georges Luis Pavarotti.

INEZ BROWN PARKINSON'S RECIPE FOR APPLE BROWN BETTY

Basic recipe.

Use as many apples as you would use making a 10 inch deep dish apple pie. Or more if you want a deeper Brown Betty. Any kind of apples you have will do, but I prefer the baking apples with a few Galas and Red Delicious added. I do not peel my apples.

Soak a box of raisins overnight in your liquid of choice. Drain the next day

Bake till crisp in a slow oven a couple packages of English muffins. (or more) Let sit overnight. Grind the next day to make even crumbs. Mix crumbs with sugar and cinnamon (as much as you like but don't go over board.) Save about a cup for topping.

Set oven to 350 degrees.

Lavishly butter deep dish (I said butter). Layer it with crumbs, apples, raisins, dot with butter. Do this over and over and over till you run out.

Cover with that cup of seasoned crumbs you saved.

Cover dish, Pop into pre heated oven for half an hour.

Remove cover, turn dish and bake another half hour- fourty- five minutes till The Brown Betty is all golden and bubbly.

My grandchildren like it served cold with warm vanilla pudding as a topping. The rest of us like it served with home made ice cream. My daughter in law Tasha Maureen O'Rourke Parkinson insists it's even better with a dab of spicy hot apple butter. To this date, Randy wants more than a dab.